NONE
OF THIS
IS TRUE

ALSO BY LISA JEWELL

NONE
OF THIS
IS TRUE

A NOVEL

LISA JEWELL

ATRIA BOOKS

New York   London   Toronto   Sydney   New Delhi

ATRIA
BOOKS

An Imprint of Simon & Schuster, Inc.
1230 Avenue of the Americas
New York, NY 10020

Originally published in Great Britain in 2023 by Century

First Atria Books hardcover edition August 2023

ATRIA BOOKS and colophon are trademarks of Simon & Schuster, Inc.

For information about special discounts for bulk purchases, please contact Simon & Schuster Special Sales at 1-866-506-1949 or business@simonandschuster.com.

The Simon & Schuster Speakers Bureau can bring authors to your live event. For more information or to book an event, contact the Simon & Schuster Speakers Bureau at 1-866-248-3049 or visit our website at www.simonspeakers.com.

Interior design by Erika R. Genova

Manufactured in the United States of America

1 3 5 7 9 10 8 6 4 2

Library of Congress Cataloging-in-Publication Data
Names: Jewell, Lisa, author. | Sagnette, Lindsay, editor.
Title: None of this is true / Lisa Jewell, Lindsay Sagnette.
Description: First Atria Books hardcover edition. | New York : Atria Books, 2023.
Identifiers: LCCN 2023000698 (print) | LCCN 2023000699 (ebook) |
ISBN 9781982179007 (hardcover) | ISBN 9781982179014 (paperback) |
ISBN 9781982179021 (ebook)
Subjects: BISAC: FICTION / Thrillers / Suspense | FICTION / Women | LCGFT:
Thrillers (Fiction) | Psychological fiction. | Novels.
Classification: LCC PR6060.E95 N66 2023 (print) | LCC PR6060.E95 (ebook)
| DDC 823/.914—dc23/eng/20230109
LC record available at https://lccn.loc.gov/2023000698
LC ebook record available at https://lccn.loc.gov/2023000699

ISBN 978-1-9821-7900-7
ISBN 978-1-9821-7902-1 (ebook)

NONE
OF THIS
IS TRUE

PROLOGUE

Stumbling from the cool of the air-conditioned hotel foyer into the steamy white heat of the night does nothing to sober him up. It makes him feel panicky and claustrophobic. A sweat that feels like pure alcohol blooms quickly on his skin, dampening his spine and the small of his back. How can it be so hot at three in the morning? And where is she? Where is she? He turns to see if the girl is behind him, and sees her wishy-washy, wavy-wavy, in double vision through the glass windows of the hotel. And then he sees a car indicate to pull over and his heart rate starts to slow. She's here. At last. Thank God. This terrible night is coming to an end. He squints to bring it into focus, to search the driver's seat for the reassuring gleam of her white-blond hair, but it's not there. The window winds down and he recoils slightly.

"What?" he says to the dark-haired woman behind the wheel. "What are you doing here? Where's my wife?"

"It's OK," says the woman. "She sent me. She'd had too much to drink. She asked me to bring you home. Come on. In you get."

He looks behind him for the girl, sees her leaving the hotel and walking quickly away in the opposite direction, her handbag clutched tight against her side.

"I've got water. I've got coffee. Come on. You'll be home in no time."

The dog on her lap growls at him softly as he slides into the passenger seat.

"I thought you'd left?" he says, fumbling behind himself to find the seat belt. "I thought you'd gone away?"

The woman smiles at him as she unscrews the lid from a plastic bottle of water and passes it to him.

"Yes," she says. "I had. But she needed me. So. Anyway. Drink that. Drink it all down."

He puts the bottle to his dry, dry mouth, and gulps it back. Then he closes his eyes and waits to be home.

PART ONE

Coming to Netflix in May:
Hi! I'm Your Birthday Twin!

Now here's a strange one, coming your way from the people behind *The Monster Next Door* and *The Serial Date Swindler*. It's a podcast within a documentary, a kind of podumentary, if you will. In June 2019, popular podcaster Alix Summer, better known for her *All Woman* series of podcasts about successful women, branched out into a one-off project, which she called *Hi! I'm Your Birthday Twin!*, about a local woman who was born on the same day as her. As the project progressed, Summer started to learn much more about her unassuming neighbor than she could ever have imagined and, within weeks, Summer's life was in shreds and two people were dead. Absolutely spine-chilling stuff, with some shocking glimpses into the darkest corners of humanity: we guarantee you'll be bingeing the whole thing in a day.

Hi! I'm Your Birthday Twin!
A NETFLIX ORIGINAL SERIES

Screen is dark. Slowly the interior of a recording studio is revealed.

The text on the screen reads:

Recording from Alix Summer's podcast, 20 June, 2019

A woman's voice fades in slowly. "You comfortable there, Josie?"

"Yes. I'm fine."

"Great. Well. While I'm setting up, why don't you just tell me what you had for breakfast this morning?"

"Oh. Erm . . ."

"Just so I can test the sound quality."

"Right. OK. Well, I had toast. Two slices of toast. One with jam. One with peanut butter. And a mug of tea. The posh stuff from Marks. In the golden box."

"With milk?"

"Yes. With milk."

There is a short pause.

The camera pans around the empty recording studio, zooming in on details: the lines going up and down on the monitor, an abandoned pair of headphones, an empty coffee cup.

"How is it? Is it OK?"

"Yes. It's perfect. We're all set. I'll count down from three, and then I'll introduce you. OK?"

"Yes. OK."

"Great. So . . . three . . . two . . . one . . . Hello, and welcome! My name is Alix Summer and here is something a little different . . ."

The audio fades and the shot goes back to darkness.

The opening credits start to roll.

SATURDAY,
8 JUNE, 2019

Josie can feel her husband's discomfort as they enter the golden glow of the gastropub. She's walked past this place a hundred times. Thought: *Not for us.* Everyone too young. Food on the chalkboard outside she's never heard of. *What is bottarga?* But this year her birthday has fallen on a Saturday and this year she did not say, Oh, a takeaway and a bottle of wine will be fine, when Walter had asked what she wanted to do. This year she thought of the honeyed glow of the Lansdowne, the buzz of chatter, the champagne in ice buckets on outdoor tables on warm summer days, and she thought of the little bit of money her grandmother had left her last month in her will, and she'd looked at herself in the mirror and tried to see herself as the sort of person who celebrated her birthday in a gastropub in Queen's Park and she'd said, "We should go out for dinner."

"OK then," Walter had said. "Anywhere in mind?"

And she'd said, "The Lansdowne. You know. On Salusbury Road."

He'd simply raised an eyebrow at her and said, "Your birthday. Your choice."

He holds the door open for her now and she passes through. They stand marooned for a moment by a sign that says "Please wait here to be seated" and Josie gazes around at the early-evening diners and drinkers, her handbag pinioned against her stomach by her arms.

"Fair," she says to the young man who appears holding a clipboard. "Josie. Table booked for seven thirty."

He smiles from her to Walter and back again and says, "For two, yes?"

They are led to a nice table in a corner. Walter on a banquette, Josie on a velvet chair. Their menus are handed to them clipped to boards. She'd looked up the menu online earlier, so she'd be able to google stuff if she didn't know what it was, so she already knows what she's having. And they're ordering champagne. She doesn't care what Walter thinks.

Her attention is caught by a noisy entrance at the pub door. A woman walks in clutching a balloon with the words "Birthday Queen" printed on it. Her hair is winter blond, cut into a shape that makes it move like liquid. She wears wide-legged trousers and a top made of two pieces of black cloth held together with laces at the sides. Her skin is burnished. Her smile is wide. A group soon follows behind her, other similarly aged people; someone is holding a bouquet of flowers; another carries a selection of posh gift bags.

"Alix Summer!" says the woman in a voice that carries. "Table for fourteen."

"Look," says Walter, nudging her gently. "Another birthday girl."

Josie nods distractedly. "Yes," she says. "Looks like it."

The group follows the waiter to a table just across from Josie's. Josie sees three ice buckets already on the table, each holding two bottles of chilled champagne. They take their seats noisily, shouting about who should sit where and not wanting to sit next to their husbands, for God's sake, and the woman called Alix Summer directs them all with that big smile while a tall man with red hair who is probably her husband takes the balloon from her hand and ties it to a chair back. Soon they are all seated, and the first bottles of champagne are popped and poured into fourteen glasses held out by fourteen people with tanned arms and gold bracelets and crisp white shirtsleeves and they all bring their glasses together, those at the furthest ends of the table getting to their feet to reach across the table, and they all say, "To Alix! Happy birthday!"

Josie fixes the woman in her gaze. "How old do you reckon she is?" she asks Walter.

"Christ. I dunno. It's hard to tell these days. Early forties? Maybe?"

Josie nods. Today is her forty-fifth birthday. She finds it hard to believe. Once she'd been young and she'd thought forty-five would come slow and impossible. She'd thought forty-five would be another world. But it came fast and it's not what she thought it would be. She glances at Walter, at the fading glory of him, and she wonders how different things would be if she hadn't met him.

She'd been thirteen when they met. He was quite a bit older than her; well, a *lot* older than her, in fact. Everyone was shocked at the time, except her. Married at nineteen. A baby at twenty-two. Another one at twenty-four. A life lived in fast-forward and now, apparently, she should peak and crest and then come slowly, contentedly down the other side, but it doesn't feel as if there ever was a peak, rather an abyss formed of trauma that she keeps circling and circling with a knot of dread in the pit of her stomach.

Walter is retired now, his hair has gone and so has a lot of his hearing and his eyesight, and his midlife peak is somewhere so far back in time and so mired in the white-hot intensity of rearing small children that it's almost impossible to remember what he was like at her age.

She orders feta-and-sundried-tomato flatbread, followed by tuna tagliata ("The word TAGLIATA derives from the verb TAGLIARE, to cut") with mashed cannellini beans, and a bottle of Veuve Clicquot ("Veuve Clicquot's Yellow Label is loved for its rich and toasty flavors") and she grabs Walter's hand and runs her thumb over the age-spotted skin and asks, "Are you OK?"

"Yes, of course. I'm fine."

"What do you think of this place, then?"

"It's . . . yeah. It's fine. I like it."

Josie beams. "Good," she says. "I'm glad."

She lifts her champagne glass and holds it out toward Walter's. He touches his glass against hers and says, "Happy birthday."

The smile fixes on Josie's face as she watches Alix Summer and her big group of friends, her red-haired husband with his arm draped loosely across the back of her chair, large platters of meats and breads being brought to their table and placed in front of them as if conjured out of thin air, the sound of them, the noise of them, the way they fill every inch of the space with their voices and their arms and their hands and their words. The energy they give off is effervescent, a swirling, intoxicating aurora borealis of grating, glorious entitlement. And there in the middle of it all is Alix Summer with her big smile and her big teeth, her hair that catches the light, her simple gold chain with something hanging from it that skims her gleaming collarbones whenever she moves.

"I wonder if today is her actual birthday too?" she muses.

"Maybe," says Walter. "But it's a Saturday, so who knows."

Josie's hand finds the chain she's worn around her neck since she was thirty; her birthday gift that year from Walter. She thinks maybe she should add a pendant. Something shiny.

At this moment, Walter passes a small gift across the table toward her. "It's nothing much. I know you said you didn't want anything, but I didn't believe you." He grins at her and she smiles back. She unpeels the small gift and takes out a bottle of Ted Baker perfume.

"That's lovely," she says. "Thank you so much." She leans across and kisses Walter softly on the cheek.

At the table opposite, Alix Summer is opening gift bags and birthday cards and calling out her thanks to her friends and family. She rests a card on the table and Josie sees that it has the number 45 printed on it. She nudges Walter. "Look," she says. "Forty-five. We're birthday twins."

As the words leave her mouth, Josie feels the gnawing sense of grief that she has experienced for most of her life rush through her. She's never found anything to pin the feeling to before; she never knew what it meant. But now she knows what it means.

It means she's wrong, that everything, literally everything, about her is wrong and that she's running out of time to make herself right.

She sees Alix getting to her feet and heading toward the toilet, jumps to her own feet, and says, "I'm going to the ladies."

Walter looks up in surprise from his Parma ham and melon but doesn't say anything.

A moment later Josie's and Alix's reflections are side by side in the mirror above the sinks.

"Hi!" says Josie, her voice coming out higher than she'd imagined. "I'm your birthday twin!"

"Oh!" says Alix, her expression immediately warm and open. "Is it your birthday today too?"

"Yes. Forty-five today!"

"Oh, wow!" says Alix. "Me too. Happy birthday!"

"And to you!"

"What time were you born?"

"God," says Josie. "No idea."

"Me neither."

"Were you born near here?"

"Yes. St. Mary's. You?"

Josie's heart leaps. "St. Mary's too!"

"Wow!" Alix says again. "This is spooky."

Alix's fingertips go to the pendant around her neck and Josie sees that it is a golden bumblebee. She is about to say something else about the coincidence of their births when the toilet door opens and one of Alix's friends walks in.

"There you are!" says the friend. She's wearing seventies-style faded jeans with an off-the-shoulder top and huge hoop earrings.

"Zoe! This lady is my birthday twin! This is my big sister, Zoe."

Josie smiles at Zoe and says, "Born on the same day, in the same hospital."

"Wow! That's amazing," says Zoe.

Then Zoe and Alix turn the conversation away from the Huge Coincidence and immediately Josie sees that it has passed, this strange moment of connection, that it was fleeting and weightless for Alix, but that for some reason it carries import and meaning to Josie, and she wants to grab hold of it and breathe life back into it, but she can't. She has to go back to her husband and her flatbread and let Alix go back to her friends and her party. She issues a quiet "Bye then" as she turns to leave and Alix beams at her and says, "Happy birthday, birthday twin!"

"You too!" says Josie.

But Alix doesn't hear her.

1 A.M.

Alix's head spins. Tequila slammers at midnight. Too much. Nathan is pouring himself a Scotch and the smell of it makes Alix's head spin even faster. The house is quiet. Sometimes, when they have a high-energy babysitter, the children will still be up when they get home, restless and annoyingly awake. Sometimes the TV will be on full blast. But not tonight. The softly spoken, fifty-something babysitter left half an hour ago and the house is tidy, the dishwasher hums, the cat is pawing its way meaningfully across the long sofa toward Alix, already purring before Alix's hand has even found her fur.

"That woman," she calls out to Nathan, pulling one of the cat's claws out of her trousers. "The one who kept staring. She came into the toilet. Turns out it's her forty-fifth birthday today too. That's why she was staring."

"Ha," says Nathan. "Birthday twin."

"And she was born at St. Mary's too. Funny, you know I always thought I was meant to be one of two. I always wondered if my mum had left the other one at the hospital. Maybe it was her?"

Nathan sits heavily next to her and rolls his Scotch around a solitary ice cube, one of the huge cylindrical ones he makes from mineral water. "Her?" he says dismissively. "That is highly unlikely."

"Why not!"

"Because you're gorgeous and she's . . ."

"What?" Alix feels righteousness build in her chest. She loves that Nathan thinks she's pretty, but she also wishes that Nathan could see the beauty in less conventionally attractive women too. It makes him sound shallow and misogynistic when he denigrates women's appearances. And it makes her feel as if she doesn't really like him. "I thought she was very pretty. You know, those eyes that are so brown they're almost black. And all that wavy hair. Anyway, it's weird, isn't it? The idea of two people being born in the same place, at the same time."

"Not really. There were probably another ten babies born that day at St. Mary's. Maybe even more."

"But to meet one of them. On your birthday."

The cat is curled neatly in her lap now. She runs her fingertips through the ruff of fur around her neck and closes her eyes.
The room spins again. She opens her eyes, slides the cat off her
lap, and runs to the toilet off the hallway, where she is violently
sick.

SUNDAY,
9 JUNE

Josie awakens suddenly from a shallow puddle of a dream, a dream so close to the surface of her consciousness that she can almost control it. She is in the Lansdowne. Alix Summer is there and calling her to join her at her table. The table is dressed with extravagant bowls of fruit. Her friends leave. The pub is empty. Alix and Josie sit opposite each other, and Alix says, "I need you." And then Josie wakes up.

It's the buses.

The buses always wake her up.

They live right next to a bus stop on a busy, dirty road on the cusp of Kilburn and Paddington. The large Victorian villas on this street were built, according to a local history website, in 1876 for wealthy merchants. The road once led to the spa at Kilburn Priory and would have rumbled with the wheels of carriages and clicked with the hooves of horses. Now every grand villa on the road is split into clunkily converted apartments and the stucco exterior walls are stained the color of old newspaper by the endless traffic that passes so close. And the buses. There are three on this route and one passes or stops outside every few minutes. The hiss of the hydraulics as the buses pull up at the stop is so loud that it sometimes sends the dog cowering into the corners.

Josie looks at the time. It is 8:12 a.m. She pulls back the heavy denim curtains and peers into the street. She is a matter of feet from the faces of people sitting on the bus, all oblivious to the woman spying on them from her bedroom window. The dog joins her, and she cups his skull under her hand. "Morning, Fred."

She has a mild hangover. Half a bottle of champagne last night and then they finished with a sambuca. Much more than Josie is used to drinking. She goes to the living room, where Walter sits at the dining table in the window overlooking the street.

"Morning," he says, throwing her a small smile before turning his gaze back to his computer screen.

"Morning," she replies, heading to the kitchen area. "Did you feed the dog?"

"Yes, indeed I did. And I also took him out."

"Thank you," she says warmly. Fred is her dog. Walter never wanted a dog, least of all a handbag dog like Fred, who is a Pomchi. She takes full responsibility for him and is grateful to Walter whenever he does anything to help her with him.

She makes herself a round of toast and a mug of tea and curls herself into the small sofa in the corner of the room. When she switches on her phone, she sees that she had been googling Alix Summer late last night. That explained why she'd been dreaming about her when she woke up.

Alix Summer, it appears, is a reasonably well-known podcaster and journalist. She has eight thousand followers on Instagram and the same on Twitter. Her bio says: "Mum, journo, feminist, professional busybody & nosey parker, failed yoga fanatic, Queen's Park dweller/lover." Then there is a link to her podcast channel, which is called *All Woman*, where she interviews successful women about being successful women. Josie recognizes some of the names: an actress, a newsreader, a sportswoman.

She starts listening to one: a woman called Mari le Jeune, who runs a global beauty empire. Alix's voice in the introduction is like velvet and Josie can see why she's pursued this particular career path.

"What's that you're listening to?" she hears Walter ask.

"Just a podcast thing. It's that woman, Alix, who I met in the pub last night. My birthday twin. It's what she does," she replies.

She carries on listening for a while. The woman called Mari is talking about her marriage at a young age to a man who controlled her. "Everything I did, he controlled, everything I ate, everything I wore. He turned my children against me. He turned my friends against me. My life was so small, like he took it and squeezed every last drop of *me* out of it. And then, in 2005, he died, quite suddenly. And it was like pressing the reboot button on my life. I discovered that all through those dark years with my husband, when I thought I was all alone in the world, there'd been a cast of people waiting in the background for me to come back to them, they'd been there all along. They picked me up and they took me with them."

Then Alix's voice is back. "And if your husband—and I hope this doesn't sound like a harsh or unfeeling thing to say—but if he hadn't passed away at such a young age, what do you think might have been your path? Do you think you might have found your way to where you are now? Do you think in any way that your success, everything you've achieved, that there was maybe some kind of destiny at play? Or do you think that it was only the tragic passing of your husband that allowed you to follow this path?"

"That's such a good question and, actually, I think about it all the time. I was thirty-six when my husband passed away. At the time of my husband's prognosis, I was nowhere near strong enough to leave, I'd been subconsciously waiting until the children were older. But I'd already spent so many years dreaming about the things I would do when I did leave that I had the blueprint for my life without him all drawn up, even if I didn't know how I would ever get away. So it's possible, yes, that I could have followed this path without losing him to cancer. But it just happened sooner, I suppose. Which gave me longer to really build the company, to know it, nurture it, grow with it. It would have been different if I'd waited. And as awful as it sounds, death is a clean break. There are no gray areas. No ambiguity. It's like a blank canvas in a way. And that proved very helpful to me in terms of negotiating the endless possibilities that opened up to me during those first few years. I would not be where I am at this very moment had he lived."

Josie presses pause. Her breath has caught slightly; she feels almost winded. *Death is a clean break.* She glances across the room at Walter, to see if he's noticed, but he is oblivious. She presses play and listens to the rest of the podcast. The woman called Mari now owns three properties around the world, employs all four of her children in her family business, and is the founder of the biggest anti-domestic-violence charity in the UK. At the end of the podcast Josie sits for a moment and lets all she has heard about this woman's extraordinary life percolate through her. Then she goes back to the Google results and scrolls through Alix's Instagram feed for a while. She sees, as she'd known she would, a large kitchen with an island, redheaded children on windswept beaches, views from London skyscrapers, cocktails and cats and rose-gold holidays. Alix's children look young, probably no older than ten, and Josie wonders what Alix was doing for all those years before; what do you do when you're thirty years old if you're not raising children? How do you spend your time?

She pauses at a photograph of Alix and her husband. He is tall, even compared to Alix, who is taller than most, and his thatch of thick red hair looks much redder under the effect of some kind of filter than it looks in real life. The caption says: "Fifteen years today since you came into my life. It hasn't always been easy, but it's always been you and me," followed by a string of love-heart emojis.

Josie has social media accounts, but she doesn't post on them. The thought of slapping a photograph of her and Walter onto the internet for people to gawp at and to judge makes her feel queasy. But she's happy for others to do so. She's a consummate lurker. She never posts, she never comments, she never likes. She just looks.

8:12 A.M.

Sunday dawns hot and sticky. Nathan is not beside her in their bed and Alix tries to pull the fragments of the night before into some semblance of a bigger picture. The pub, the champagne, the tequila, the walk home around the park, talking to the ducks in the petting zoo through the fence, *wack wack*, Nathan pouring Scotch, the cat curled on her lap, the smell of the scented reed diffuser in the downstairs toilet mixed with the smell of her vomit, peering into the kids' rooms, eyelashes touching cheeks, night-lights, pajamas, Nathan's face in the mirror next to hers, his mouth against her neck, hands on her hips, wanting sex, NO ARE YOU ACTU-ALLY MAD, then bed. But the pillow on Nathan's side of the bed has not been touched. Did they have a row? Where is he sleeping?

She gingerly climbs off the bed and peers into the en suite. He is not there. She takes the stairs down to the hallway and hears the sound of her children. The television is on in the kitchen, and Eliza is lying on the sofa in front of it with the cat lying on her chest. Leon is on the laptop. Breakfast detritus is scattered across the long cream kitchen counter.

"Where's Dad?"

Eliza glances up. She shrugs.

"Leon. Where's Dad?"

He removes his headphones and squints at her. "What?"

"Where's Dad?"

"I dunno."

Alix wanders into the garden. The flagstones on the back terrace are already warm underfoot. Nathan is not in the shed; nor is he in the studio. She pulls her phone out of her pajama pocket and calls him. It rings out.

"Did you see him earlier?" she asks Eliza as she walks back into the kitchen.

"Nope. Mum?"

"Yes."

"Can we go to the bookshop today?"

"Yes. Of course. Of course we will."

Alix makes coffee and drinks water and eats toast. She knows what's happened and she knows what to expect. It hasn't happened for a few months, but she remembers the shape of it, the awful, grinding nightmare of it. The pleasure of her birthday night lies already in tatters in her memory.

As she sits with her second coffee, she remembers something from the night before.

The woman in the toilets who shared her birthday. What did she say her name was? Or maybe she hadn't.

She wonders what she's doing this morning. She wonders if her husband has disappeared silently in the night, leaving her to wake alone. No, she thinks, no, of course he hasn't. That's not what other husbands do. Only hers.

He reappears at 4 p.m. He is wearing the same clothes he was wearing the night before. He brushes past her in the kitchen to get to the fridge, from where he pulls out a Diet Coke and drinks it thirstily.

Alix eyes him, waits for him to talk.

"You were out cold," he says. "I was still . . . buzzing. I just needed to . . ."

"Drink some more?"

"Yes! Well, no. I mean, I could drink here. But I just wanted to be, you know, *out*."

Alix closes her eyes and breathes in hard. "We were out all night. All night, from six until midnight. We saw all our friends. We drank for six solid hours. We had fun. We came home. You had whisky. And then you wanted more?"

"Yeah. I guess. I mean . . . I was very drunk. I wasn't thinking straight. I just followed my urges."

"Where did you go?"

"Into Soho. Giovanni and Rob were there. Just had a few more drinks with them."

"Until four in the afternoon?"

"I took a room in a hotel."

Alix growls gently under her breath. "You paid to sleep in a hotel rather than come home?"

"I wasn't really capable. It just seemed the best option at the time."

He looks appalling. She tries to imagine him stumbling around Soho in the middle of the night, tipping drink after drink down his throat. She tries to imagine what he must have looked like reeling into a hotel at four in the morning, his bright red hair awry, breathing the putrid breath of a long night of alcohol and rich foods into the receptionist's face, before collapsing into a hotel bed and snoring violently in an empty room.

"Didn't they kick you out at midday?"

He rubs at the salt-and-pepper stubble on his chin and grimaces slightly. "Yeah," he says. "Apparently, they made quite a few attempts to get me up. They, erm, they had to let themselves in in the end. Just to check I wasn't, you know, dead."

He smirks as he says this, and Alix realizes that fifteen years ago this would have been something they would have joked about.

It would have been funny, somehow, a grown man drinking for nearly twelve hours, going AWOL in Soho, forcing hotel staff to enter his room because they thought he might be dead, finding him, no doubt, spread-eagled and half-naked on the bed, oblivious, hungover, revolting.

She would have laughed.

But not anymore.

Not now she's forty-five.

Not now.

Now she's simply disgusted.

Josie listens to nearly thirty episodes of Alix's podcast over the following week. She listens to stories of women bouncing back from a hundred different kinds of crud: from illness, from bad men, from poverty, from war, from mental health issues, and from tragedy. They lose children, body parts, autonomy; they are beaten, they are humiliated, they are downtrodden. And then they rise up, each and every one of them, they rise up and find goals they didn't know they had. The podcast series has won awards and Josie can see why. Not only are the women's stories inspiring, but Alix's approach is so empathetic, so intelligent, so human that she would make an interview with anyone she chose to talk to sound moving. Josie tries to uncover more about Alix from the internet, but there's very little to go on. She has rarely been interviewed, and when she is, she gives little away. Josie assumes her to be a self-made woman, in control of her life. She assumes she has a similar tale to tell as the women whom she interviews, and Josie entertains fantasies about crossing paths with Alix again, swapping their own stories, Alix maybe mentoring Josie somehow, showing her how to be the person she thinks she was always meant to be.

Then one afternoon there is a new photo on Alix's Instagram

feed. It's a birthday party for one of the children. There are balloons with the number eleven on them and the daughter with the red hair is dressed as a punk fairy and the father stands behind her watching proudly as she purses her lips to blow out the candles on a huge pink cake and other people stand behind, their hands cupped halfway to applause, faces set in smiles. And then Josie zooms in to the background at the sight of something familiar. A school photograph on the sideboard behind the group, the two children in crested polo shirts, pale blue with a dark blue logo. And she realizes that Alix Summer's children go to the same school that Roxy and Erin went to when they were small, and suddenly she feels it again, that strange wire of connection, that sense that there is something bringing her and Alix Summer together, something in the universe. She pictures Alix Summer in the same playground that she had spent so many years of her life standing in, going into the same overheated office to pay for school trips and lunches, sitting squashed on the same benches at the back of the same small hall to watch assemblies and nativities, hanging out the same navy-and-sky-blue uniforms to dry.

Born on the same day.

In the same hospital.

Celebrated their forty-fifth birthdays in the same pub, at the same time.

And now this.

It means something, she's sure it does.

MONDAY, 17 JUNE

Alix watches her husband in the kitchen, his hair still wet from the shower, the back of his shirt stuck to his skin—she's never understood why he doesn't dry himself properly before he gets dressed—drinking coffee from his favorite mug and nagging the children to move faster, eat up, get their shoes on. He's acting as if it's a normal Monday, but it is not a normal Monday. It is the Monday after his second bender in a row. The Monday after he failed to come home yet again and appeared once more, bedraggled and pitiful, on a Sunday afternoon stinking of the night before. It is a Monday when Alix has started seriously wondering about the future of their marriage again. If she keeps wondering about the future of their marriage in this way, this could well be the Monday that marks the beginning of the end. Nathan has always been a walking list of pros and cons, from the very first time she met him. She'd even written a list after their third date to help her decide whether or not she should carry on seeing him. His behavior these last two weekends has suddenly added a huge weight to the cons column, which is bad because the pros have always been quite slight. Being a good dancer, for example. Great on a second date, but not so important fifteen years down the road with two children, two careers, and a future to worry about.

At eight fifteen Nathan leaves. He calls out his goodbyes from the hallway. It's been a long time since they habitually kissed when leaving the house. Ten minutes after that, Alix walks the children to school. Leon is grumpy. Eliza is hyper.

Alix walks between them, looking at her phone, checking her emails, looking at websites for the puppy she has promised they will get some time this year, an Australian shepherd that should, ideally, have mismatched eyes and hence is proving impossible to find, about which Alix is secretly relieved. She hasn't got space in her head right now for a puppy, as much as she misses having a dog in the house.

She's just finished recording the thirtieth episode of *All Woman*; it's launching next week and then after that she wants to try something new. The theme has run its course and she's ready for a new challenge, but she's still waiting for inspiration to strike and her diary is empty and an empty diary is as stressful as a full diary when it comes to a career.

The children are gone a few minutes later, sucked into the maelstrom of the playground, and Alix turns to head home. After a cloudy morning, the sun suddenly breaks through and dazzles her. She delves into her handbag, looking for her sunglasses, and then, when she's found them, she looks up and sees a woman standing very close to her. The woman is immediately familiar. She thinks for a brief moment that she must be a mother from the school and then it hits her.

"Oh," she says, folding down the arms of her glasses. "Hello! You're the woman from the pub. My birthday twin!"

The woman looks surprised, almost theatrically so. "Oh, hello!" she parrots. "I thought you looked familiar. Wow!"

"Are you—do you have children here?" Alix gestures at the school.

"No! Well, at least, not anymore. They did come here but left a long time ago. They're twenty-one and twenty-three."

"Oh. Proper grown-ups!"

"Yes, they certainly are."

"Boys? Girls?"

"Two girls. Roxy and Erin."

"Do they still live at home?"

"Erin does, the oldest. She's a bit of a recluse, I suppose you might call her. And Roxy—well, she left home when she was quite young. Sixteen."

"Sixteen. Wow! That is young. I'm Alix, by the way." She offers her hand to shake.

"Josie," the woman replies.

"Nice to meet you, Josie. And who's this?" she asks, noticing a tiny caramel-and-cream-colored dog on a lead at Josie's feet.

"This is Fred."

"Oh, he's adorable! What is he?"

"He's a Pomchi. Or at least, that's what they told me. But I'm not so sure now he's full-grown. I think he might be more of a mix than that. I do wonder about the place we got him from—I'm not entirely sure they were kosher, you know, now I think back on it. I keep meaning to get one of those DNA tests. But then, you know, I just look at him and I think, whatever."

"Yes," Alix agrees. "He's gorgeous whatever he is. I love dogs."

"Do you have one?"

"No. Not at the moment. We lost our girl three years ago and I haven't quite been able to get my head around replacing her. But I have been looking. The kids, you know, they're at that age where I think having a dog will be really good for them: coming into adolescence, the teenage years. Teeny was my dog, the dog I had before I had kids. This one would be for them. But we'll see."

She reaches down to pet the dog, but it backs away from her.

"Sorry," says Josie, overly apologetically.

"Oh," says Alix, "he's shy. That's fair enough."

Alix glances at Josie and sees that she is staring at her meaningfully. It makes her feel uncomfortable for a moment but then Josie's face breaks into a small smile and Alix sees that she is, as she'd thought on the night they met in the pub, quietly, secretly pretty: neat teeth, rose-petal lips, a small Roman nose that gives her face something extra. Her hair is hazel brown and wavy, parted to the side and tied back. She's wearing a floral-print T-shirt with a blue denim skirt and has a handbag also made of blue denim. Alix notices that the dog's collar and lead are blue denim too and senses a theme. Some people have that, she ponders, a repeat motif, some defining aesthetic tic that somehow makes them feel protected. Her friend's mother only bought things that were purple, she recalls. Everything. Purple. Even her fridge.

"Anyway," Alix says, unfolding her sunglasses and putting them on. "I'd better get on. Nice to see you again."

She turns to leave, but then Josie says, "There's something I'd like to talk to you about actually. If you've got a minute. Nothing important. Just . . . to do with us being birthday twins. That's all." She smiles apologetically and Alix smiles back.

"Oh," she replies. "Now?"

"Yes. If you have a minute?"

"I'm so sorry, I can't really now. But maybe another time."

"Tomorrow?"

"No, not tomorrow."

"Wednesday?"

"Oh God, Josie, I'm sorry, I really am. But I'm busy pretty much the rest of the week, to be honest."

She starts to leave again but Josie places a hand gently on her arm. "Please," she says. "It would really mean a lot to me."

There is a sheen of tears across Josie's eyes; she sounds desperate somehow, and Alix feels a chill pass through her. But she sighs softly and says, "I have a spare hour tomorrow afternoon. Maybe we could grab a quick coffee."

Josie's face drops. "Oh," she says. "I work afternoons."

Alix feels a sense of relief that maybe she has swerved the commitment. But then Josie says, "Listen. I work at that alterations place, by Kilburn tube. Why don't you come along tomorrow—we can chat then? It won't take longer than a few minutes, I promise."

"What is it that you want to chat about?"

Josie bites her lip, as if considering sharing a secret. "I'll tell you tomorrow," she replies. "And if you've got anything that needs altering, bring it along. I can give you a twenty percent discount."

She smiles, just once, and then she walks away.

6 P.M.

Josie works part-time: midday to five thirty, four days a week. She's worked at Stitch for nearly ten years, ever since it originally opened. It was her first-ever job, at the age of thirty-five. She'd always made clothes for the girls when they were little, and given that she left school at sixteen with virtually no exams and then spent the next ten years looking after her husband and raising children, she didn't have many skills to draw on when she finally decided it was time for her to do something outside the house. She could have worked with children—in a school, maybe. But she's not great with people and this job is not public-facing. She sits behind her sewing machine next to a huge sash window which overlooks the tube tracks and rattles in its frame every time a train goes past. She chats with the other women occasionally, but mainly she listens to Heart FM on her earphones. She spent the whole of today sewing large fake-fur beards onto printed images of a groom's face on twenty stag night T-shirts. They were all off to Riga apparently. But usually it's just hems and waistbands.

Walter is sitting at the dining table in the window when she gets home, staring at the laptop. He turns and hits her with a single smile when he hears her. "Hello," he says. "How was work?"

"Work was fine." She thinks about telling him about the fake-fur beards but decides that, really, it would lose in the telling.

"How was your day?" she replies, scooping the dog into her arms and kissing his head.

"Quiet. Did some research into the Lake District."

"Oh, that's nice. Find anything good?"

"Not really. Everything seems so expensive. Feels like one big rip-off."

"Well, remember, I've had my windfall. We could probably stretch it a bit further this year."

"It's not about whether we can afford it," he says. "Don't like feeling ripped off."

Josie nods and puts the dog back on the floor. Half the reason the dog is not a real Pomchi is that Walter refused to pay the going rate for a real Pomchi and was determined he could get a bargain. She'd just gone along with it.

"What shall we have for dinner?" she says. "There's loads in the fridge. Some of those ready-made meatballs. I could make a pasta?"

"Yeah. That'd be great. Put some chili in it. I fancy something spicy."

Josie smiles. "I'm just going to get changed first," she says. "Then I'll start."

She walks past Erin's room to get to hers. The door is shut as it always is. She can hear the squeak of the gaming chair in Erin's room, the expensive one they bought her for her sixteenth birthday that's held together with duct tape these days. Walter puts WD-40 on the base every few months, but it still squeaks when she moves. Josie can hear the click of the buttons on the controller and the muted sound effects leaking from Erin's headphones. She thinks about knocking on Erin's door, saying hi, but she can't face it. She really can't face it. The stench in there. The mess. She'll check in on her tomorrow. Leave her to it for now. She touches the door with her fingertips and keeps walking. She acknowledges the guilt and lets it pass away like a cloud.

But as soon as the guilt about Erin passes, her concern about Roxy turns up; they always come in a pair. She picks up the photo of Erin and Roxy that sits on top of the chest of drawers in her bedroom, taken when they were about three and five. Fat cheeks, long eyelashes, cheeky smiles, colorful clothes.

Who would have guessed? she thinks to herself. Who would ever have guessed?

And then she thinks of Alix Summer's children this morning in their Parkside Primary uniforms: the girl on a snazzy scooter, the boy scuffing his feet against the pavement, their smooth skin, and their hair that she knows without going anywhere near them will smell of clean pillowcases and children's shampoo. Young children don't exude smells. That happens later. The shock of scalpy hair, of acrid armpits, cheesy feet. And that's just the beginning of it. She sighs at the thought of the sweet children she once had and resets the photo on the chest.

She changes and washes her hands, heads back to the kitchen, opens the fridge, takes the meatballs from the fridge, a can of chopped tomatoes and some dried herbs from the cupboard, chops an onion, watches Walter tapping at the buttons on his laptop in the window, sees a bus pass by, registers the faces of the passengers on board, thinks about Roxy, thinks about Erin, thinks about the way her life has turned out.

When the meatballs are simmering in their tomato sauce, she covers the pan and opens another cupboard. She pulls out six jars of baby food; they're the bigger jars for seven-month-plus babies. They're mainly meat-and-vegetable blends. But no peas. Erin will not countenance peas. Josie takes off the lids and microwaves them. When they're warm, but not hot—Erin will not eat hot food—she stirs them through and places them on a tray with a teaspoon and a piece of paper towel. She takes a chocolate Aero mousse from the fridge and adds that to the tray; then she takes the tray to the hallway and leaves it outside Erin's room. She doesn't knock. Erin won't hear. But at some point between Josie leaving the food and Josie going to bed tonight the baby-food jars will reappear empty outside Erin's room.

Another bus passes by. It's empty. Walter closes his laptop and gets to his feet. "I'll take the dog out, before we eat?"

"Oh! That's OK, I can do that."

"No. It's good for me. Fresh air. Exercise."

"But are you all right picking up after him?"

"Just kick it in the gutter."

"You can't do that, Walter."

"Course I can. His shits are like rabbit droppings anyway."

"Please pick it up," she beseeches. "It's not nice leaving it there."

"I'll see," he says, taking the dog's lead from Josie's outstretched hand. "I'll see."

She watches them leave, from the front window. Fred stops to sniff the base of a tree and Walter pulls him along impatiently, his eyes on his phone. Josie wishes she the one walking Fred instead. Dogs need to sniff things. It's important.

She stirs the meatballs on the hob and then adds a few flakes of dried chili. She pours water into a pot and puts it on to boil. She turns on her phone and goes to the browser and types in "Roxy Fair." Then she goes into "Tools" and sets the timings to "Past week" so that she only sees the most recent results. She does this twice a day, every day. Every time there is nothing. Roxy has most probably changed her name by now, she knows that. But still, you can't stop looking. You can't just give up.

At 8 p.m. Walter returns with the dog.

"Did he poo?"

"No."

"Are you sure?"

"Very sure."

He's lying, but Josie isn't going to push it.

They eat their spaghetti and meatballs in front of the TV. Walter makes out it's really spicy and knocks back his pint of water theatrically and Josie laughs indulgently. They get up to go to bed at ten o'clock. The empty baby-food jars are outside Erin's room. Josie takes them to the kitchen and rinses them for the recycling. Walter is brushing his teeth in the bathroom, naked from the waist up. He looks like an old man from behind. It's easy to forget what he once was. Josie gets into her pajamas and waits for Walter to finish in the bathroom, then she goes in and brushes her teeth, brushes her hair, washes her face, smooths cream into her skin and onto her hands. In bed she picks up her book, opens it, and reads for a while.

At 11 p.m. she turns off her bedside light and says good night to Walter.

She closes her eyes and pretends to sleep.

So does Walter.

After half an hour she feels him leave the bed. She hears his feet soft against the carpet. Then the creak of the floorboards in the hallway. Then he is gone, and she stretches out across the empty bed, knowing that it is hers for the rest of the night.

Hi! I'm Your Birthday Twin!
A NETFLIX ORIGINAL SERIES

The screen shows an empty floral armchair in a large open-plan studio.

From the side of the screen a young woman appears.

She wears green dungarees over a cropped black vest top and has tattooed sleeves on her arms.
She sits on the armchair, crosses her legs, and smiles at the camera.
The text at the bottom of the screen says:

Amy Jackson, Josie and Walter Fair's neighbor

Amy, laughing: "We called her Double Denim."

Interviewer, off-screen: "And why was that?"

Amy: "Because everything she wore was denim. Literally. Everything."

Screen switches briefly to a photo of Josie Fair in a denim skirt and jacket.

Interviewer: "When did you move into the flat next door to Josie and Walter Fair?"

Amy: "I suppose it was late 2008. The same year I had my first baby."

Interviewer: "And what did you think about Josie and Walter, as neighbors?"

Amy: "We thought they were really kind of weird. I mean, he was OK. We thought he was her dad, when we first moved in. He always nodded and said hello if we passed him in the hallway. But she was really unfriendly, acted like she was a bit better than anyone? But then sometimes I wondered if maybe she was just being standoffish because she was trying to keep people out of her business, you know? If maybe there was stuff going on, behind closed doors."

Interviewer: "Did you ever meet their daughters?"

Amy: "Yes. When we first moved in we used to see both the girls quite a lot. I guess Erin was about twelve; Roxy must have been about nine, ten? It was a loud household. A lot of shouting. A lot of slammed doors. And then one day, I guess about five or six years ago, it suddenly went really quiet. And we never really knew why. Until all this happened."

Interviewer: "All this?"

Brief pause.

Amy: "Yes. All this. All the killings. All the deaths."

Screen fades to black.

TUESDAY, 18 JUNE

S titch is a lovely, bright place, formed inside the skeleton of what was once a Victorian haberdashery. It still has the original curved bow windows at the front and a huge sash window at the back overlooking the tube tracks. In between are six sewing machines in two rows. Alix spots Josie at the machine nearest the back. She has earphones in, and her hair is tied back into a low ponytail. Alix takes her canvas bag to the desk and smiles.

"Hi," she says, "is Josie in today?"

The woman calls over her shoulder to Josie, who looks up and then pulls out her earphones and smiles widely when she sees Alix. She holds up a finger and mouths "Just one minute" and then finishes what she's doing.

"Hi, Alix," she says, brushing bits of thread and lint off her jeans, "you came!"

"Yes! You reminded me that I had things I've been meaning to get altered since literally before I had children."

She opens the bag and shows Josie two dresses, one of them a maxi dress with straps that are too long, another a maternity dress she's always wished she could still wear because the print is so pretty.

"You'll need to put this one on," Josie says, holding out the maxi dress. "So we can see how far to take the straps up. Here." She pulls back the curtain on a changing cubicle. "I'll just be out here, when you're ready."

Alix takes the dress from Josie and steps into the cubicle, slips out of her summer dress, and puts on the maxi dress. It's odd to feel Josie's hands against the skin on her shoulders and her upper arms as she fiddles with the straps. "Strange cut," she says. "Given that you're already quite tall. You'd think the straps would be perfect on you. Can't imagine anyone shorter standing a chance with this dress. It's like they think all women are meant to be built like giraffes."

She slides pins into the fabric and then stands back and smiles. "That OK?" she asks, turning Alix toward the mirror.

Alix nods. "Perfect."

Then Alix changes into the maternity dress and she and Josie chat about pregnancy as she pins the waist into shape. Her hands are fluttery around Alix's midriff, and she smells like dust overlaid with body spray.

Alix redresses and waits while Josie rings the work through the till, applies the 20 percent discount with a flourish, and presents her with the bill. "So," Alix says. "What was it you wanted to talk to me about?"

Josie glances quickly about herself, checking that nobody is listening in, and then says, "I saw that you're a podcaster. I mean, I heard you saying your name in the Lansdowne that night and thought it sounded familiar so I googled you and realized why I'd heard of you. I'm not like a stalker or anything. And I listened to some of your podcasts. So inspiring. Those women! I mean, the things they've been through. It's just incredible. And I . . ." She pauses and checks around herself again. "I hope this doesn't sound strange, but I wondered, have you ever thought about doing a podcast about someone who's about to change their life, rather than someone who already has?"

"Oh!" says Alix, in surprise. "No. No I haven't. But I could see how that could be interesting."

"Yes. That's what I thought. You could follow someone's progress as they break through their barriers and achieve their goals. As they're doing it."

"Yes. Absolutely. But I suppose the problem is that people often don't realize that their lives are changing for the better until after the event, when they stop to look back."

Josie frowns. "I'm not sure that's true. Because listen, it's happening to me. It's happening to me, right now. I've been living the same life for thirty years. Thirty years. Been with my husband since I was fifteen years old. Nothing has ever changed. I have worn the same clothes, had the same hairstyle, had the same conversations at the same times, sat on the same side of the same sofa every single night of my life for thirty years. And the things . . ." She pauses and Alix sees a red flush pass from her collarbones up to her neck and cheeks. "The things that have happened to me. Bad things, Alix. Really bad things. My marriage . . ."

She pauses, takes a breath. "My husband is . . . He's very complicated. And our family life has been quite traumatic at times and I just . . . I don't know, listening to your podcasts, those amazing women—I'm forty-five, if I don't break free of the past now, then when will I? It's time. It's time for me to change everything and I'm not asking you to help me, Alix, I just want you to . . ." She stops as she tries to find the right words.

"You want me to tell your story?"

"Yes! That's exactly what I want. Because I know I look quite ordinary, but my story is extraordinary and it deserves to be heard. What do you think?"

Alix is silent for a moment, not sure how to respond. Her instincts tell her very strongly to walk away, but she came here for a reason. She came here because the journalist inside her couldn't resist the tantalizing essence of the words "There's something I'd like to talk to you about." She wanted to hear what Josie was going to tell her. And now she's heard that Josie has an extraordinary story to share, and even though Alix is slightly repelled by Josie's intensity, she is also sickeningly drawn to the idea of finding out what it is.

"I think," she says, "that it sounds like a very interesting idea indeed. What are you doing tomorrow?"

———————

Alix walks home through the back streets between Kilburn High Road and Queen's Park. The June breeze is cool, and she walks on the sunny side of the street. She has two hours before she has to collect the children from school, and she can't face going back to work on the edits for the final podcast of the *All Woman* series. She's bored of listening to women who made good decisions and ended up exactly where they wanted to be and feels strongly and sharply that what she wants right now, as dark clouds begin to gather across the light in her own life, is to bear witness to the dark truth of another woman's marriage. Alix feels the buzz of anticipation build inside her. She's been doing the same thing for so long. The thought of doing something completely different is stimulating.

She takes a detour to the boutique on Salusbury Road and spends an hour leafing through clothes she doesn't need before leaving with a pair of forest-green-framed sunglasses that she also doesn't need. She goes to a delicatessen and buys expensive antipasti to eat in the garden tonight so that she doesn't have to cook. She buys brownies from Gail's and a cactus plant from the trendy florist's. The money she spends is Nathan's money; Nathan's money that he earns selling leases on glamorous high-rise office space in various corners of the city. He works so hard. He earns so well. He's so generous. He never looks at bank statements or makes snidey comments about clusters of designer carrier bags. His money, he always tells her, is her money. The money she earns is also her money, but he doesn't expect her to contribute to family expenses, and as she thinks about these things, she feels the pros and cons list in her head start to shift a little, swinging back toward the pros. The memory of the empty bed on Sunday morning starts to fade away. The thought of him unconscious on a hotel bed diminishes. The hum of low-level anger and resentment mutes. She will open wine tonight. They will eat the expensive food on the terrace and sit and marvel at the way the midsummer sky is still light at ten and let the children stay up past their bedtimes and listen to music on Spotify and have the sort of night that people expect someone like her to have.

WEDNESDAY, 19 JUNE

Josie stares at herself in the mirror the next morning. Her skin looks nice; it's hereditary, nothing to do with expensive creams or treatments. Her hair needs a trim; it's far too long and splitting at the ends. She unzips her denim makeup bag and takes out a tube of mascara. She never normally wears makeup to walk the dog, but then, she never normally meets a famous podcaster halfway through walking the dog. She colors her face with bronzer using a huge fluffy brush and puts on some tinted lip balm. Then she pulls on her favorite dress; it's made of denim and buttons up the front to a shirt collar and ties up at the waist with a matching belt. She wears it with her denim Vans and appraises herself in the full-length mirror.

Walter is in the window overlooking the street, staring at his laptop. She tries to avoid his gaze as he will wonder about the makeup and the smart dress, and she doesn't want to tell him about the meeting with Alix until it has happened and she knows what it means.

She stands in the hallway and puts the dog's harness on. "Taking Fred out now," she calls out. "See you in an hour or so."

Walter nods and says, "See you soon."

She turns to leave and pauses for a moment outside Erin's room. Erin will be sleeping now; she sleeps late, until at least lunchtime. She could open the door a crack, just grab a glimpse of her baby, but she knows what else lies on the other side of that door and she doesn't have the stomach for it. Not now. Maybe later.

Halfway to Salusbury Road, Fred starts dawdling so she picks him up and tucks him into his dog carrier. She loves the feeling of having him there, close to her chest; it reminds her of carrying her babies in slings—BabyBjörns they were called. Walter had thought they were for hippies, sneered at her clipping the babies into them, said, "What's wrong with a pushchair? Worked fine for my other two."

She spots Alix immediately, by the beacon of her white-blond hair and angular face and shoulders. She waves and Alix waves back and then they do a kissing thing that takes Josie by surprise as she never really kisses anyone. She follows Alix to one of the trendy coffee shops on Salusbury Road, the ones she walks past all the time and never stops at, and she tries to insist on buying the drinks but Alix won't let her, says it's a business expense, which makes Josie get goose bumps.

"So," says Alix a moment later, pushing her coffee cup to one side and sliding an iPad across in its place. "I've been thinking a lot about your idea. And at first, I wasn't sure. You've listened to my podcasts, so you know the format. They are fully fledged stories with a beginning, middle, and end, which means that even before I start recording, I know what the format will be. I've done it twenty, thirty times and I know what I'm doing, I know how to get the story onto tape and how to edit it to make it gripping for the listener. But this would be very different. I have no idea how your story is going to end, but you're promising me it will be worth following and so I'm already kind of hooked. I want to know too. And if I want to know, then maybe my listeners will want to know. So I think we could give this a bash, you know. It won't be for my *All Woman* series, that's finished now. This will be something completely new and different, a one-off. The interviews would be mainly studio-based but I'd also love to talk to you in various locations that tie in with your story—where you were brought up, where you went to school, where you met your husband, all that kind of thing. And then we can take it forward into the traumas you mentioned, and what you're going to do next to escape the trap you've found yourself in. I thought I might call it *Hi! I'm Your Birthday Twin!* I don't know if you remember but those were your first words to me in the ladies at the Lansdowne. I feel like it signifies the beginning of a journey that could go in absolutely any direction. The very first moment of me colliding with you. The spark, if you like? How does that sound?"

Josie realizes she has stopped breathing and moving. Her teaspoon is still suspended over her Americano, the sugar she'd added still unstirred at the bottom of the cup. She stares at Alix and nods. "Yes. It sounds good."

Alix smiles. "Great!" she says. "It would mean spending a fair bit of time together, but you work part-time and your children are fully grown. So maybe you'd be able to squeeze it in. An hour or two, here and there?"

"Yes," says Josie. "Yes. Definitely. Where do you do it? Where do you record?"

"At my house. I have a studio." Alix's fingertips clutch her golden bee pendant and slide it back and forth along the chain. "We could make a test episode. Just you and me chatting for an hour, in my studio. I'll edit it and get something back for you to listen to, no obligation, you'd be totally free to walk away from it if you don't like how it sounds. I promise."

Josie thinks of Alix's eight thousand followers on Instagram. In

her mind's eye she sees a sea of white-blond women with broad shoulders and oversize sunglasses all listening to her through expensive
AirPods as they cook healthy dinners for their red-haired children in
open-plan kitchens. She shakes her head slightly to dislodge it. It's too
much. Instead, she zooms in on the central pinprick notion of sitting
in Alix's studio for an hour, just the two of them, talking. She has so
much she needs to share.

She picks up her coffee cup and takes a sip, then carefully places it
back in the saucer. "I suppose we could give it a bash," she says. "We
could at least try."

Walter is in the kitchen when she gets back from coffee with Alix.
He's making tea and offers to make her one too and she says, "No
thanks, I just had a coffee."

He raises an eyebrow at her. "Oh yeah? On your own?"

"No!" she says, taking Fred out of his carrier and putting him
down on the floor. "No. I—" She freezes. She can't. He would be
horrified. He would talk her out of it. "I bumped into a mum from
Erin and Roxy's old primary school. We just had a quick catch-up."

She turns away but recovers herself quickly. It wasn't even a lie.
It was true.

"Nice?"

"Yes. Very nice. We might meet up again."

She knows he won't ask anything else. Walter didn't really have
much to do with the girls' schooling, especially after all that business
with the social services when Erin was in year six.

"I'm going to get ready for work," she says, hanging Fred's harness back on the coat rack. Walter nods and then does a double
take as he comes out from behind the kitchen counter with his tea.
"You look all dressed up," he says, gesturing at her button-down
dress.

She looks down at her dress. "Yes," she says. "All my other summer stuff needs a wash. And I thought, why not?"

"You look lovely," he says, nodding approvingly. "Very slim."

"Thank you," she says, touching her stomach. "Just a flattering cut, I suppose."

He appraises her once more and nods. "Lovely."

He smiles, but there's no warmth in his voice.

THURSDAY,
20 JUNE

lix's studio is at the bottom of the garden. It was Nathan's fortieth birthday present for her, in recognition of how well her newly launched podcast was doing. He'd sent her away on a girls' weekend, had it all professionally fitted, then wrapped the shed in an oversize ribbon and guided her to it blindfolded on her return. Is it any wonder that Alix is so torn about her marriage, when her husband is capable of such acts of generosity and affection, whilst also capable of making her want to die?

She switches on the power for the Nespresso machine at the wall and places a vase of flowers on the desk. At ten o'clock the doorbell rings and Josie is on her doorstep with her little dog in a shoulder bag.

"I hope it's OK to bring Fred," says Josie. "I should have checked."

"No problem at all," Alix replies. "I have a cat but as long as he's in the studio with us, she won't bother him. Come on through."

"Your house is beautiful," says Josie as she follows Alix through the open-plan kitchen at the back of the house and out into the garden.

"Thank you so much."

"My house was probably beautiful once. It's one of those big stucco villas. You know. But the council chopped them into flats in the seventies and now they're ugly."

Alix smiles and says, "So sad. London's full of places like that."

Josie oohs and aahs about Alix's studio, runs her hands over the gleaming recording equipment, pats the fat foam head of the microphone. "Will I be talking into that?" she says.

"Yes."

Josie nods, her eyes wide.

She lets the little dog out of its carrier and it trots around, sniffing everything.

Alix makes Josie a cup of tea and herself an espresso. They pull on their headphones and face each other across the recording desk. Alix does a test run with Josie, asks her the standard question about what she had for breakfast, and then they begin.

"Josie, first of all, hello and thank you so much for giving me your time so generously. I cannot tell you how excited I am to start this project. For listeners coming across from my regular podcast series, *All Woman*, welcome and thank you for taking a punt on me doing something new. For new listeners who've come upon this podcast from some other angle, welcome. So, let's kick off with an easy question, Josie. Your name. What is it short for? If it is in fact short for anything?"

Josie shakes her head. "No," she says. "No. Just Josie. Not short for anything."

"Named after anyone?"

"No. Not that I know of. My mum is called Pat. Her mum was called Sue. I think she just wanted to give me a pretty name, you know. Something feminine."

"So, just to set up the premise for everyone, the story behind the title of this podcast, *Hi! I'm Your Birthday Twin!*, is that those were Josie's first words to me when we met in our local pub the night we both turned forty-five. Josie and I are not just birthday twins but were born in the same hospital too. And now we live less than a mile apart in the same corner of northwest London. So, before we get into your life story, let's talk about your birth story. What did your mum tell you about the day you were born?"

Josie blinks. There's a ponderous silence that Alix already knows she might need to edit out. "Well," she says, eventually. "Nothing much really. Just that it hurt!"

Alix laughs. "Well," she says, "yes. That's a given. But what did she tell you about the day itself: the weather, the midwife, the first time she saw you?"

There follows another silence. "Like I said. Nothing. She never said anything. Just that it hurt so much she knew she'd never do it again."

"And she didn't?"

"No, she didn't."

"So, no siblings?"

"No siblings. Just me. What about you? Oh." Josie stops and puts her hand against her heart. "Sorry. Am I allowed to ask you questions?"

"Yes! Absolutely! And I am one of three girls. The middle."

"Oh, lucky you. I'd've loved a sister."

"Sisters are the best. I'm very lucky. And tell me about your mum, Pat. Is she still around?"

"Oh God, yes. Very much so. She lives on the same council estate where I was born, runs the community center, looks after the old people, shouts at the politicians, works with the anti-gang unit, all of that. Larger than life. Louder than life. Everyone knows her. It's like she's famous."

"What about your father?"

"Oh, he was never in the picture, my dad. My mum got pregnant by accident and then went off and had me without even telling him. I've never met him."

Alix shuts her eyes and mentally loops back to the man in the pub on her birthday who she had assumed to be Josie's father. "So, in the pub, on the night we met—the man you were dining with. That was your . . . ?"

"That was my husband. Yes. Not my father. And no, you are not the first person to make that mistake. My husband is a lot older than me. I've been with him since I was fifteen." Josie pauses and glances up at Alix.

Alix tries to hide her surprise. "Fifteen," she repeats. "And he was . . . ?"

"Forty-two."

Alix falls silent for a moment. "Wow. That's . . ."

"Yes. I know. I know how it seems. But it didn't quite feel like it sounds at the time. It's hard to explain." Josie purses her lips and shrugs. "There's power in being a teenager. I miss that power in some ways. I would like it back."

"In what way was there power?"

Josie shrugs again. "Just in the way that you have something a lot of people want. A lot of *men* want. And a lot of them want it. They want it so much."

"It? You mean youth?"

"Yes. That's exactly what I mean. And when you meet someone who is very *clear* about what they want and you know that the only thing that stands between what they want and what you have is your consent . . . Sometimes, as a very young girl, there's a power in giving that consent. Or at least, that's how it felt at the time. That's how *they* make you feel. But really, it's not, is it? I can see that now. I can see that maybe I was being used, that maybe I was even being groomed?

But that feeling of being powerful, right at the start, when I was still in control. I miss that sometimes. I really do. And what I'd like, more than anything, is to get it back."

Alix leaves a brief silence to play out, to allow Josie's words the space they need to hit home to her listeners. She maintains her composure, but under the surface her blood races with shock. "And you and Walter, how did you meet?"

"He was a contractor, doing the electricals on our estate. He was the project leader and my mum, of course, made it her business to get involved with it all, so one day, when I was about thirteen, I was sitting in my room and the doorbell rang, and I looked out and he was standing there. Had his high-vis vest on, holding his hard hat in his hand. That was the first time I saw him."

Alix says, "And what did you think?"

Josie issues a small laugh. "I was thirteen. He was forty. There wasn't much more to think really. It wasn't until my fourteenth birthday that I could tell there was something else going on. He walked into the house when I was blowing out the candles on my birthday cake. I was there with my best friend, Helen. And my mum invited him to stay for a slice of cake and he sat next to me and it was . . ." Josie exhales and makes a sound like she's been punched in the throat. "It was just there. Like an invisible monster in the room."

"A monster?"

"Yes. That's what it felt like. His interest in me. It felt like a monster."

"So, you were scared of him?"

"Not of him. No. He was nice. I was scared of his wanting me. I couldn't believe that nobody else could see it. Only me. It was so big and so real. But my mother didn't see it. Helen didn't see it. But I saw it. And I was scared of it."

"So, it didn't feel like power then?"

"Well, no. And yes. It felt like both things at the same time. It was confusing. I became obsessed with the idea of him. But it was another year until anything happened."

Hi! I'm Your Birthday Twin!
A NETFLIX ORIGINAL SERIES

The screen opens with a woman pulling a small suitcase through an airport. She is tall and heavily built, with her dark hair pulled back into a small bun.
The next shot shows her sitting in a café, with a cappuccino on the table in front of her.
The text beneath her reads:

Helen Lloyd, Josie Fair's schoolfriend

Helen starts to speak.

"Josie and me were best friends. From when we were about five years old. From primary school."

Helen pauses.

There is a short silence.

Then she says: "She was always a bit odd. Controlling? She didn't like it when I had other friends. She always wanted to make things about her. 'Passive aggressive' is the term these days. She would never just come straight out and tell you what was bothering her. She made you go all around the houses to get to it. She was a sulker too. The silent treatment. We'd already started to grow out of each other when she met Walter."

The interviewer asks a question off-mic: "So what was that like, when she met Walter?"

"Weird. I mean, he was an old man, virtually. And that was that. From her fourteenth birthday, she just disappeared. Into this *other world*. With an old man."

The interviewer interjects: "Would you say Walter Fair groomed Josie?"

"Well, yes. Obviously. But . . ."

Helen's eyes go to the interviewer. She touches the rim of her coffee cup.

"As bad as it sounds. As weird as it sounds. It was a two-way street, you know? She wanted him. She wanted him, and she made him want her."

11 A.M.

Josie walks home from Alix's house an hour later. Her head spins with all of it.

She thinks of Alix's home: from the front, a neat, terraced house with a bay window, no different to any other London Victorian terraced house, but inside a different story. A magazine house, ink-blue walls and golden lights and a kitchen that appeared weirdly to be bigger than the whole house with stone-gray cabinets and creamy marble counters and a tap that exuded boiling water at the touch of a button. A wall at one end reserved purely for the children's art!

She remembers pinning the girls' artwork to the fridge with magnets and Walter tutting and taking it down because it looked messy.

Then the garden with its fairy lights and winding path and the magical shed at the bottom that contained yet another world of wonder. Even the cat; a cat unlike any she'd seen before. A Siberian, apparently. Tiny and fluffy with the huge green eyes of a cartoon Disney princess.

Her hand goes to the inside pocket of her handbag, where she touches the smooth skin of the Nespresso pod she'd taken when Alix wasn't looking. There was a huge jar of them on the shelf behind the recording desk, all different colors, like oversize gemstones. She doesn't have a Nespresso machine at home, but she just wanted to own a little bit of Alix's glamour, tuck it into a drawer in her shabby flat, know it was there.

Walter is at his laptop in the window when she gets home. He looks at her curiously, his eyes huge through the strong prescription of his reading glasses. She'd told him she was seeing the school mum again. He'd raised an eyebrow but not said anything. Now he says, "What's really going on?"

A spurt of adrenaline shoots through her.

"What do you mean?"

"I mean," he says, "you've been gone ages. You can't have been drinking coffee all this time."

"No," she says. "I went to see my gran after. At the cemetery." A preplanned fib.

"What for?"

"I dunno. I just had a really weird dream last night about her and it made me want to go and see her. Anyway, I need to get ready for work. I'll be back in a tick."

She walks toward her bedroom, hears the sound of Erin's gaming chair, through her bedroom door, *squeak squeak*, notices that the smell from Erin's room is starting to drift out into the hallway now. She can't put it off for much longer. But not now. Not today. Tomorrow, definitely.

She touches Erin's door with her fingertips as she passes, then kisses them.

In her bedroom she picks up the photograph of her small girls from the top of the chest of drawers and kisses that too.

Then she takes the Nespresso pod from inside her handbag and tucks it into her underwear drawer, right at the very back.

Hi! I'm Your Birthday Twin!
A NETFLIX ORIGINAL SERIES

The screen shows a leather chair in an empty City pub.
Muted light shines through a dusty window.
A man walks in and sits down. He wears a white shirt and jeans. He smiles.
The text on-screen reads:

Jason Fair, Walter Fair's son

He starts to talk; he has a Canadian accent.

"The last time I saw Dad? I guess when I was about ten?"

The interviewer interjects off-mic: "And why is that?"

Jason: "Because he left my mum for a teenager and my mum was so disgusted that she emigrated us out of the country."

Interviewer: "And that teenager was . . . ?"

"That teenager was Josie Fair. Yes."

Jason shakes his head sadly and drops his gaze to the floor.

When he looks up at the camera again, he is seen to be crying.

"Sorry. Sorry. Could we just . . ."

The screen fades to black.

8 P.M.

Nathan doesn't come home from work that night. Alix feels the dreadful inevitability of it in her gut from the minute the clock ticks over from 8 p.m. to 8:01 p.m. He said he'd be home at seven. Even accounting for last-minute delays or phone calls or problems on the tube, eight o'clock marks the cut-off point for explainable lateness and tips it into something darker. She texts him. He doesn't answer. At eight thirty she calls him. It goes to voicemail. And she knows. Alix knows.

When the children are in bed at nine, Alix takes a glass of wine into the studio and listens back to her interview with Josie from that morning.

They had talked for over an hour, but hearing it now, Alix suspects that the whole conversation will be edited down to about ten minutes. And those ten minutes will be the ones that Josie had spent talking about how she met her husband.

Alix had been barely able to breathe. She'd merely nodded, her eyes wide, not interjected with questions, just listened and absorbed.

A fourteen-year-old girl.

A forty-one-year-old man.

Alix thinks of the man she'd barely noticed in the restaurant on

Saturday night, the man she had assumed to be Josie's father: non-descript, balding, faded, bespectacled.

They'd stopped recording before Alix had been able to uncover more about what had happened after the birthday-cake moment on Josie's fourteenth birthday, what had led to Josie and Walter becoming a couple. They will discuss that at their next meeting. But the tiny prickle of excitement that she's been feeling since the first moment she decided to make a show about Josie is growing by the minute. She can sense something bigger than her here, something dark and brilliant, with every fiber of her being.

———————

Back indoors, Alix looks at her empty wineglass and considers for a moment the possibility of topping it up. But no, it is gone ten o'clock and she is tired, and she wants a clear head tomorrow when she wakes up in what she already knows will be an empty bed and has to deal with the aftermath of Nathan's latest bender so soon after the last, and this one on a school night. Her message to him remains unread and her final attempt to call him goes through to voicemail again. She feels adrenaline pulsing through her and she knows she won't sleep, but she goes to bed anyway. She tries to read a book, but her heart races. She scrolls through the news on her phone, but it swims in front of her eyes, and she feels suddenly, strangely, that she wants to talk to Josie, Josie with her waxy skin and haunting voice and her dark, dark eyes, Josie who doesn't know Nathan, who didn't dance at their wedding, who has no investment in the mythical mirage of their marriage.

She sends her a message:

It was lovely talking to you earlier. Thank you so much for your time. I just listened to the recording, and I can see how this is going to take shape and I'd really like to continue

*with the project if you're happy to do so? Maybe next time
we could visit the estate where you grew up, where you first
met Walter. What do you think?*

She presses send and stares for a few minutes at her phone, looking for a sign that Josie has seen it, that she is replying. But ten minutes pass and there is nothing. She finally turns off her screen and lies herself flat, tries to lull herself into a sleep that she knows will not come for many hours.

10 P.M.

Josie rests her open book against her chest and looks at the message on her phone screen.

It's from Alix. The sight of her words on her screen sparks something inside Josie. A kind of childish delight. Something like a crush. She opens it and reads it in a rush and then again more slowly. She pictures herself on her Kilburn estate with Alix and she feels a shiver of delight. She could introduce her to her mum, watch her mother's face as it dawns on her that someone like Alix is interested in her daughter. She could picture the confusion followed by, yes, no doubt, a flicker of jealousy. She would think that Alix should be making a podcast about *her*, the legendary Pat O'Neill. And no doubt Alix would have questions for her mother, but they would be questions related only to Josie, questions to help Alix find out more about Josie, not more about Pat. Her stomach flips, pleasantly. She doesn't reply immediately, but goes instead to her browser and googles Alix Summer, spends half an hour flicking through photos of Alix, looks at her Twitter feed, at her Facebook page, which is set to private but has a couple of posts visible, at her Instagram feed. She reads listeners' reviews of Alix's podcasts and sees photos of her at award ceremonies in swirling satin dresses. When Josie has had her fill of Alix Summer, she returns to the message but realizes that it is gone eleven, that it is too late to politely reply. She sighs, turns off her screen, and picks up her book.

From somewhere else in the flat she hears the muted sounds of her husband's voice. She tucks in her earplugs and turns the page of her book.

FRIDAY, 21 JUNE

Nathan finally replies to Alix's message at 6 a.m. She hears her phone buzz on the bedside table, yanks down her sleep mask, grabs her phone, and squints at it.

Fuck. Sorry. Don't know what happened. At Giovanni's. Blacked out. Please don't kill me.

She lets the phone fall back onto the bedside table and tugs her mask back down over her eyes. She has thirty minutes before her alarm goes off—she's not wasting it. She didn't get to sleep until after two in the end and her head is thick with tiredness and despair. She tries to claw back the stolen half hour, but her adrenaline is pumping again; her husband went somewhere last night and has woken up in his friend's flat and doesn't know what happened in between. Her husband, who has a career and a mortgage and two children to think about. Her husband, who is forty-five.

A second later her phone buzzes again. She groans and picks it up.

On my way home now. Please don't hate me. I love you. I'm sorry. I'm a dick.

Once again she puts the phone down and pulls her sleep mask over her eyes. But now there is even more adrenaline pumping through her. She is enraged. *Please don't hate me.* Like a whiny little boy.

She gives up on salvaging the last half hour of sleep and sits up in bed. She stares for a moment at the messages on her phone and wonders what to do. She decides not to reply, not yet, not until her rage has subsided. But a moment later her phone buzzes again and it's him with a plaintive: *Alix???*

Her hands shake slightly with rage as she presses call on his number.

"Hi." His voice is small, and it makes her even angrier.

"I didn't get to sleep until two a.m., Nathan. Two a.m., waiting to hear from you. Wondering where the fuck you were. And then you message me at six a.m. and wake me up, and you know my alarm goes off at six thirty yet you couldn't even wait for half an hour because you're too fucking selfish. So yes, thanks a lot, Nathan. I've had four hours' sleep and now I have to get our kids up and get them ready for school and then do a full day's work and you don't even know where you've been."

"Alix, I am so sorry. It's just—"

"Fuck off, Nathan."

She turns off her phone and slams it down.

Then she gets out of bed and has an extra-long shower.

By the time she gets the children to school at 8:50, she is calm again. Nathan has messaged three more times, professing his dismay at his own behavior and promising her that it will never ever happen again. It is Friday and the weather is forecast to be beautiful this weekend and Alix is having lunch with her sisters on Sunday and she doesn't want to hold on to the terrible dark feelings that had her in their nightmarish grip all of last night and so she forces herself to let them go.

After saying goodbye to the children at the school gates she is about to turn and leave when she remembers that she has a form that needs to be handed into the school office. She goes to the side gate of the school and rings on the bell, is buzzed in a moment later.

"Hi, Alix!"

It's Mandy, the office manager.

"Hi, Mandy. This form is for the Natural History Museum trip tomorrow. I'm really sorry, it's been in my handbag for weeks and I keep forgetting to drop it in. Sorry, it's a bit scrunched up."

She passes the scruffy piece of paper across the desk toward Mandy, who smiles and says, "No problem, lovey. I have seen worse, I can assure you."

And as she says this, Alix looks at her and thinks, Mandy has been working here for twenty years; there was a celebration for her last year to mark the anniversary. The longest-serving member of staff.

"Oh, Mandy. By the way. I've just started talking to a mum whose kids used to be at this school, a long time ago. They're in their early twenties now. I wonder if you remember them?"

"Oh. Try me! I always pride myself on never forgetting any of my children."

"Roxy and Erin? Fair?"

A strange shadow passes across Mandy's face. "Oh," she says. "Yes. I remember Roxy and Erin. They were . . ."

Alix inhales and waits.

Mandy glances behind her at the door to the head teacher's office, and then from left to right, before leaning toward Alix and lowering her voice. "They were a strange family, I suppose you could say. I mean, Roxy was wild. Oppositional, you know. Turned over furniture. Threw things about. Had to suspend her a couple of times. But Erin was the sweetest thing. The total opposite to her sister. So quiet. Had some issues, possibly on the autism spectrum? But wasn't statemented as far as I can remember. And there was this one time, I think when Erin was in year six, just toward the end of her time here . . ." Mandy pauses and looks around herself again before continuing in a semi-whisper, "She came in with a broken arm. And there was all this talk about how she'd fallen out of bed and then one day she told a friend that it was Roxy."

"Roxy?"

"Yes. Her younger sister. Said that she'd done it to her. Had to get the social services involved. It was all very messy."

"And had she? The younger sister? Had she broken Erin's arm?"

"I don't think it was ever proved. But the parents were livid. There were some horrible scenes. Only time I ever met their dad. Big man. Big temper. And the mother . . ."

Alix nods, her breath held again.

"She was really very odd. Wouldn't say boo to a goose. Just stood there with this sort of blank look on her face. Let it all play out as if it was nothing to do with her, you know? And then they took Roxy out. Homeschooled her until she went to secondary school, I seem to recall."

"Which secondary school did they go to?"

"Queen's Park High, I think. But yes. Funny family. Always wondered what happened to them. And you're friends with the mother now, are you?"

"Well, I wouldn't say friends. No. Acquaintances."

"And the girls? Have you met them?"

"No. No, not at all."

"Would love to know what they're both up to now. I never had a good feeling for either of them, do you know what I mean?"

Alix nods and smiles.

SUNDAY, 23 JUNE

O n Sunday Josie makes a roast. She and Walter eat it quietly at the table in the window overlooking the street. It's the only meal of the week they eat at the table. Afterward she liquifies the leftovers with her stick blender and spoons them into a bowl for Erin. She covers it with a plate to keep Fred's snout away and puts it on a tray outside Erin's room alongside a chocolate-flavor Müller Corner and two teaspoons. She still hasn't been in there. The longer she leaves it, the harder it gets. She will go in. Next week. She will go in and clean. Walter said it's not so bad. But she doesn't know that that can be true, given the smell.

She washes up slowly and cleans the kitchen thoroughly. By three o'clock it's spotless, as if nothing ever happened. She looks at Walter and says, "Taking the dog out now. Want to come?"

She hopes he'll say no, and he does.

Sunday afternoon, and the area around Queen's Park is full of the flotsam and jetsam of other people's summer days: half-drunk plastic pints of honey-gold lager left to go warm outside pubs, crumpled picnic blankets in the park, discarded beer cans and pizza boxes overflowing from bins, melted ice-cream puddles on the pavement that she has to drag Fred away from. Other people have been out here all day, enjoying themselves, enjoying the weather, enjoying their friends and their children. Other people have been living.

At the thought of the extraordinariness of other people's lives, she finds her feet leading her subconsciously around the park and toward Alix's road.

She keeps her distance. She would be mortified, completely mortified, if Alix were to see her standing here in her scruffy leggings and her denim jacket, loitering around her house on a Sunday afternoon. But she just needs a glimmer, nothing more, of Alix's existence, and then she can return to her flat ready to deal with the long Sunday evening ahead of her.

The view through the front window is obscured by white wooden shutters. The front door is painted a milky-blue color that reminds Josie of a particular dress she had when she was small. On either side of the door is a pair of plants in matching milky-blue pots, cut into puffballs. She wonders who did that to them, or if you could buy them like that. She glances up at the two windows on the first floor: more wooden shutters. The house is a blank face. Not like her flat with its huge windows that let in the faces of all the people on the bus who can virtually see what they're eating for their dinner. After a minute or two she turns to leave, but at that moment she sees a group of women walking toward her from the other direction. They are all tall and angular and a split second later she realizes that one of them is Alix and the other two look just like her and that they must be her sisters: one has dark blond hair down to her waist; the other has strawberry-blond hair in a top knot. They are a mass of hoop earrings, big leather bags with tassels, flip-flops, black nail polish, long skirts that swish when they move, suntans from other countries. They are loud, even from here; one of them says something and the other two tip back their heads and laugh—so many teeth, such big, wide mouths. She watches as they move toward Alix's front door. She recognizes the smaller one now from the night of her birthday at the pub. Zoe. Alix removes a set of keys from inside the bag that is looped over her arm and puts one in the lock, and then there is the hallway and the cat just visible, and a child, and she hears Alix say, "We're back!" and then there is the husband, Nathan, with his thick red hair, greeting her distractedly, and they all pile in and the door closes and Josie pictures wine being pulled from the big chrome fridge and olives being tipped into bowls, a water sprinkler flip-flopping lazily over the lawn in the back garden. She pictures it and she wants it. She wants it more than anything.

Confident now that Alix and her family are all firmly ensconced inside the house, she crosses the street. She walks past Alix's house as if she is simply walking past her own house, but as she does so, she lets her fingertips trail across the climbing plant that graces Alix's front wall. She glances down and sees the remarkable purple-and-lime-green face of a passionflower staring up at her from between the leaves and her breath catches. She pulls it toward her, plucks it, and holds it in her hand the whole of the way home.

TUESDAY,
25 JUNE

Alix stands outside the housing estate where Josie was brought up. It's a low-level estate, no blocks higher than four stories, built around a playground and several winding pathways. Josie appears a moment later. She is wearing jeans and a chambray top with puffed sleeves. The dog peers out over the top of the denim dog carrier.

"Sorry I'm late," Josie says. "Couldn't get away."

Alix leans toward her with a kiss and feels the same awkwardness emanate from Josie she'd noticed the first time she'd greeted her this way.

"No problem! Not at all." Alix turns to survey the estate and says, "So, this is where you grew up?"

"It certainly is. My mum's going to meet us in the community hall. Is that OK? Then you can get yourself all set up."

"Perfect," says Alix.

She follows Josie through the estate toward a squat building at the back.

Inside, a woman with dyed brown hair and trendy black-framed glasses is pulling chairs around a table. She's wearing a bright-print summer dress and strappy sandals. She looks up at Alix and Josie and beams. "Welcome! Welcome! I got some juice in, and some pastries."

She is not what Alix was expecting. Where Josie is stiff and unanimated, her mother is all expansive hand gestures and chatter. She's glamorous too, clearly takes care of her appearance, sees herself as a woman worthy of attention and respect. She sends Josie to make them teas and coffees in the kitchenette and invites Alix to sit down.

"So," she says, eyeing her frankly. "I went and listened to some of your podcasts, when Josie told me about you. So inspiring. I would have had a career to talk to you about, but I devoted all my life to this estate. This estate has been my career, I suppose you'd say. Not that I get paid for it. I do it for love."

Alix turns slightly to look at Josie. She has her back to them, waiting for the kettle to boil.

"Of course," Pat continues, "my first question has to be—why Josie?"

"Oh!" Alix laughs nervously. She glances again at Josie's back. Josie has asked her not to mention the truth to her mother about why Josie wanted to do this. "Just tell her you're making a series about birthday twins," she suggested. "Make it sound harmless."

"Well. Why not Josie?" Alix says now. "That was really my starting point. A woman, born on the same day, in the same place as me. I guess it was a case of the 'swapped babies' scenario, but the other way round. We weren't swapped. We went home with the right parents. But what would have happened if we hadn't? What would it have been like for me if you'd taken me home? If I'd been brought up here, by you? And Josie had been brought up a mile away by my parents?"

"Nature/nurture?" says Pat.

"Well, yes, to an extent."

"You know, I studied social anthropology for a while. At Goldsmiths. But then I got pregnant." She sighs. "Had to drop out. So yes, there's another what-if scenario for you. What if I hadn't got pregnant? What if I'd finished my degree? I'd have got off this estate, wouldn't I, for a start. And then someone else would have to be here doing what I do. Except they wouldn't, would they, and then this estate would be a disgrace, like the others round here. So yeah, maybe that's it. I got pregnant for a reason; I got pregnant so that I could sacrifice my ambitions and save this estate." Pat trails off and stares dreamily into the middle distance for a minute. "Funny, when you think about it. Strange. But I guess maybe everyone has a purpose. Though some are harder to fathom than others." She directs this point toward her daughter as Josie pulls out the chair next to Alix and sits down. Alix squirms. This woman, she strongly suspects, loathes her daughter.

"So, talking of getting pregnant with Josie—and given that you gave birth to her in the same hospital and on the same day that my mother gave birth to me—what are your memories of that day?"

"Oh God. I try not to think about it. I was twenty years old. I wasn't married. I'd been in denial throughout my whole pregnancy—drinking, smoking. I know that's horribly frowned upon now, but back then it barely mattered. And I didn't look pregnant. Not until the very end. Was still wearing my size ten jeans. So I just kind of carried on. And then the contractions kicked in and I tried to pretend it wasn't happening because I wasn't ready. I really wasn't. I had so much I wanted to do. I was halfway through this essay, and I wanted to finish it. And I nearly did, even through the contractions. But then it got too much and my mum got us a taxi to St. Mary's and four hours later, the baby arrived. What happened in those four hours is not something I ever want to think about or talk about ever again."

"What time was she born?"

"God. I don't know. I suppose about eight in the morning."

"And how did you feel, when you first saw her?"

"I felt—" Pat stops. Her eyes go across the community hall and stare for a moment, blankly. "I felt terrified."

Alix feels Josie flinch slightly in the chair next to her.

"Just terrified. Didn't know what to do. Kept going on about this bloody essay. Finished it."

"You finished it?"

"Yes. Well, newborns, they just sleep, don't they? Finished it. Submitted it. Got an A. But after that . . . I suppose I just surrendered to motherhood. Let it *subsume* me. Always thought I'd go back, finish my degree. But"—she spreads her hands around the room—"here we are. And in fact, I've probably learned more about life, more about *people*, through my experiences here than I ever could have in a lifetime of studying books. So, it all worked out in the end."

Alix narrows her eyes slightly and clears her throat. "And at the hospital, that day, when Josie was born, do you remember any of the other women there? Do you remember this woman?" She pulls from her bag the photograph that she'd tucked in there last night: her mother, in a gray sweatshirt and jeans, her blond hair cut into a bob and permed, holding newborn Alix (or Alexis as she had been named by her parents) in her arms, beaming into the camera. "I'm about four days old here, just home from the hospital."

Pat glances at the photo and smiles drily. "God," she says, "Elvis Presley could have been there that day and I wouldn't remember. It's all a blur. It really is. How old's your mum there?"

"Thirty-one."

"Not young."

"No. Not young. She was building a career."

Alix sees a sour look pass across Pat's face. "Well," she says. "Nice if you can plan it that way, I guess."

Alix blinks. She wants to ask Pat why she didn't plan it that way. She was clever and had ambitions. Why did she get pregnant at twenty? Why didn't she go back to university afterward? But she doesn't. Instead, she slides the photo back into her handbag and says, "Is it OK if we take a look around the estate? You can show me where Josie was brought up, memories, et cetera."

"Finish your tea first," says Pat, and there's an edge to her intonation that makes it sound more like a command than a suggestion. Alix drinks the tea and gets to her feet. For half an hour Pat guides them around the estate and the entire half hour is a running commentary from Pat about her achievements: what she did, when she did it, how hard it was for her to do it, and how grateful other people were to her for doing it. And it is impressive, the sort of life's work that could ultimately lead to an honor from the Queen, and Alix can picture Pat in a smart two-piece suit and a slightly eccentric hat, bobbing on one knee in front of the monarch, a haughty smile on her face.

But it is clear to Alix that Pat is actually a raging narcissist, and that no child of a narcissist ever makes it out into the world unscathed. This knowledge adds nuance to her view of Josie, helps make more sense of her.

Pat leads them to her flat, where Josie lived when she was a child. It's on the ground floor, with a flower bed outside. Pat lets them in.

"Here," says Josie, opening the door into a room that is painted pink and dressed for a young girl. "This was my room. And this was where I first saw Walter, through the window."

Alix stands for a moment and absorbs the energy of the room, pictures a young Josie peering through the slats in the wooden venetian blinds that had once covered this window. Back in the kitchen she touches the top of the dining table. "Is this where you were sitting? When Walter ate your birthday cake?"

Josie smiles. "Yes. Not this table—this one is new—but yes, right here."

Alix turns to Pat. "Did you know?" she asks. "That day. Josie's fourteenth birthday. Did you know what was going to happen?"

"You mean with Josie and Walter? No, of course not. I mean, come on. He was older than me! How could I have thought? How could I have known?"

"And what did you think? When you found out? You must have felt quite shocked?"

"Well, what do you think?" Pat issues this with a note of dark fury.

Alix looks at Josie. Her face is pinched, and Alix takes a breath and stops herself from asking her next question.

8 P.M.

Nathan has been extra nice since the events of Thursday night. Not that Nathan isn't always nice. It's his default setting. But he's been getting back from work early enough to enjoy time in the garden with the kids, to help make dinner, to watch a show and look at homework and chat and be part of the family. He had no explanation for Thursday night, other than that he "lost control." He has promised that he won't do it again, and for now, bathed in the warm waters of marital harmony, Alix is choosing to believe him.

Now, as they clear the kitchen together, he says, "Oh, by the way, I'll be working from home tomorrow."

"Oh," she says. "How come?"

"Just have a ton of paperwork to catch up on and no appointments in the diary, thought I'd make the most of it. Maybe I can take you out for a cheeky lunch?"

She pauses. She hasn't yet told him about her new podcast project with Josie. But she will be here tomorrow morning at nine thirty and Alix will need to explain her to him. She says, "I've got an interviewee coming in the morning."

"Oh, OK. I thought you'd finished your series. Is this something new?"

"It is. . . . It's, well, it's kind of an experiment, I guess. It's the woman from the pub the other night, the one who was my birthday twin. I'm doing a thing about, erm, birthday twins, you know, the randomness of life, the otherness of strangers, nature/nurture, that sort of thing." Her face flushes with the white lie and she turns away from Nathan so that he can't see it.

Nathan looks at her skeptically. "Sounds . . . different."

"Yes. Exactly. Different."

"Difficult to pull off?"

"Maybe. But actually, there're a couple of compelling things going on with her already."

"What sort of compelling things?"

She draws in her breath: a husband who groomed her as a fourteen-year-old child; a narcissistic mother; two problematic children; and brushes with social services. But the compelling things feel precious somehow, half-formed and delicate, not yet ready for the judgment of her husband. "Well," she says, "you'll have to listen to the podcast to find out."

Nathan raises an eyebrow humorously. "Fair enough," he says. "Fair enough."

Alix pulls a full bag out of the bin, ties a knot in it, and takes it to the front garden. She stops after she's dropped the bag in the wheelie bin and stares into the inky summer sky, waiting for some time to pass. She doesn't want to talk about this with Nathan. Not right now. He doesn't deserve her confidences. He doesn't deserve to know every last thing she does.

Nathan has his own priorities, his own secrets. She should have some too.

WEDNESDAY, 26 JUNE

Josie is breathless by the time she arrives on Alix's doorstep the next morning. It's all she's wanted to do, the only place she's wanted to be, and she's walked extra fast to get here. She pulls a tissue from her bag and wipes the sweat from her forehead and upper lip before ringing the doorbell.

She is all primed for the soothing, beatific face of Alix Summer as the door opens, but instead, there is the husband. His features are rough and raw, the sort of man who is attractive only because of some base, elemental factors to do with chemicals and attitude. There is not one thing on his face that Josie could pick out for special mention; even his eyes are a sludgy, indefinable color. He has stubby eyelashes and a two-day beard growth that contains every shade that hair can be, from silver to red to blond. His mouth is tight and thin. He wears a sloppy T-shirt and gray joggers and peers at her curiously over the top of a pair of horn-rimmed reading glasses. He clicks his fingers and says, "Josie?"

She nods and says, "Hi. Alix is expecting me."

He lurches toward her suddenly and for a terrible moment she thinks he's going to kiss her but then she realizes he is aiming for Fred's head, poking out of the dog carrier. "Well, hello!" he says, recoiling slightly when Fred begins to growl at him. "Aren't you a feisty little dude? He? She?" He offers Fred the backs of his fingers to sniff, which he does, gingerly.

"He," says Josie. "Fred. He's a Pomchi."

"A Pomchi," says Nathan. "Well I never. Anyway, come in. Alix is just in the kitchen."

She appears from behind her husband then, her face betraying some regret that it was he who met Josie at the door, and not her. Josie smiles at her and bypasses Nathan, her arm just brushing against the cotton of his T-shirt, close enough to feel the clean heat emanating from his flesh.

They walk through the kitchen, where the cat is sitting on the kitchen island looking like a pretend cat. The dog growls quietly as they pass it.

"We'll be about an hour," Alix calls over her shoulder to Nathan, who is still loitering in the hallway.

"Okey-dokey," he calls back, distantly.

This time Josie tries to absorb every last detail of the kitchen. The fridge, she now realizes, is not chrome at all. It is hidden away inside cabinetry that matches the rest of the kitchen. There is a huge cake mixer on the counter that's the same milky blue as the front door. There's an upholstered window seat overlooking the garden scattered with cotton-covered cushions in numerous shades of ocean blue. There's a row of plastic shoes and boots lined up by the back door. The cat's food bowls are made of copper and the chairs around the kitchen table are all different shapes and sizes.

"How are you?" Alix asks her as they cross the lawn.

"Oh. I'm fine, I suppose."

"You seemed a bit . . . stressed yesterday?"

"Yes. I was a bit. My mum always makes me feel like that. I mean, I know she looks very together. I know she gives off this vibe of being a decent person, all her talk of saving the estate and everything. But believe you me, she's not what she seems at all. She was a terrible mother, Alix. A terrible, terrible mother to me."

"Actually, I could see that, Josie. And I'd like to talk about it today, if that's OK with you?"

Josie shrugs. "I suppose so. I don't really know. If you think it will be good for the podcast, then yes."

"I think it will be great for the podcast. But of course you'll get final approval before it goes to air and if there's anything you don't like, I won't put it in."

In the studio, Alix makes Josie a cup of coffee from the Nespresso machine and Josie stares at her from behind. She's wearing a long filmy top over leggings. Through the fabric, Josie can see the knuckled impression of her spine and the outline of a sports bra. "How was your weekend?" she asks her.

"Oh. Goodness. That feels like a long time ago now. But yes. It was nice. I saw my sisters on Sunday. That's always a good thing."

"What are their names?"

"Zoe and Maxine."

"Nice names. What did you do?"

"Long boozy lunch."

Long boozy lunch. The words wash through Josie like a dream. She nods and smiles and says, "That sounds good."

Alix places Josie's coffee in front of her and then sits down. She tucks her hair behind her ears and smiles at Josie. "Right," she says. "Let's get these headphones on and start, shall we? And I wanted to start where we left off last time. With Walter. And how you two became a couple."

Hi! I'm Your Birthday Twin!
A NETFLIX ORIGINAL SERIES

The screen shows Alix's empty recording studio.
The camera pans around the details of the room.
Josie's voice plays over the footage in conversation with Alix.
The text on-screen reads:

Recording from Alix Summer's podcast, 26 June, 2019

"Ah, yes. So now we're at my fifteenth birthday. Me and Walter were sort of friends, by that point. He always stopped and had a chat with me if we crossed paths on the estate. He always waved, said something nice to me. You know. And on the day I turned fifteen Walter ran after me when I was walking to school. He'd remembered my birthday from the year before and he'd bought me a present."

"What did he get you?"

"A bracelet. Look. This one."

"You're still wearing it. Wow."

"Well, why wouldn't I? We're still together."

Josie sighs heavily.

"And then my friends took me to the park after school that day, to the rec, and there was this boy, he was called Troy? I think? And Helen really wanted me to, you know, kiss him. I hadn't had a boyfriend yet and she was always trying to get me to go with a boy and I did not want to go with a boy because they were all disgusting, honestly. And he'd been drinking cider and his breath—I can smell it, even now. The sourness of it, rancid, in my face as he came toward me, and I just got up and left and as I left I knew, I knew that

I was done. Done with being that sort of teenager. I went home.

"My mum said, 'You're back early.' I told her I wasn't feeling well. She asked me if I'd been drinking. I told her about the cider and the boy and she told me I had good friends, that I should make more of an effort with them. I said, 'I do make an effort. But then they do things I don't want to do, and there's not much I can do about that.' She said, 'What do you want to do, Josie?' I said, 'I don't know. How am I supposed to know? What did you want to do when you were fifteen?' She stared at me like she couldn't believe I was anything to do with her and she said, 'I wanted to take over the whole world, Josie. That's what I wanted to do.' I said something like, 'Well, I'm not going to take over the whole world drinking cider in the rec, am I?' and she said, 'You're not going to do it sitting in here with me, either. On your birthday.' So I said, 'Fine then. Fine. I'll leave.' And I slammed the door and stormed through the estate, down to the cabin where Walter worked.

"I was just going to thank him for the bracelet, but I knew, I think, I knew what was going to happen. I felt powerful then. And he took me to the pub. I sat in a pub with a forty-two-year-old man and I was fifteen and he poured a shot of vodka into my lemonade and he kissed me and I remember looking down at my hands, at the pen scribbles on them from school, and looking down at my shoes, these battered old Kickers with the little leather tags that everyone wore back then, and thinking, This is it. I'm jumping. I'm going. I'm leaving this world. I'm entering another. It was almost as if I knew, even then, that there was no way back. That once I'd befriended the monster, that was it. For life."

MIDDAY

"Oh my God," Alix whispers to herself an hour later, after closing the front door behind Josie. She stands with her back against the door, her arms behind her. "Oh my God," she whispers again.

She closes her eyes and tries to gather herself, but her head is spinning. She'd hidden her shock when Josie was talking. Nodded furiously. Made encouraging noises of interest. Interjected with neutral questions. All the while resisting the temptation to say, *Fuck, Josie, you married a pedophile.*

She goes back to the shed to tidy up her studio, gather the cups and saucers, lock it up behind her. In the kitchen she loads the cups and saucers into the dishwasher and then she heads to the downstairs toilet, the one tucked under the stairs. After she's used the toilet, she turns on the tap to wash her hands and then stops when she realizes there's no hand wash. She looks behind her, she looks on the ledge that runs along the floor covering the water pipes, she looks inside the cupboard under the sink. She washes her hands without soap and then asks Nathan when she walks back into the kitchen, "Did you do something with the hand wash in the downstairs toilet?"

"Like what?"

"Like, move it? Get rid of it? I only put it in there a couple of days ago."

"No," he replies. "Of course not. Maybe it was your weird friend?"

Alix scowls at him. "Don't be ridiculous. It must have been one of the kids. I'm sure it'll turn up."

1 P.M.

Josie tucks the hand wash into the back of her underwear drawer with the Nespresso pod. It came in such a pretty bottle: dark gray with a cherry-blossom print on it, like Japanese art. And it smells like Alix.

The experience of being at Alix's house again has given her a strange kind of energy. Meeting the husband was a bonus, although she doesn't know what Alix sees in him. And using their beautiful toilet with the mottled glass mirror and crazy wallpaper with peacocks on it. The posh hand wash. The soft black towel hanging from a golden ring. And the interview itself: reliving the early days of her relationship with Walter; telling her about her terrible mother; the look on Alix's face of rapt fascination, as though Josie were the most interesting woman she'd ever met in her life.

Buoyed up, she walks to Erin's bedroom door and puts her ear to it. She can hear the chair squeaking, the buttons clicking, the tinny noises from her earphones. She can smell the layers of her room. But she can't keep ignoring it. It's not going to go away. She pulls down the handle and pushes the door. It goes only a few inches before it stops, wedged up against the piles on the floor. She calls through to Erin, but Erin can't hear her. She pushes a little harder, another couple of inches. She can see a bit of Erin now, the side of her face, her threadbare sheepskin slippers, her hands clutching the controller, pale and bony. She decides that she can't do it. Not today.

Josie brings Alix's kitchen into her mind's eye. The brightness of it. The sweetness of it. The children's drawings pinned to the special wall. Then she remembers the way that Erin's room used to look, when she shared it with Roxy. It used to have two pink beds in it and a white wardrobe with hearts cut out of it. Where Erin's gaming desk is, there used to be a chest full of dolls and toys. In her head she hears the sound of two small girls laughing together at bedtime.

She closes her eyes and pulls the door shut again.

SATURDAY, 29 JUNE

Alix searches the chest by the front door for her pull-on rain cape, the one she bought to take to a festival a few years back when rain had been forecast for the whole weekend. The warm, dry spell is over for now, and the next few days are predicted to be cool and wet. She finds the cape, puts it on over her clothes, and then calls for Eliza. She's walking her to her friend's house for a birthday party, about half a mile away.

The pavements are full of puddles and the traffic makes hissing sounds as it passes by. Alix barely notices Josie, at first, through the overhanging hood of her rain cape. She notices the dog first, looks at it and thinks, Oh, a Pomchi like Josie's! Then she notices the denim slip-on shoes, stained wet from the rain, a denim jacket tied at the waist with a matching belt, and an umbrella printed with a denim-effect pattern, and she says, "Josie!"

Josie blinks at her. "Alix! What a surprise!"

"Not exactly dog-walking weather," she says.

"No. It's not. But I could wait all day for it to stop raining and then Fred wouldn't get any kind of walk. Where are you off to?"

Alix puts her hands on Eliza's shoulders and says, "Taking this one to a birthday party. Just a couple of roads down."

She sees Josie's eyes mist over with some sort of longing. "Oh, that's nice," she says. "How old?"

"Eleven."

"Well, have a wonderful time, won't you? Enjoy every minute."

"She'll be home in a couple of hours bouncing off the walls on sugar and TikTok."

"Well, enjoy. And have a good weekend, Alix. See you next week."

"Yes. See you next week."

As they carry on down the street, Eliza looks up at Alix and says, "Who is that lady?"

"Oh, she's the lady I'm interviewing for my podcast."

"Why? She seems quite boring. Apart from her dog."

"Well, yes. But that's sort of the point. That people who seem boring can sometimes have the most interesting stories to tell. You just need to get it out of them somehow."

Alix stays awhile at the party, long enough to have a cup of tea and swap some school-gate gossip with a couple of the other mothers. Then she makes her way back through the puddles and the umbrellas toward home. As she passes the spot where she saw Josie on her way here, she stops with a start. She is still there.

"Oh," says Alix. "Josie. What are you doing still out in the rain?"

"I don't really know. I was just . . ."

She trails off and she looks strangely as if she might be about to cry.

"Are you OK?"

"Yes. Yes. I'm fine. I just . . . What we're doing, it's making me feel a lot of things. A lot of things I haven't felt for a long time. You know? It's making me feel like I've been numb. And when I saw you just now, with your lovely little girl . . . I just . . . I don't really know, to be honest, Alix. I don't really know. I just sort of couldn't get my feet to work. Does that sound mad?"

"No, Josie. No. It doesn't sound mad at all. It sounds completely understandable. And listen, let's get out of the rain, shall we? Come on. I'll buy you a cup of tea. Or something stronger?"

Alix guides Josie into the nearest café and sits her at a table while she goes to the counter and orders them both cappuccinos. She adds two chocolate cookies to the order and then brings them back.

But Josie is nowhere to be seen.

4 P.M.

Josie is soaked to the bone when she gets home. She wraps the dog in a towel and rubs him dry, then she makes herself a cup of tea to warm herself up and pads barefoot into the living room, where Walter is on the sofa watching football.

"You're drenched."

"Yeah. Don't know what I was thinking going out in that."

The dog looks longingly at the sofa and Walter looks at him and says, "No chance. You stink. Not having you up here."

Josie scoops him up and holds him to her chest. She doesn't like it when Walter talks sternly to the dog.

She sits on the other end of the sofa from Walter and stares numbly at the football. She hates the sound of football—the dull bass monotone of male calls, the incessant up and down intonation of the commentators, the whistles and the drums; it sounds like the backdrop to a nightmare, an oncoming army of bloodless killers. It's been the soundtrack of her weekends for twenty-seven years, since she first moved into Walter's flat. She'd watched with him in the early years, professed her enthusiasm for the game, shouted when their team scored, pretended to be devastated when they lost. Although, no, not pretended. It had been real, at the time. Everything she thought, did, wanted, cared about back then had been through the filter of Walter. All she had wanted, from the moment they first got together, was to please him, to be the person he thought she was, to be his dream come true.

She finishes her tea and takes the mug into the kitchen. "I'm going to get into bed," she says. "I'm feeling a bit shivery."

Walter looks up at her, concern shining in his eyes. "Oh, love. I hope you're not coming down with anything?"

"No. I'm sure I'm fine."

"I'll bring you in a Lemsip?"

"Oh, no. But thank you. I love you."

"Love you too—" but the "ooh" of his final word is torn in half as something exciting happens on the screen and his attention is gone from her.

She carries the dog into the bedroom and closes the door behind them. She feels poleaxed, beaten-up. She doesn't know what happened to her. The last hour is a blur. The rain that descended down upon her, then Alix in her plastic poncho, her daughter staring curiously at her from under the hood of her raincoat, and then . . . a blank. Then sitting in the coffee shop, watching Alix at the counter, the beads of rain gleaming on her plastic poncho; then she'd seen something through the window—what was it? She's not sure. At the time, she'd thought it was Roxy. Had been convinced it was her. Collected the dog, her bag, run out onto the pavement. No sign of Roxy. Was it real? Or was it a memory? A shadow? Maybe just someone who looked like her?

In bed, she searches for Alix's podcast channel on her phone and selects one at random, lets the sound of Alix's voice wash away the black noise of the mooing football fans from the living room.

MONDAY, 1 JULY

Josie listens to Heart FM through headphones. Behind the glorious crashing crescendos of "Greatest Day" by Take That lies the buzz of sewing machines, the rumble of the tube trains, the chatter of her colleagues, the loud voice of the current customer, but she focuses on the music, the way it makes her feel, filling up her senses with rightness and certainty. The weekend feels like a blur. She spent most of it in bed. Walter diagnosed her with a summer cold and brought her food and beverages. He took Fred out for her and fed him. But this morning she'd awoken feeling fresh and normal, and headed into work despite Walter's protestations that she should stay home, take care of herself.

On her break at three o'clock, she makes herself an instant hot chocolate using powder from a jar, and she writes Alix a message.

I am sorry about Saturday. I had a summer cold. Spent the weekend in bed, shivering. Think I had a touch of deliria!

I'm fine now though and looking forward to our next
meeting. I can do tomorrow morning.

Alix's reply comes a moment later.

> *Oh no! I'm so sorry you were unwell.*
> *You did seem a bit out of sorts.*
> *Please come over tomorrow,*
> *if you're feeling up to that?*

Josie replies with alacrity.

I would love that. See you then.

TUESDAY, 2 JULY

"What does Walter do, now he's retired?" Alix asks as they begin their recording.

Josie sighs. "Good question," she says. "Not a lot. He's quite happy just being at home, reading the news online, watching sport, emailing family."

"What family is he emailing?"

"Oh, his sons. They're in their thirties. They live in Canada."

"Both of them?"

"Yes. Their mum immigrated there when she and Walter split up. He's not seen them again since."

"And they were how old?"

Josie shrugs. "Ten and twelve, when they left."

"He hasn't seen his sons since they were children?"

"No. It's very sad. But his ex wouldn't let him anywhere near them."

"Why?"

Josie shrugs again. "I guess she was just really unhappy about what happened with me."

Alix registers this uptick in the already strange narrative of Josie's relationship with Walter. "So," she begins gently. "Josie. I'd love to hear more about this, but only if you're comfortable talking about it. Remember, anything you're not happy about can be deleted before this goes out."

Josie nods her assent.

"So, Walter was married? When you met him?"

There is a tiny pulse of silence, long enough for Alix to read Josie's discomfort with the answer she is about to provide.

"Yes," she says. "He was. But obviously I didn't know. Obviously he didn't tell me. Otherwise, I never would have got together with him. I mean, of course I wouldn't."

"So, hold on. After that day, your fifteenth birthday, when he took you to the pub, how long was it before you found out that he was married?"

This time the silence is even longer. "Quite a long time," she says eventually. "I'd say a few years."

"A few years?"

"Yes. I didn't find out he was married until I was eighteen."

"So he was still living with her? Right up until then?"

"No. He wasn't. That's why I didn't know. Because he had his flat in London, that he had from his dad. But his ex and the boys lived out-side London, somewhere in Essex. He went home at the weekends. It was all—it was a bit messy, I suppose."

Alix nods but stays silent.

It's raining when their session ends a while later and Alix offers to drive Josie home. After she drops her back, Alix watches from her car as she walks round the corner, to see which house she goes into. Alix knows this road. She's been down it a thousand times: an unprepossessing rat run connecting Paddington with Kilburn.

And there, just as Josie had described, a long sweep of huge Victorian villas in semidetached pairs, all built close to the pavement and shabby and faded with no trees to protect them from the dirty fumes. She watches Josie unlock the door of a house set right behind a bus stop. She sees Walter in the window and is taken aback once more by how old he looks. She tries to imagine the handsome forty-two-year-old Josie had described kissing her in a pub when she was a girl, but it's hard to do. He has not worn the passage of time well. She sees him turn as Josie enters the room and a small smile break over his face. He mouths something at her and then turns back to his laptop. Josie appears briefly by the window, holding her dog and looking behind her, before disappearing again. There is another window next to the bay in which Walter is sitting. This one has denim curtains which are half-opened. Alix can see the shape of a wardrobe and a door. Somewhere beyond that door, she supposes, is Erin, the older girl, the one who still lives at home, the one who had her arm broken by the little sister who left home when she was sixteen.

And then a bus pulls up in front of the house and snaps Alix out of her peculiar reverie. She puts her car into gear and drives home.

———

At the kitchen counter she opens her laptop and googles Josie's address. She adds the name "Walter Fair," but nothing comes up. She adds the names "Josie Fair," "Erin Fair," and "Roxy Fair," but still nothing comes up. As she'd suspected. Anonymous, like 90 percent of the population of the world. Even in these days of ubiquitous sticky fingerprints all over social media, most people aren't traceable on the internet. She puts the address into Google Maps and stares at the Street View for a while, scrolling up and down Josie's road, looking for something, she's not sure what.

THURSDAY,
4 JULY

Josie puts her denim jacket on over her T-shirt and joggers and looks at herself in the mirror. It's the same denim jacket she's had since she was a teenager, the one she was wearing on her fifteenth birthday in the pub with Walter. It's worn on the elbows and at the cuffs, but she has kept it in one piece over the years, kept it looking smart enough to wear. It's her lucky jacket, the jacket she was wearing when her life turned around, when she went from being the sort of girl who drank warm cider with rough boys to the sort of girl who had the love of a real man, who had beautiful babies and a two-bedroom flat. But that girl . . . that girl is starting to feel like a shape-shifter, a fraud, a one-dimensional paper doll. She's blurring in her mind's eye into a human puddle. She rips the jacket off and looks at herself again. She has kept her figure, somehow, without trying. She looks nice. She could probably wear similar clothes to Alix and look good in them. She flicks through her wardrobe, looking for something that's not denim—why does she have so much denim?—and something that's not gray. She finds a floaty black shirt that she'd bought to cover up her swimsuit once when it was really hot in the Lake District. She puts it on over her T-shirt and joggers and turns this way and the other. She decides she looks nice and she hangs her denim jacket back in the wardrobe. She gets some sunglasses out of her chest of drawers and tucks them into her hair and then she takes out her dangling turquoise earrings and replaces them with a pair of hoop earrings Walter had bought her for her birthday one year.

Walter glances at her as she gets the dog ready for his walk.

"You look like you're on holiday."

"Do I?"

"Yes. You do."

"Well, it's nice out. Thought I might hang out in the park for a bit. Get some ice cream."

Walter looks out the window and then back at her. He says, "You know what, that sounds nice. I'll come with you."

Josie reels slightly. "Oh," she says. "No. I mean, I'm meeting my friend there. The school mum. You know."

Walter narrows his eyes at her. "Are you sure it's not a school dad you're meeting?" He has a playful tone to his voice, but she knows that beneath it there is a thin blade of anger.

She matches his playful tone and says, "God, Walter, you clearly never saw any of the school dads for you even to say that!"

He nods slowly and then puts his glasses back on and turns back to his screen. "Well," he says, "have fun. See you soon."

She clips the dog's lead onto his collar and leaves the flat.

———

"Oh!" says Alix, eyeing Josie up and down on her doorstep fifteen minutes later. "No denim!"

"No," Josie replies brightly. "Not today. I wasn't in the mood."

"I'd love to talk to you one day, maybe, about the denim? Would that be OK?"

"Yes. I think I'd like to talk about it too."

Josie glances about Alix's house, looking for signs of the red-haired husband, but he is not here today; the house feels silent and still. Just the two of them.

"Husband back at work?"

"Yes." Alix nods and smiles. "He hardly ever works from home."

"What does he do?"

"He's a leasing agent for commercial property. Mainly in the City."

"Sounds stressful."

"Well, yes, I suppose it is in a lot of ways. Hard work."

"But clearly it pays off." Josie arcs her gaze around the open-plan kitchen.

"Yes. Yes, it does. We're very lucky. Most people work hard, don't they? But not everyone gets to live in a house like this."

"I love this house."

"Thank you."

"Not just because it's beautiful, which it is. But because it's so homely. It's not just like a house in a magazine. It's a proper home. It's . . . very *you*." Josie runs her hands over the creamy marble of the work surface as she says this. "My flat," she continues, "it's never really felt like my flat. It's always felt like Walter's. It's all his furniture. His things. And of course it's council so we can't really spend any money on it. I look around it and all I see is other people's things. And Walter doesn't like stuff on the walls. Or clutter. You know. It would be a dream come true to have a place like this that I could just fill with things I like."

"And what things do you like?"

"Well, yes, that's half the problem. I don't know. I really don't know. I've just . . . lost my way. Or in fact, I'm starting to realize, I never even *had* a way in the first place. I handed my life over to Walter when I was a child and never gave myself the chance to find out who I really was."

Josie pulls herself up straight when she realizes she might be about to start crying. She looks up at Alix and smiles as brightly as she can.

"It's not too late for you to find out," says Alix. "Come on." She guides her toward the studio. "Let's start right now."

Hi! I'm Your Birthday Twin!
A NETFLIX ORIGINAL SERIES

Screen shows a reenactment of a young woman following an older man into a large white house.
She wears a denim jacket.
The soundtrack over the images is Josie's voice, taken from Alix Summer's podcast. The text on-screen reads:

Recording from Alix Summer's podcast,
4 July, 2019

"He first invited me to his apartment when I was sixteen, exactly a year after our date in the pub on my fifteenth birthday. He said we'd have pizza and he'd give me my present. I'd never been there before. We always met in public. Or in his Portakabin on the estate after his team had all gone home. We just kissed. Talked. And I'd known, all along, that at some point he'd want more from me and I made it very clear that when it did happen, it had to be perfect. So he had champagne. He had music. He drew the curtains, lit a candle. He gave me an engagement ring and he asked me to marry him. I said yes. Of course. Of course I said yes. And then, roughly twelve hours after I turned sixteen years old, he took my virginity."

FRIDAY, 5 JULY

There is a young man standing on Alix's doorstep. It takes a moment for Alix to realize who it is and then she says, "Oh! Harry! Hi! How are you?"

Harry is their next-door neighbor's son. Alix has known him since he was a child, but now he's an adult, in his last year at university, and she hasn't seen him for a long while.

"I'm good. How are you?"

"Not bad. Everything OK?"

"Well, no. I just got back, and Mum's out and she won't be back until, like, this evening. And I haven't got a key. She said that you might have a spare?"

"Oh," she says, turning behind her to look at the console where she keeps things like neighbors' keys. "Yes, I think actually I do, hold on just a second."

She feels through the drawers in the console, but they're not there. "Come in," she says. "Come in. I think they might be in the kitchen."

Harry follows her through the hallway and stands awkwardly in the entrance to the kitchen while she goes through more drawers. Eventually she finds them, in an envelope with her neighbor's name scrawled on it. "Aha!" she says triumphantly. "Here they are. I think you were about ten years old when she gave us these. It's when you were off on your American road trip. Remember that?"

"Ha," says Harry, taking the envelope from her outstretched hand. "Yes, I do. And thank you."

"No worries at all." She leads him back down the hallway and then, just before they get to the door, she remembers something. "Oh, Harry. By the way. You and your brother went to Queen's Park High, didn't you?"

"Yes, we did."

"And you're how old?"

"I'm twenty-one."

"So, do you remember two sisters at your school—Erin and Roxy Fair?"

She studies his face carefully as he forms his response. "Oh, shit, yes. I certainly do," he says with a wry smile. "Roxy was in my year. She was insane."

"Insane?"

"Yes. Scary as shit."

"Oh, that's interesting. In what way?"

"Just scary. You know. Hard. Aggressive." Harry cocks his head and looks at her. "Wait," he says, "do you know her?"

"No. No, I've never met her. I know her mother though."

"Right."

"Apparently Roxy left home when she was sixteen."

Harry throws her another look. "Left? Or ran away?"

"Ran away? Why do you say that?"

"I don't know. There were a lot of rumors about her. About both of them. About their home life. Like, dark stuff."

"Like . . . ?"

"I dunno. Abuse, I guess? The older one, Erin. She was so weird. Literally the weirdest person I have ever met. I never spoke to her, but I would see her around, with these really dark brown eyes, and she was so thin. You know, apparently, she never ate solid food. That's what I heard. Never in her life. Only soft food." He tips the envelope from one hand to the next and then beams at Alix. "Well, thanks for the keys. I'll get them back to you later. In case we need them again in another eleven years from now. See you."

"Yes," says Alix, closing the door as he leaves, "see you."

SATURDAY,
6 JULY

Josie returns to the same spot where she'd bumped into Alix the week before, just outside the coffee shop from which she'd run in a state of certainty that she'd seen Roxy on the street. She buys a coffee and sits outside with it. It's a cool, cloudy day, the beginning of July, but it feels more like September and the air carries the sad feeling of the end of summer although it is still in its full stride. Josie knows that it wasn't Roxy she saw last week. She knows it with 99 percent of her soul. But there is still 1 percent that thinks: Why not? Why wouldn't it be Roxy? Roxy had once existed in three dimensions; there is no reason why she shouldn't exist in three dimensions still, and no reason furthermore why those three dimensions should not be here, on Salusbury Road, inches from where she sits.

She sips her coffee and stares across the street, her eyes taking in the form and shape of every young woman who passes. The dog sees a standard poodle and starts yapping madly at it. "Shhh," Josie whispers into his ear. "Shush now."

She makes the coffee last as long as she can and then she sighs and gets to her feet.

She has not seen Roxy.

The emptiness of this realization scoops out the base of her belly.

But then relief quickly takes its place.

It is nearly midday, and Alix's house looks still, it looks empty. Josie scans the street for Alix's car, but it isn't there. Emboldened, she walks up the front path and peers through the edges of the shutters. She sees a living room that she's never seen before. Alix always takes her straight through from the front door to the kitchen and into the garden. She sees the cloud-cat, curled on a chair. She peers through the window to the side of the milky-blue door. There is a pile of mail on the stairs, shoes in a managed heap under a console table, a spiky flowering plant in a brass pot. She stares for a moment more, relishing the luxury of time, of not being rushed, of taking in details. A photo of the four of them, on a beach, in raincoats. Alix's hair is under a hat, just one strand escaped, kicked across her forehead by the wind. Nathan looks ruddy and faintly ridiculous.

Josie hears a car slowing on the street behind her and turns. It's not them. But the adrenaline rush reminds her that they could be back any minute and she is loitering on their doorstep with no good reason to be there. She casts around desperately for something to take, some shred of Alix to fill her up until they meet again. She lifts the lid of Alix's recycling box and sifts through it until she comes upon a glossy magazine called *Livingetc*. She flicks through it and sees that it is full of beautiful photographs of houses. She slides it into her shoulder bag, and she heads home.

4 P.M.

"Erm, Alix?"

"Yes," Alix calls back to Nathan, who is sitting at the kitchen table staring at his phone with a frown on his face.

"Isn't this your friend Josie?"

Alix stops what she's doing and takes a step toward Nathan. "What?"

He turns his phone toward her. "The Ring app. It showed movement at the front door at about midday when we were at my dad's. So, I just looked at it. And it's her, isn't it?"

Alix draws up beside him and takes the phone from his hand. And yes, it is, clearly. It's Josie, staring first through their shutters into the living room, and then through the small side window in the hallway. Her face looms in and out of shot of the camera. At one point Josie turns slightly and the dog's face comes right into focus, his funny bug eyes looking even buggier.

"She must have dropped by, on the off chance," she says to Nathan.

"But look," he says, pointing at the screen. "Look how long she's standing there for. Staring through the window. I mean, what the fuck is she doing?"

Alix continues watching the footage and the seconds pass by slowly and still there is no obvious explanation for what Josie is doing outside her house.

"But *this*," says Nathan. "This is the weirdest thing. Look what she does next."

Alix watches but can't make sense of what she's seen. "Wait," she says, "rewind that bit." Nathan rewinds and she watches again and yes, there it is, Josie opening the lid of their recycling box and taking out a magazine, stuffing it in her handbag, and then leaving, very, very quickly.

"Oh my God," she says breathlessly. "Oh my God."

7 P.M.

Alix sits next to Nathan in the back of an Uber that evening, on their way to a friend's birthday dinner in Acton. She wants to talk to him about Josie, but she also doesn't want his opinion to cloud her view of how to handle things. Her project feels simultaneously thrilling and terrifying. She has opened a physical and metaphorical door to this woman, a pure stranger; she has brought her into her home, made her feel that she is somehow party to Alix's inner life. She takes full responsibility for the decisions she has made to this point and now she needs to decide if she is prepared to take full responsibility for anything untoward that may happen to her or her family as a result. If she discusses this with Nathan, she knows what he will say. He will say, "Bin it. Tell her it's off. Get rid," and then if she ignores him and this project turns out to be a disaster, he will tell her that he'd told her, he will tell her that she was wrong and he was right, and Alix does not want to make professional or personal decisions based on what her husband will think if she makes a mistake.

Because if she is right and he is wrong, this podcast could be the making of Alix's professional career.

She watches Nathan that night over the dinner table. The friends are his friends; Giovanni is Nathan's best friend from college; his partner is Nathalie, who Alix knows only in relation to Giovanni. When Nathan is with his friends, he is bombastic, he is high-octane, he engages every element of his being in the act of producing the sort of persona that his friends expect from him, and in order to tap into these elements, he drinks twice as fast as he does when he's with Alix's friends or with his family.

She feels a sense of unease pass through her as she sees Giovanni head to the cocktail cabinet for a second bottle of vodka, the careless, loose-wristed glugging into guests' glasses, the glaze across Nathan's eyes, the loudness of him, the babble of bullshit, the overloud laugh, and she knows already that this will be one of those nights and she doesn't want to be *that wife*, the purse-lipped, stick-up-the-butt wife, the wife who can't relax and can't have fun and spoils it for everyone else. She wants to down tequila shots and sing and dance and laugh like a drain. But she can't take on that role because Nathan has already staked his claim on it and one of them has to remain sentient and together; one of them has to be the grown-up.

At eleven o'clock she whispers into Nathan's ear, "We need to get back for the babysitter," but even as she does so she knows that he isn't really listening and that even if he were, he has no intention of heading home, that he has entered the stage of inebriation where time has no meaning, when consequences have no meaning, and so she calls herself an Uber and she leaves.

In bed an hour later, she looks at her phone. Emboldened by drink, she types a message to Josie.

> *Hey, Josie. We saw you at the house earlier,*
> *on our doorbell camera. Is everything all right?*

The ticks turn blue immediately and Josie is typing.

> *Everything's fine. I was just passing.*
> *I thought I'd say hello. Sorry to worry you.*

Alix stares at the message for a moment. There is more to it than her innocuous reply would suggest. But it is late, and if there is more to Josie's peculiar behavior at her front door earlier today than she is letting on, then maybe it is a topic of conversation better kept for their next face-to-face meeting.

No problem, she replies. *Sleep tight.*

You too Alix, replies Josie, followed by a sleeping emoji and a love heart.

Alix turns off her phone and picks up her book, waits for sleep to take her away from the weird, swirling sensations of alcohol-induced paranoia, edginess, and very slight dread.

MIDNIGHT

Josie switches off her screen and puts down her phone. She picks up the magazine that she'd been studying before Alix's message came through and returns to the article she'd been reading about a lakeside house near Cape Town lived in by a handsome architect, his beautiful mermaid-haired wife, and a dog called Rafe with dreadlocked fur. Also to hand she has a notepad in which she is writing down the things in the magazine that she would like to buy. Her grandmother left her three thousand pounds in her will in May. She also has about six thousand pounds in savings built up over the years because she barely spends the money she earns as they mostly live on Walter's pension. She could afford the lamp with a base in the shape of an owl, or the blue rug with textured stripes that look like ripples on the surface of the sea. She could afford a velvet bed throw the color of overripe raspberries and the huge silky cushions printed with abstract streaks of ink blue and clotted cream. She could afford other things as well, but she doesn't want to go crazy.

She glances across at Walter's side of the bed. He is not there. She swallows back the dark feeling this gives her and turns her attention to the magazine. As she flicks through it, something falls out from between the pages. It's a paper receipt. It's dated 8 June. Her birthday. Alix's birthday. It's from Planet Organic, 10:48 a.m. Sunflower oil. Sourdough olive loaf. Alpro chocolate milk. Oatly milk. Organic pinot grigio. A 200-gram stick of unsalted butter for £3.99.

This suggestion of what Alix had been doing in the hours before they first met seems strangely magical, weighted down with some essence of fortune, of posterity. She holds it to her mouth and kisses it, then slides it back inside the pages of the magazine.

MONDAY,
8 JULY

"So," says Alix, smiling at Josie across the desk in her studio. "Denim. Are you happy to talk about that today?"

"Yes. Sure."

"So, I've noticed that most things you wear are made of denim and I'm curious about that. For example, today you are wearing a denim skirt, with a pale blue top and denim plimsolls. Your handbag is made of denim and your dog is in a denim dog carrier. Do you have a story, or a theory? About your love of denim?"

"Yes. I wasn't sure at first when you mentioned it last week. I wasn't sure what the reason was. I think I always just thought I liked it because it's practical, you know. Easy. But you're right. A denim jacket is one thing—everyone has a denim jacket. But denim accessories are another thing completely and you know, in my bedroom I actually have denim curtains. So clearly there's something going on. And I think it's got something to do with the early days of my relationship with Walter, you know. I was wearing a denim jacket the first time I went out with him. I wore it a lot during the first couple of years we were together and it became, for me, almost a part of our love affair. Always there. On the back of a chair. Or hanging off my shoulders. He'd put it there for me, if the sun went in and I got cold, just put it there. Like I was a princess or something. And then one day he picked it up and cuddled it and sniffed it and said something really cheesy like: "This jacket is you, it's just you." Something to do with my essence being inside it? Something to do with the smell? And he made the jacket sound so powerful and important and it made me feel like the jacket was maybe lucky, in some way? Had brought us together? I don't know, it all sounds so stupid when I try to explain it. But after that I think I always made sure I was wearing something denim, so that maybe the way Walter felt about me then might last forever."

Alix leaves a stunned moment of silence, and her mind fills with the image of the old man in the window of Josie's flat.

"I believe you brought some photos along today, of you and Walter, when you were both younger. Shall we have a look at those now?"

Josie nods and pulls an envelope from her shoulder bag. "There aren't many," she says. "Of course, this was pre-smartphones, so we only took photographs with cameras and obviously, back then, well, we were kind of still a secret, so we weren't exactly snapping each other here, there, and everywhere. But I found a couple. Here."

She passes them across the desk to Alix. Alix looks at one and then the other. Her eyes widen. "Wow," she says. Then she laughs drily and gazes at Josie. "Wow! Walter was quite a hunk."

She sees Josie flush pink. "He really was," she says.

Alix looks again, studying the two photos more carefully. In one, Josie wears a denim jacket and baggy jeans. Her chestnut hair is mid-length and clipped back on one side. She appears to be wearing lipstick. She stands a foot away from Walter, who is beaming down at her from his elevated height, wearing a hoodie and jeans and a baseball cap. In the other, Josie sits on his lap, her hair in a ponytail, her head resting back against his chest, smiling widely into the camera, which is being held aloft by Walter. His hair is thick and shiny, his skin is clear and smooth, he looks young for his age, more early thirties than early forties. His forearms are big and strong. His eyes are madly blue. Alix feels a sick swoop in her stomach as she acknowledges that if she were to bump into forty-something-year-old Walter today, she would be attracted to him. And she gets it. She gets it. And the fact that she gets it sickens her. Because Josie was a child, and he was a grown man, and he may not have looked like a pedophile then, but he looks like one now, and whether he looks like one or not, he was, and he is.

"You look so young," she says, handing the photos back to Josie. "So very young."

"Well," she replies. "I was. I was young. I was . . . It's crazy, when you think about it."

"So, if you could go back to thirteen-year-old Josie, just before she met Walter, what would you say to her?"

She watches Josie's face. She sees it fall slightly before lifting again, almost with an effort. "I don't know," she says, her voice tight with emotion. "I really don't know. Because in some ways, being with Walter all these years has been the making of me, you know. Having the babies young. Having something solid in my life. Having something real, when other girls my age were running round being fake and ridiculous, searching for things. But on the other hand"—Josie looks up at her with glassy eyes—"on the other hand, I do wonder, I wonder quite a lot, especially now that the girls are grown, especially now I'm middle-aged and Walter is getting old and . . ." Josie pauses and sighs. Then she looks straight at Alix, something sharp and clear suddenly shining from her nearly black eyes, and she says, "I wonder what it was all for, you know? I wonder what else might have been. And actually, all things considered, I'd probably tell thirteen-year-old me to run for the hills and not look back."

11 A.M.

"What's your cat called?" asks Josie as they pass back through the kitchen an hour later.

"Skye."

"Skye. That's a beautiful name. Are you still looking for a puppy?"

"Hm. Not really. It seems a lot right now, you know? I have other issues that seem more pressing than house-training and sleepless nights."

"What sort of issues?"

"Oh. Just . . ." Alix pauses and gazes at the floor for a moment. She hasn't told anyone about Nathan's recent behavior, not even her sisters. They would judge him, and they would judge her for putting up with him. They would tell her to fix it, to deal with it, to do something. She thinks of all that Josie has shared with her these past few days and finds herself saying, "Nathan. You know—he's amazing. Obviously, he's amazing. But he has . . . he has a drink problem."

She sees Josie flinch.

"Like, not all the time. Most of the time, he's fine. But when he's not fine, he's really not fine. He goes on benders. Doesn't come home."

Benders.

It sounds like such an old-fashioned word. It must surely have been superseded by now by something more modern? But it's the only word Alix can find to explain what her husband does. What he did on Saturday after Giovanni's dinner party. What it now seems he will keep doing from here on in unless she starts issuing ultimatums and threats.

Josie sucks in her breath. "Oh," she says. "That's not good."

"No," says Alix. "No. It's not good."

"And does he cheat on you? When he stays out all night."

Alix starts at the question. "God. No! Nothing like that. No. I don't think he'd be capable of doing anything like that, even if he wanted to. Which he wouldn't. Because it's not his style." But even as she says the words, an image flashes through her mind: her reflection in the bathroom mirror on the night of her birthday party, Nathan's arms around her waist, his smile buried into her neck, her brusque rejection—*Are you actually mad?*—and his subsequent disappearance into the petrol-dark Soho night.

She shakes the image from her mind.

Josie stares at her intensely. "What are you going to do about it?" she says.

Alix sighs. "I have no idea. He used to do it a lot before the children were born, and I did have my concerns back then. Did wonder if he was going to be the right father for my children. But then Eliza arrived, and he changed, overnight. I thought that was that. You know. But then, a couple of years ago, it started up again. It feels almost as if he thinks that we've got to the end of the intense bit of parenting, that we're on the home run, that he's, well . . . *free again.*"

Both women fall silent. Then Josie sighs and says, "Men."

And there it is, the point which it all boils down to eventually. The point where there are no words, no theories, no explanations for behaviors that baffle and infuriate and hurt. Just that. *Men.*

"Alix," says Josie. "I've been thinking, about the denim. It's weird. I know it's weird. It's like I've been holding on to something for so long and there's no meaning to it anymore. Walter doesn't feel that way about me anymore. He hasn't for a long time. Walter barely sees me, you know? So what's it for? And I have a little money, an inheritance, and I want to, I suppose, *refresh* my life? My clothes? The flat? And I hope this doesn't sound strange, but you . . ." She waves her hand toward Alix. "You always look so nice and I wondered if maybe you might want to go shopping, one day? Help me?"

Alix blinks at Josie. And then she smiles. "Of course!" she says. "I'd love to!"

She glances at the time on the clock above the hob. It's not even midday. "Do you know the boutique, on the corner, the Cut?"

"Yes. I think so."

"It's on your route home. We could go in there now, maybe?"

Josie glances at the time too. "OK," she says. "Sure."

MIDDAY

Josie has walked past this boutique a hundred times and never set foot inside the door. *Not for her.* She'd imagined the clothes inside to cost hundreds of pounds, the sales assistants to be snooty and rude, the other customers to be entitled and sour. But as she pulls the price tag on a black jersey dress closer to inspect it she sees that it is only £39.99. And then a young girl appears at her side and makes baby noises at the dog and says, "Oh my God, so cute! What's her name?"

"Oh," says Josie. "Him. He's a him. He's called Fred."

"Fred! Oh my God. Cute name. Sophie, look!" She beckons over her colleague, another very young girl, who coos and clucks and says, "How old is he?"

"He's one and a half."

"Oh my God, he's a baby!"

Josie wills Fred not to growl or snarl at the girls and he doesn't. "Did you want to try that on?" the girl called Sophie asks.

"Er, yes. Sure."

"I'll just hang it in the changing room for you. Let me know if you need any help."

"Here," says Alix, heading toward Josie with a handful of summer dresses, some knitwear, a blazer-style jacket in red. "Try these on too."

Josie hands Fred to Alix and heads into the changing cubicle. She tries on the black jersey dress first, the one she'd chosen. It hangs loose and shapeless on her and she immediately takes it off and puts it back on its hanger. Then she tries on one of the dresses that Alix chose for her, soft floral jersey with a V-neck, fitted to the knee, and she checks the price tag and sees that it is £49.99 and that she can afford it and then feels a shiver of excitement because the dress is exquisite and because it makes her look pretty and shapely and young and because it is not made of hard-wearing denim but of a soft, silky fabric that feels beautiful to touch, and she takes it off and then tries on another and another and another and all of them make her look like a woman she has never met before and would like to know better, and she takes all three dresses, both pieces of knitwear, and the red cotton blazer to the till and watches in breathless awe as all six items are rung through by one assistant while the other assistant wraps them in tissue and the total is £398.87 and that is more than Josie has ever spent in one go on anything ever in her life but the atmosphere feels celebratory, somehow, as if Alix and the sales assistants are all cheering her on, as if the purchase is an achievement of some kind, a reward, an award, a prize for good behavior.

She tries to hold on to that feeling as she says goodbye to Alix outside the boutique, lets Alix bring her in for one of the hugs that come so easily to her but that still feel so strange to Josie, tries to hold on to it as she walks the ten minutes from the boutique to her flat, tries to hold on to it as she enters the flat, sees Walter's eyes turn toward her, questioningly, smells the stench from Erin's room even from here, sees the faces of the people on the bus at the stop outside staring numbly through her grimy windows, wondering about the people who live in here and never, she is sure, coming even halfway close to the reality of it.

She takes the bag straight into the bedroom and hangs the dresses in her wardrobe, puts the tissue-wrapped knitwear in a drawer, and then, from the inside pocket of her handbag, she takes the bracelet she'd seen sitting on Alix's console table by the front door. She holds it in the palm of her hand and stares at it. It's gold with tiny little diamond droplets, like a little puddle of glitter. She puts it to her lips and kisses it before putting it in the back of her underwear drawer.

Then she goes to Pinterest, to the page she started a few days ago for inspirational quotes about being single. She thinks of Alix's husband disappearing for hours and days, leaving his beautiful wife alone at home, scared and angry and unhappy. Josie recognizes that Alix has shown some vulnerability in sharing this with her, and thinks that maybe Alix needs this today, needs to know she has options. Josie scrolls through the memes, chooses one, and WhatsApps it to Alix.

A WEAK MAN CAN'T LOVE A STRONG WOMAN.
HE WON'T KNOW WHAT TO DO WITH HER.

Underneath the image, she types in a row of love-heart emojis interspersed with strong-arm emojis. She presses send.

TUESDAY, 9 JULY

Alix looks at the image on the screen of her phone that Josie sent her yesterday. A black square with the words "A weak man can't love a strong woman. He won't know what to do with her" in white capitals. Underneath are some emojis and for a few seconds Alix squints at it trying to work out what it means and why Josie has sent it to her. And then she realizes that Josie is using memes and quotes to bolster her resolve to change her life, so she types in a thumbs-up emoji and presses send. Then she carries on getting ready to leave the house with the kids.

"Nathan, have you seen my bracelet? The one you bought me for my birthday?"

She hears his disembodied voice coming from somewhere else in the house. "No. Wasn't it by the front door?"

"Yes. That's what I thought." She opens the drawers and goes through them again. She calls out to Eliza, who also has no idea where it is. Alix sighs and closes the drawers. She'll look again later. Now she needs to get the kids to school.

Josie is wearing one of the dresses she bought at the boutique yesterday when she arrives at Alix's door at nine thirty. She looks almost like a completely different person and there's a second of dissonance, before Alix smiles and says, "Josie! Hi! I didn't think we'd . . ."

"Didn't we?"

"Not that I . . ." Alix scrolls through her mental diary and fails to find the moment that they agreed to another interview today. "Not that I remember. But that's OK. I'm not busy. Come in. You look great, by the way."

"Thank you! Walter nearly had a coronary."

"What did he say?"

"Oh, Walter doesn't say much. Man of few words. Asked how much it cost, *obviously*. First thing they all ask, isn't it?"

Alix laughs. Nathan never asks her how much things cost. "So true!" she says.

"But yes. I think he liked it. But the important thing is that I like it, isn't it?"

There's a brittle note of uncertainty in her tone and Alix recognizes the need to bolster her.

"Absolutely," she says. "That is absolutely right. Come through."

"No Nathan?" Josie asks, peering into the living room as they pass.

"No. Like I said, he rarely works from home."

"And all OK? You know, with what you were telling me about yesterday?"

Alix blanches. She's beginning to wish she'd never said anything to Josie. "I guess," she says. "I mean, we haven't really talked about it."

"It's really shitty, you know, that sort of thing. You deserve better. That's what we both need to start to understand. We're forty-five, Alix. We can do better. We *have* to do better."

Josie's words sting slightly. Alix knows that she deserves better than being abandoned by her husband twice a week while he gallivants around spending money on tequila shots and hotel rooms, that she deserves her messages to be replied to, her calls answered, a proper explanation for the absence of her husband for twelve straight hours. She knows it, but somehow the pendulum of pros versus cons keeps swinging back to the pros.

"Do you love him?"

Alix spins round to face Josie.

"Nathan. Do you love him?"

"Oh," she says. "Well, yes. Yes. Of course I do."

"Because, you know, lately I've been thinking a lot about love. About what it is, what it's for. And I feel like maybe I have no idea. That I've got to forty-five years of age and I really don't know. And people talk about it all the time like it's, you know, something real, something you can touch—like when we talk about love, we're all talking about the same thing. But we're not, are we? It isn't a real thing. It isn't anything. And sometimes I make myself imagine what it would be like if Walter died, to see if maybe that will make me know if I love him or not, and I really do think, if he died, everything would be better. And surely, if that's the way I feel, then I don't really love him? Do I?"

Alix says nothing.

"And I have to wonder, then, what it was all for, at the end of the day. All the *smallness* of everything. All the *quietness*. And you don't know yet, Alix. You're still in the middle of it all—your kids, they still need you. But after they've gone, then what? Will you still want this? Everything you've built? Will you still want Nathan?"

"I . . ." Alix puts her hand to her throat and clasps her bumblebee pendant. "I really don't know," she says. "I used to think that I couldn't live without him. But recently, with all the, you know, the benders, I do sometimes wonder if life would be easier on my own."

"But when you think about Nathan dying, how does it make you feel? Really? Inside? Does it make you feel sad? Or does it make you feel . . . *free*?"

Alix looks inside herself, for something true to give to Josie. She pictures Nathan dead, the children fatherless, her future alone, and she says, "No. It doesn't make me feel free. It makes me feel sad."

There's a harsh silence and Alix can feel judgment in it. Josie stares at her dispassionately. "Oh," she says, and the atmosphere chills by a degree. "Anyway," she says coolly, "if you're busy, I'll let you get on."

"No!" says Alix, feeling strangely as if she needs to win back Josie's approval. "It's fine. I don't have anything on right now. We can do another session, if you want?"

Josie's demeanor softens and she smiles. "Sure," she says. "OK."

Alix leads her to her studio.

Hi! I'm Your Birthday Twin!
A NETFLIX ORIGINAL SERIES

The screen shows a dramatic reenactment of a young girl sitting at a kitchen table.
To her right is an older man.
Standing by the kitchen sink is an older woman, the girl's mother.
The text on the screen reads:

Recording from Alix Summer's podcast, 9 July, 2019

Josie's voice begins.

"We told my mother on my eighteenth birthday. Told her we were engaged. Told her we were going to get married.

Told her I was moving out. Walter was there. He said there was no way he'd let me do something like that unsupported. And I genuinely had no idea how my mother was going to react. No idea if she'd laugh or cry or scream or call the police. But she just sighed. She said to me, 'You're an adult now. I can't make your choices for you. But, Josie, I don't like this. I don't like it at all.' And then she took hold of my face, like this, inside her hand, so hard it almost hurt, and she stared hard into my eyes and said, '*Remember you have choices.*' Then she let go of my face and left the room, slammed the door behind her. Me and Walter just looked at each other. Then he took me out for dinner to an Italian restaurant on West End Lane. Went back to his after and never went home. My life had actually begun. Or at least that's what I told myself. That's what I believed. It's only now that I can see how wrong I was. That I was just handing myself from the hands of one controlling person to another."

The screen changes to a young couple sitting on a sofa in an empty apartment staged with vintage furniture and spot-lights.

The man holds a small dog on his lap. He lifts the dog onto its back legs by holding his front paws and turns it to face the camera.

"Say hello, Fred," *he says, waving the dog's front paw.*

The dog wriggles from his hold and jumps across to the woman's lap.

Both of them laugh.

The text beneath them on the screen says:

Tim and Angel Hiddingfold-Clarke, current owners of Josie's dog, Fred

An interviewer asks them, off-mic: "Tell us how you and Fred got together?"

Tim and Angel exchange a look and then Tim speaks.

"This woman approached us a couple of years ago. We were on honeymoon in the Lake District, summer 2019, eating lunch on a bench. And she just appeared in front of us. She looked kind of scared. Haunted in a way. And it was hot but she was wearing her hood up, dark sunglasses, a jacket done all the way up to her chin. She said, 'Please, please help me. I can't take care of my dog anymore. Please, will you take him to a rescue center? Please. Please help me.' And then she just handed him to us, in this, like, dog-carrier thing and passed us a carrier bag with food in it. She said, 'He's lovely once he gets to know you. The loveliest, loveliest boy.' And then she sort of kissed him and left and it was literally the weirdest, weirdest thing that ever happened. And of course we had no idea at the time who she was. No idea whatsoever. It was only a few days later that we saw that it was her. That it was Josie Fair."

"But you kept the dog?"

"Oh my God, yes. Of course we did, I mean, look at him. Just look at him!"

11 A.M.

Josie sits outside the café where she once thought she'd seen Roxy. She has a cappuccino, and the dog sits on her lap. Her hands shake slightly and her mind pulses and twitches with contradictory thoughts. She thinks of Alix's stupid-faced husband, with his mud-colored eyes, leaving Alix and his children to go out drinking to the point of stupefaction. She thinks: At least Walter has never done that. She thinks: Walter has always been there for me and the children. But then she thinks: Walter is always, always there. Walter is never anywhere else. She would like it if Walter could be somewhere else. She would like it if *she* could be somewhere else. Forever. But then she thinks: What is my alternative? And she thinks: Alix. She thinks Alix is the answer to everything, somehow, but then, Alix "loves" her stupid-faced, cheating husband, which makes Josie think that Alix is maybe every inch as stupid as she is. And Josie *needs* Alix to be cleverer than her. Josie has always needed people to be cleverer than her. And she doesn't know how she feels about Alix anymore. She also doesn't know how she feels about Walter. As her eyes scan the pavement for the daughter she hasn't seen for five years, her thoughts spiral back to the day Roxy disappeared and the reason why she left and she feels a nauseating darkness envelop her, and as it begins to smother her, her breathing grows labored and panicky and she knocks her coffee cup as her hand goes to the pocket of her jacket and she pulls out the teaspoon that had rested on the side of her coffee cup in Alix's studio.

She caresses it gently and slowly brings her breathing back to normal. She checks around her to see if anyone is looking her way, and when she is sure they are not, she puts the teaspoon to her lips and kisses it.

———————

She gets home an hour later. Walter turns and smiles at her from the table in the window.

"Never see you anymore," he says.

"Don't be silly. Of course you do."

"What's going on with you and this school mum?"

"Nothing. We're just getting to know each other."

"Where do you go?"

"Here and there. Cafés. Her house. The park."

"What's her name?"

"Alix."

"Alix? Isn't that the name of the woman, when we were at that pub on your birthday?"

"Yes."

"Is it her?"

"Yes."

She sees Walter's face crumple with confusion. "Why didn't you say?"

"I don't know. I thought you might think it was weird."

Walter's right eyebrow lifts slightly, and he turns back to his laptop with a sigh. "Like I'd ever think you were weird," he says drily.

Josie's wiring is all off after talking to Alix. Instead of ignoring Walter, as she normally would, she feels the nauseating darkness fall upon her again and she folds her arms across her chest and says, "What is that supposed to mean?"

"Oh, nothing, love. Nothing. Obviously."

"No! Walter! Seriously. What is that supposed to mean? Just say it."

Walter slowly removes his reading glasses and rubs away the sweat at the bridge of his nose. Then he turns to her and says, "Josie. Leave it."

"I'm not going to leave it, Walter. If you've got something to say, then say it."

"No. I'm not doing this, Josie. I'm not going there."

Suddenly she finds herself striding across the room, propelled by pure adrenaline. She stops a foot from Walter and breathes in hard and then slaps him, ringingly, hideously hard, across his face. "I FUCKING HATE YOU," she screams. "I FUCKING HATE YOU!"

She stops, recoiling slightly in the wake of her own violence.

Walter blinks at her, touches the side of his face with his fingertips. Then he slowly returns his glasses to his face and turns back to his computer.

2:30 P.M.

"Alix? Isn't it?"

Alix turns to locate the source of the greeting.

It takes a second for her to recognize Josie's mother, Pat O'Neill, and then she says, "Oh, Pat. Hello!"

Alix is on Kilburn High Road, on her way to the bank to pay in the check that her great-aunt sends on her birthday every single year. It's for twenty-five pounds and she's been putting it off for too long, risking causing offense to her great-aunt, who will be watching her bank account to see the money being cashed and, if it isn't, will send a message to her via her mother to check that it hasn't got lost in the post.

Pat is wearing an apple-green linen shirt with skinny jeans and strappy sandals. She looks vibrant and glamorous; her aura is busy and important.

"How are you?"

"I'm great," Pat replies. "Just getting some paperwork sorted for one of my ladies on the estate. Sally. She's nearly ninety. Still thinks she can do everything, bless her. How are you?"

"Oh, yes, fine. Just heading to the bank."

"Seen Josie lately?"

"Yes! Saw her earlier today, in fact."

"So, this podcast thing. It's still happening?"

"Yes. Yes, it is." Alix pauses. She feels the need to dig just a little. "What do you think about it?"

"I think it's weird, to be honest. If you didn't seem so completely normal, I'd be wondering about what your motivation was. As it is, I can tell you're straight up. I googled you and I saw your credentials. You're proper. But this birthday twin thing—I still don't really get it?"

Alix cocks her head to one side and glances upward briefly. "Yes," she says. "It's not really so much about that now. It's evolving into something else, something that's more about being women at a very particular age, on the cusp of menopause, not young but not quite old, questioning our choices, wondering about our paths, our futures. Looking at the similarities between us, but also . . ." She pauses, choosing her next words carefully. "Well, Josie—she's very different to me too."

"That's for sure." Pat's mouth purses at the end of her sentence. "You're polar opposites. You're the sort of woman I'd always assumed a daughter of mine would be. You know, grit and talent and get-up-and-go."

Alix ignores the slight against Josie and says, "What do you think of Walter?"

"She's told you, has she? How they met?"

Alix nods.

Pat eyes her disparagingly. "Well then—what do you think I think about Walter? A forty-five-year-old man hooking up with an eighteen-year-old girl. Disgusting. And God knows how long it had been going on before they told me about it. Have you met him?"

"No. Just seen him, from a distance. Is he . . . is he controlling?"

Pat considers the question for a moment and then says, "They're both as bad as each other if you ask me. They're what you call a toxic combination. And those poor girls . . ."

"Yes. Tell me about the girls. Josie doesn't mention them much. Just that one still lives at home and the other left home when she was sixteen. I couldn't help feeling that there was more she wasn't telling me."

Alix sees immediately that she has crossed a line. Pat's face closes down and she takes a step back. "Probably best you talk to Josie about that sort of thing," she says. "Not my place to say. But listen. Good luck with it all. You're going to need it."

Then she hitches her bag up onto her shoulder, musters a weak smile, turns, and walks away.

———————

Alix messages Josie when she gets home:

> *I think it is really important that I meet Walter and talk to him about his side of the story. Would he be open to the idea of coming to the studio? Or I could even come to yours and talk to him at home? Let me know what you think.*

A reply appears a few seconds later.

> *I'm not sure Walter would want to do that. He's very private.*

Alix stares at the message for a moment. Then she types a reply.

> *Does Walter know about this project?*

> *Sort of. He knows I'm talking to you.*

> *OK. Well, I do think I really need to talk to him. It could be off the record if he'd prefer. How do you think we could persuade him?*

There's a short delay then before Alix sees that Josie is typing a reply. She stares at her screen waiting for the message to appear.

If it was social he'd probably come?
As long as your husband was there?
Maybe dinner?

WEDNESDAY, 10 JULY

"I was thinking of inviting Josie and her husband over for dinner this weekend? For my project."

Alix has been gathering the nerve to make this pronouncement for over an hour, since she and Nathan woke up this morning. She'd been awake half the night, oscillating between feeling utterly convinced that it was a perfectly good idea and just another way of doing her job and feeling utterly convinced that it was the worst idea she'd ever had. Right up until ten seconds ago she had still been uncertain which way she was going to go. But the words are out now, and she bites her lip as she waits for his response.

"Jesus Christ."

"I know," she says. "I know. It'll be weird as fuck. But I really think it's going to move this project along."

"But do *I* have to be there?"

"Yes. Yes, I think you do. Sounds like he's a man's man. I don't think he'd want to hang out with only two women. And I could just interview him, but I get the feeling I'd get more out of him in a social setting. With alcohol. You know."

She throws Nathan a pleading look and his faces softens. "Sure," he says. "Anything for you, my love." He says this with sarcasm, but also, Alix knows, with a touch of sincerity, an awareness of how much he currently owes her.

Alix exhales with relief. "Thank you," she says, then picks up her phone and texts the invitation to Josie.

8:30 A.M.

Josie glances at her phone and, seeing Alix's name, snatches it up from the kitchen counter.

> *How about you and Walter come to*
> *my place for dinner on Friday night?*
> *Let me know! And see you tomorrow*
> *for another session?*

Josie stills. Her gaze flicks across the room to Walter, sitting on the sofa, watching *BBC Breakfast* and eating toast, in his dressing gown. She returns her gaze to the message again and then lets it percolate for a while, as she waits for her toast to cook. Occasionally her eyes go back to Walter, to the thatch of wiry white hair on the back of his neck that grows horizontally, to his fluffy earlobes and patchy stubble.

"Walter," she says. "You need to go to the barber's."

"I know," he says. "I was going to go on Saturday."

"We've been invited for dinner on Friday. At Alix's house. You need to go before Friday."

He turns briskly and narrows his eyes at her. "What?"

"Dinner. At Alix's. We're going. OK?"

NONE OF THIS IS TRUE

"The woman with the same birthday as you? The woman you've been seeing so much of?"

"Yes."

"Why the hell does she want to have us for dinner?"

"I told you. We're friends. That's what friends do."

"Where does she live?"

"One of those roads that runs between the park and Salusbury Road."

His left eyebrow shoots up. "Bloody hell."

"Seriously, Walter. This is important. You need a new outfit too. I can't take you in any of your clothes. When was the last time you bought anything new? Eh?"

The atmosphere in the flat shifts into a new realm with every word that she utters. It's like she's smashing a fist through a sequence of invisible walls with each one, getting closer and closer to something approaching the truth of everything.

Walter puts up his hands into a gesture of surrender. "Jesus Christ, Jojo. Chill out. I'll sort it, OK?"

"Hair? Clothes?"

"Yes. Hair. Clothes. Jeez."

He turns off the television and brings his plate through to the kitchen. He has a smell about him, probably his dressing gown needing a wash. Also stale stubble and morning breath. The smell of decay. Of defeat. It sits at the back of her throat and makes her feel enraged.

"I don't know what's got into you lately, Jojo," he says as he heads toward the bathroom for his morning shower. "I really don't."

———

At work that afternoon, Josie feeds the hem of a dress through the overlocker, her hands moving mechanically while her brain whirls and weaves chaotically through the new universe of things she thinks about these days. She's obsessively planning an outfit for Friday whilst anxiously picturing Walter in a rotating range of clothes that don't suit him. Inside her head there plays a grainy movie of them all sitting around the table in Alix's kitchen with the mismatched chairs, the red-haired children running about in colorful pajamas, wine being poured into huge glasses by the annoying red-haired husband, cool music through a speaker, the cloud-cat curling around their ankles, the light dying in the sky as the conversation flows. And then her spiraling thoughts bring her back to Walter and his old-man teeth, his irritating monotone, his defeated air, and she is fourteen again, sixteen, eighteen, a young mum spending her husband's money frugally in Sainsbury's, a middle-aged woman in a quiet flat, and in every incarnation she is the same person: a girl in stasis. And now, just as she'd hoped would happen when she first thought about asking Alix to make her the subject of a podcast, someone else is breaking through her carapace. Another person entirely. And that person is bigger than her, louder than her, harsher than her, older than her. That person is ready finally to tell her truth.

She cuts the ends of the thread from the overlocking machine and turns the dress over, ready to hem the other side. A tube rumbles along the tracks beyond the big window and Josie sees her face as a blurred reflection in the glass. She looks like a half-finished painting, she observes, waiting for the artist to come back and add the detail.

Her phone buzzes with a message from Alix. She experiences the endorphin rush she always gets when she sees Alix's name on her phone, the sense that something good is happening to her.

Can you bring a photo tomorrow of the girls?
Would love to see what they look like.
See you then!

A chill goes through Josie. *The girls.* How can she talk to Alix about the girls? she asks herself. But then she looks again at the blurred version of herself in the big window and suddenly she sees that the half-finished portrait is that of a queenly woman, not a gauche girl, and she knows that finally, after all these years, it is time to hold her life up to the light.

THURSDAY, 11 JULY

"Here." Josie pushes a fan of photographs across the table toward Alix. "My girls."

Alix lifts her gaze to Josie and smiles. "Oh," she says. "Amazing. Thank you."

The first photograph shows two chubby toddlers in thick knitted sweaters and jeans holding hands and standing in what looks like the big sand pit in Queen's Park. The older girl has hair the same color as Josie's, but more vivid in tone. The younger one has sandy blond hair with the type of ringlets at the ends that will never grow back after her first haircut.

"Which one is which?" she asks.

"This one"—Josie points at the one with the ringlets—"is Roxy. That one"—she indicates the one with chestnut-brown hair—"is Erin."

"They're adorable," Alix says. "Just adorable."

Josie nods and smiles and watches as Alix moves on to the next photograph. It's the two girls, side by side, outside the school where

Alix's children go, wearing the same sky-blue polo shirts and navy bottoms that her children were wearing when they left the house this morning.

"Roxy's first day," says Josie, a note of pained nostalgia in her voice. "I cried for about four hours that day."

Alix glances at Josie. "Oh God. Really?" She thinks back to Leon's first day at school, returning to an empty house for the first time in seven years and the euphoria of knowing that it could be about her again for a while. She'd never understood the weeping mums outside the playground.

"I was bereft. I didn't know what I would do. Suddenly, all this time. Suddenly, all this silence."

Alix thinks of her conversation with Mandy in the school office and says, "And the girls. How did they get on at primary school? Did they like it?"

She notices Josie tense slightly, her shoulders lifting toward her ears. "Oh, you know," she says. "Not really. You see, Erin, my oldest, she's always had some problems. Not quite sure how you'd describe it, really. The teachers called it global developmental delay? But I didn't agree with that. She was just a bit lazy, I think. A bit passive? Hard to get a reaction out of her. Hard to know what she was thinking. And then Roxy was the opposite. Oppositional defiant disorder, the teachers called it. I think I did agree with that. You could never tell Roxy anything. She would never, ever comply. She was always angry. Used to hit me. Hit her sister. Just the angriest, angriest child." Josie shudders at the memory. "So between them, with their problems, no, it wasn't the happiest of times. And high school was no better, of course."

Alix doesn't respond, just goes to the last of the three photographs.

"This is the last one I have of the two of them," says Josie, touching the edge of the photo gently. "Just before Roxy left home."

Alix holds her breath as she absorbs the image. It is not what she was expecting at all. She cannot relate the girls in this photograph to the girls in the other photographs. She cannot believe that they are the same people.

The girl who once had sandy ringlets is now a stocky girl wearing her hair scraped back hard from a wide greasy forehead with rings pierced through both of her nostrils and her septum. Erin, who had once been a glowing, sweet-faced child with an air of shy vulnerability, is stony-faced and scrawny to the point of emaciated, with dark circles around her eyes and her hair hanging limp on both sides of her face.

"Look different, don't they?" Josie says with a brittle edge to her voice.

"Yes. Yes. They do."

There's a tart silence before Josie shuffles the three photographs back together and slides them into her shoulder bag. "Please don't judge me."

Alix flicks her eyes toward Josie. "Sorry?"

Josie opens her mouth, words waiting on the tip of her tongue but not being spoken. Then she smiles, tightly, and says, "Nothing! Nothing." She places her bag on the floor, pulls her headphones toward her, and says, "Shall we start?"

Hi! I'm Your Birthday Twin!
A NETFLIX ORIGINAL SERIES

Screen shows a pink wooden chair with a heart shape cut out of the back.
The chair has been modified with straps and belts.
It stands in an empty room, lit by rays of daylight shining through grubby windows.
The text under the shot reads:

**Recording from Alix Summer's podcast,
11 July, 2019**

Josie's voice begins.

"Walter couldn't cope with them. He was away a lot. He'd
been made redundant by the company he'd been working for
in London and ended up getting a much better job with an
electrical company that worked mainly out of Scotland and
the North East. So he'd be away for days on end, just back for
the weekends. I have to say, I liked it. For so many years I'd
existed only as half of a couple and as a mother. I had never
been alone, not really. You know, before the girls were born,
I didn't even have a key to our flat. I just used to have to wait
in for him to get home from work. Just wait in, all day . . . so I
liked those years when Walter worked away during the week,
when it was just me and the girls. We were happy. We were
free. I let the girls be themselves, gave them room to breathe.
But then Walter would get back at the weekends and, well,
everything would change. And not in a good way."

The shot of the pink chair with the leather straps fades away.

The screen goes black.

11 A.M.

Walter has been to the barber's and, to Josie's great disappointment,
looks almost exactly the same. She masks her dismay and thanks him
for making the effort. He grunts in response, and she knows that she's
pushing him very close to the precipice of his own tolerance of her.

Their marriage sometimes feels like a huge ship that left harbor
facing one way and has slowly, lugubriously, turned 180 degrees,

headed off in the wrong direction, and then stalled. Somehow, Josie had taken control of the deck, but it had turned out that she was as bad at steering the ship as Walter had been, and ever since, they'd been going round and round in circles, staring disconsolately into the middle distance, waiting to be rescued.

Until Alix.

Josie takes three jars of baby food from the cupboard and heats them up for Erin. She places them on a tray with a spoon and a pouch of Ella's Kitchen pureed mango and apple. She leaves the tray outside Erin's room. She kisses her fingertips, puts them to the door, and then goes to her bedroom to get ready for work.

When Josie gets back from work, Walter has been clothes shopping. He doesn't do her a fashion parade. He merely cocks his head at the Primark bags and says, "Go on, then. Have a look."

He's done quite well. A nice navy-blue casual long-sleeved shirt, and a pair of camel-colored chinos. He's even got some new socks.

"Good," she says to him, with a nod. "Very nice."

He grunts. She can sense him shutting down.

She gets started on a shepherd's pie. It's Walter's favorite of her small repertoire of dishes, and even though she's trying to be more experimental with food these days (yesterday she made a dish with couscous, Halloumi, and chickpeas), today Walter deserves something he likes. Then she takes the dog for a walk around the block. She thinks she sees Roxy three times in the ten minutes she's out of the house and the second she gets home she opens up her laptop and searches for her in the places she always searches for her on the internet. But, as always, she is not there.

Normally Josie doesn't talk to Walter about Roxy; they never talk about the girls at all, it's just made everything easier, somehow. But later on, as they sit side by side on the sofa eating the shepherd's pie, Josie turns to Walter and says, "Do you ever think you see her? Roxy?"

He throws her a look. She knows he'd planned not to talk to her tonight; he's still smarting from how horrible she's been to him the last few days. But this isn't the sort of question you can ignore because you're in a huff, and she sees his guard fall, and then another take its place. "What do you mean?"

"I mean, when you're out. Do you see someone on the street and think it's her, for a minute? And then realize it's not?"

He's silent for a second before nodding. "Yeah. Sometimes."

"Do you ever wonder if she's dead?"

"Course I do. All the time."

They fall silent for a moment and eat their food, but the air is filled with things they both want to say, and Josie gets in first.

"You know, I'm probably going to tell Alix about the girls."

His head snaps toward her. "What do you mean, tell her?"

"I'm going to tell her. What happened. What we did."

He narrows his eyes at her. "Are you mad?"

Josie recoils slightly. She hates it when Walter says things like that. "It's time. That's all. She'll be able to help us."

"Help us? Fuck, Josie. She'll call the fucking police."

"Good."

"Oh my God. Oh Jesus. Josie. You actually are, aren't you? You're actually mad. Genuinely. We've been through all of this. I thought we agreed—"

"No. No, we did not agree. We did not agree anything. We need to—"

"We need to do *nothing*, Josie. We need to do nothing. Fucking hell . . ." He slaps his forehead with his hand and pushes the tray of food off his lap so he can stand up.

He starts to stride away from Josie and she pulls him back by his arm and then flinches when she sees his hand arcing toward her. He brings it back quickly to his side and carries on walking toward the bay window.

"It's happening, Walter. Whether you like it or not. I'm going to tell Alix everything. I can't live like this anymore. We're moving on."

"I can't talk to you. You're insane. You're literally insane. I'm married to a fucking nutter."

"And I'm married to a *fucking pedophile!*"

The air in the room freezes. For a second, neither Josie nor Walter breathes or moves.

Finally, Walter speaks. "I'm sorry?"

She wants to say it again. And then again and again. She wants to pummel her fists against his chest and spit the word into his face until he's choking on it. But she can't. It's gone.

She collects their half-eaten plates of food, scrapes some into the blender for Erin, throws the rest into the bin.

She purees the pie for Erin and spoons it into a bowl. She puts it on a tray with a strawberry-flavored Müllerlight. She leaves it outside Erin's room, her spare hand clamped over her mouth and nose to mask the smell. She is about to touch the door and then kiss her fingers, but she stops herself.

She's starting to feel that Erin is part of the problem here. She's starting to feel like Erin is no longer on her side.

FRIDAY,
12 JULY

Nathan texts Alix at 6:30 p.m.:

I'm just having a quick one with Gio.
Should be back before 7:30.
Need me to pick anything up?

Alix sighs heavily, her thumb over the keyboard, thinking of and discarding a dozen ripe responses, before simply typing *OK*, turning off the screen, and putting the phone down. She returns to the onion she'd been slicing for the dish she's cooking for Josie and Walter, turns it round to dice it, then slides it into the casserole dish, where it sizzles in a pool of melted butter.

Eliza is at her friend's house for a sleepover. Leon is watching TV in the living room. Alix thinks about the half-open bottle of wine in the fridge, thinks about pouring herself a large glass right now and glugging it. But she mustn't. She has to hold it together.

She slices chicken breasts into strips and adds them to the frying onions.

Nathan is still not home at seven thirty. She stares at her phone desperately, even though she knows there won't be anything there. She sends a prayer out to the universe that Josie and Walter will be late, but at 7:32 the doorbell rings and she dries her hands, tidies her hair, and heads to the front door.

"Hi!"

Josie stands on the top step in one of the dresses they'd chosen together at the boutique, her hair held back in a French braid on one side of her head, clutching a bunch of pink roses and a bottle of expensive champagne. She beams at Alix brightly and slightly unnervingly; Josie does not usually beam. And then she leans into her and kisses her firmly on both cheeks. "Hi! You look lovely!"

Then Josie turns and pulls Walter to her gently by his elbow. "Alix, this is Walter. Walter, this is Alix."

Walter smiles shyly at Alix and gives her his hand to shake. He has had a brutal haircut since the last time Alix saw him and is wearing brand-new clothes with sharp crease marks down the legs and sleeves. Alix feels a stab of tenderness toward him, but then remembers that he is not the innocent old man that he appears to be.

"Come in! Come in! I'm afraid Nathan isn't back from work yet. But he should be here any minute."

She takes the pink roses from Josie and thanks her profusely. Then she puts the room-temperature champagne in the fridge and offers them drinks, seats them on stools at the kitchen island, pushes bowls of crisps and nuts and dips toward them, and checks on the pasta sauce.

"You have a very nice home," says Walter, his fingers wrapped around the bottle of Peroni Alix has just passed to him.

"Thank you!"

"How long have you lived here?"

Walter has a monotone voice which makes him sound as if he's being sarcastic.

"Oh," she replies. "About ten years. We were in a flat in Kensal Rise before that."

"Is that where you come from? Kensal Rise?"

"No. I was brought up in Paddington, actually. Nathan and I moved here after we got married. And talking of Nathan"—she locates her phone and touches the screen—"let me just see if he's sent an update."

There is no update from Nathan and it is nearly quarter to eight. She calls him and the call goes straight through to voicemail. She smiles tightly and says, "Gone straight through to voicemail. He must be on the tube."

"After-work drinks?" says Walter.

"Yes. I'd imagine."

"What does he do, your husband?"

"He leases high-end commercial space to big companies."

Walter nods thoughtfully, as if considering the legitimacy of this claim, and then grabs a handful of nuts from a bowl and tips them directly from the palm of his hand into his mouth.

"How are you, Josie?" Alix asks, her voice sounding too high in her ears.

"Great, thanks."

"I love your hair like that." Alix gestures at the very professional French braid. "Did you do it yourself?"

"Yes. I used to do the girls' hair like this. I was always quite good at hairstyles."

"I just can't," says Alix. "It hurts my brain trying to work out how to do it!"

"I suppose I'm what you'd call 'dexterous.' Sewing, dressmaking, knitting, crochet, all that kind of thing."

Alix sees Josie throw a quick glance at Walter, who is staring unhappily at the label on his beer bottle.

"I've always been good at things like that," Josie says, flicking another look at her husband. "Haven't I?"

Walter nods, his fingertips pulling at the beer label. "Yes. You have."

Alix turns to Walter. "Tell me about yourself, Walter. Are you from around here originally?"

"No. I was brought up in Essex, then my parents split up when I was fifteen and I came and lived in Kilburn with my dad."

"In the flat where you live now?"

"Yes. That's right."

"And you raised your family there too?"

"Yes. Erin and Roxy."

"And what's Erin up to tonight?"

"Oh, she'll just be in. Gaming."

"Oh! She's a gamer?"

"Yes. Hard-core." He laughs drily and Alix sees a strange look pass across Josie's face. Why hasn't Josie mentioned this aspect of Erin's existence to her? she wonders. She glances at the kitchen clock and sees that it is nearly eight o'clock. She apologizes to Josie and Walter and calls Nathan again. This time it doesn't go through to voicemail, it rings out, and she feels a surge of hope that maybe he is, right now, halfway down the street, his tie loosened, his mood softened by a couple of pints, ready to bring fresh energy to this strange gathering of people. More than anything in the world she wishes Nathan were here—Nathan with his loud voice and high-octane ways. She doesn't care how drunk he is, she just wants him here.

"So," Walter says. "You and Josie. That's an odd thing, isn't it?"

"What, you mean . . . ?" She gestures at herself and then Josie.

"Your friendship. Yes."

"Friendship?" Alix replies. "I thought you meant the podcast."

"Podcast?" he says. "What podcast?"

"Oh, come on, Walter," says Josie. "I told you. I told you this."

"I don't think so."

"I told you that Alix does podcasts."

"Well, you might have mentioned it, but you didn't say she was doing one about you."

"Oh, it's not about me. It's about us being birthday twins. Me and Alix."

Alix feels an awkward cloud of dishonesty pass through the room. She'd been surprised by the fact that Walter had agreed to come along and essentially make himself a part of the project and thought that maybe he was more evolved than Josie had made him sound. But no, this was, Alix realized, a classic Josie maneuver, like buying a Pomchi without checking that it really was a Pomchi, or allowing herself to be groomed into a lifelong relationship by a man old enough to be her own father: a sort of blundering, thoughtless, aimless approach to life. A "do the thing and worry about it later" approach. And so now Alix has to go along with the subterfuge.

She clears her throat and smiles. "Can I top you up?" she asks brightly, before excusing herself to get something from the larder. When she comes back, Walter and Josie are sitting in silence, chewing crisps. Alix looks at the time. It's been ten minutes since she tried calling Nathan and he should be home by now. She calls him again. It goes to voicemail. She sighs and brings up Giovanni's number. She wouldn't normally, but she cannot do this by herself. She simply cannot.

"Oh, Gio! Hi! It's Alix. I'm sorry to bother you, but are you still with Nathan?"

The background of the call is frenetic with the sounds of laughter and music.

"Oh, hi, Al! Yeah. Hold on. Here he is."

A moment later Nathan is on the line. "Fuck," he says, drawling already, and it's not even eight thirty. "Fuck. Alix. Fuck. I'm leaving. Right now. Literally leaving right this second. I'll get a cab, OK? I'm so sorry. I'll see you in . . . *half an hour*. Start eating without me, though, if you need to."

Alix forces a stiff smile as she ends the call.

"Everything OK?" asks Josie.

"Yeah, he's on his way. Lost track of time. Said to start without him. So I'll get this pasta on now, shall I?"

"I'm sorry, Alix, but I think that's disgusting."

Alix stops halfway to the tap with the pasta pan and turns back to Josie. "I—"

"Seriously. I'm sorry. But I could hear him, on the phone, slurring. And here you are, slaving over a nice meal for him, entertaining guests, looking so nice. Who does he think he is?"

Alix feels her breath catch in the back of her throat. Suddenly, she feels threatened. It's the deathly tone of Josie's voice, the other-ness of her, Walter by her side breathing so heavily through his nose that Alix can hear it. She thinks of Leon next door in his big head-phones, his legs tucked up under him on the sofa that still makes him look tiny even now he's getting big and she wonders what she has done. She thinks of Josie on her doorstep, rifling through her recycling box, taking home the old magazine. She thinks of Wal-ter keeping Josie locked up at home as a young woman without a key, waiting for him to get home from work. And then she thinks of Josie's daughters with the dead eyes and she suddenly wants to scrap the whole thing; get the champagne out of the fridge and hand it back to them, hustle them down the hallway, out of the front door, and forget that she had ever allowed Josie Fair into her life.

But it is too late now. They are here, on her kitchen stools, eating Sweet Chili–flavor Kettle chips, waiting for her chicken, bacon, and spinach alfredo, insulting her husband. She can feel Josie's eyes boring into her and she brings the stiff smile back to her face and says, "Oh, it's no big deal. Friday night, you know. I'm sure he's not the only man out there losing track of time. Anyway, what else can I get you? Another beer, Walter?"

He nods and thanks her and she passes him a cold beer. Then Josie says, "Why don't you show Walter your amazing recording studio, Alix. He loves stuff like that."

Alix throws Walter an uncertain glance. But he nods at her and says, "Yeah. I'd like that. If it's all right with you?"

"Yes. Absolutely. You coming, Josie?"

Josie smiles. "No," she says. "That's OK. You go. I've already seen it."

Alix leads Walter through the garden, which is all lit up with solar lamps and fairy lights. She unlocks the studio door and flicks on the switches.

"Wow," says Walter. "This is pretty cool." He eyes every detail of the room and asks her questions about the wiring and the electrics which she cannot possibly answer.

"You'd have to ask Nathan," she says. "He was the one who had it all done for me."

They share a dry exchange about the general lack of Nathan and then, finally, Alix finds the impetus to ask Walter the question she's wanted to ask him since the day she met Josie.

"May I ask you, about you and Josie? About how you met?"

She sees Walter blanch slightly, before recovering himself and taking a slow sip from his beer bottle. "Depends what she's told you, really."

"Well, I'd really like to just hear it from your side."

He shrugs and sighs. "I knew Jojo from when she was a kid. I was friends with her mum at first. Then Jojo and I started hanging out a bit. She was too mature for people her age, you know?

Found them tedious. Comes from being an only child, I think. I was the same. Always preferred the company of grown-ups. And yeah, one thing led to another, and it turned out that somewhere along the line we'd fallen for each other. And I suppose it must look weird to some people, me being so much older than her. But it's never felt weird to us. Not once."

Alix nods, slowly, hypnotized slightly by the bass monotone of Walter's voice, the way he makes opinion sound like fact, the lack of nuance, space, dichotomy in the way he speaks. Yes, she thinks, yes. I can see that. I can see how that might happen between two people. But then she snaps out of it, remembers that this man bought a fifteen-year-old girl a gold bracelet for her birthday, took her to the pub, and poured vodka in her lemonade. All while married to somebody else.

"And your ex-wife," she continues. "Was she much younger than you?"

"No. Not really. She was ten years younger than me."

"And how old were you when you met her?"

"Oh God." He scratches at the back of his neck and screws up his eyes. "I must have been late twenties, I suppose."

Alix lets the maths of this pronouncement float between them, unremarked upon.

"You know," Walter says, thoughtfully, peering at Alix through narrowed eyes, "she's a tricky one, my Jojo. She gives this impression, doesn't she . . . of being . . . simple."

"Simple?"

"Yes. You know. Like there's not much going on in her head. And if there's one thing I've learned about her over the years it's that there is actually *too much* going on in her head. She's not who she makes out to be. Not at all."

His words sit there, like ticking bombs. Alix nods and says, "Yes. I think there is more to her than meets the eye."

"That's putting it mildly," he says.

"Would you . . ." Alix begins, uncertainly. "How would you feel about talking to me a little? For my podcast?"

"This birthday twins one?"

"Yes." Alix pinches her bottom lip between her thumb and fore-finger and eyes him anxiously.

"But what would it have to do with me? I'm not your birthday twin."

"Well, no. You're not. But you're married to one. And you've shared most of her life journey with her. It'd be great to get a few nuggets of insight from you. Just for context."

She watches him for a reaction. It comes slowly, as a shake of the head. "No," he says. "I think not. But for what it's worth from my side—Jojo's got what you might call an *elastic* relationship with the truth."

"Elastic?" she repeats.

"Yeah. She, er . . . how can I put it? When she doesn't like the reality of things, she finds a reality she prefers."

"You mean, everything she's been telling me about herself, about her life, is untrue?"

"Well. No. I wouldn't go that far. But you can't believe everything she says. Just keep your wits about you."

Alix narrows her eyes at Walter, assessing how much he is trying to manipulate her. She says, "Ah. OK. I'll bear that in mind."

"Probably best not to say anything to Jojo. About this conversa-tion. You know?"

"Why not say anything to Josie?"

"Just . . ." He pauses. "Josie just likes to control things. You know? If she knew that I'd been talking to you, she would feel like she was losing control of you."

"Of me?"

"Yes. Of you and the whole situation." He sighs. "Believe

me, I know Josie better than anyone, and she's a control freak. And you don't even realize you're being controlled until it's too late."

Alix stares at Walter for a moment. Once again, she is struck by the sheer blandness of him, the impenetrable wall of nothingness between his physical being and the rest of the world. Yet he is clearly a master gaslighter. Behind the dead eyes lies the soul of a groomer and a liar and an abuser. She feels a bolt of ice shoot through her core and shivers slightly.

———————

She serves the pasta half an hour later at the kitchen table. Nathan has still not returned. The conversation limps on. They discuss the primary school that they have in common, working out which teachers are still there, and which have left. They discuss the state of the world, in a stolid, one-dimensional way. Leon walks in at one point, and Alix is able to leave the table for a couple of minutes to get him a snack and a drink, and to locate a charging cable for him. They discuss how delicious the food is and Alix manages to stretch out the description of the recipe into a five-minute spiel.

"Anyway," says Josie, after a somewhat painful silence. "Where's that husband of yours? Maybe you should give him another call?"

"Yes," says Alix. "Maybe. I'll give him another ten minutes."

"Hardly worth him coming back now," Josie says. "I mean, dinner's over." Josie shakes her head sadly and tuts under her breath. "Terrible," she says. "I'm so sorry, Alix. You poor thing."

Alix feels herself tense up with a weird, defensive anger. "I'm not a poor thing," she replies tersely. "I really am not." She gets to her feet, the chair scraping noisily against the floor tiles, then collects the plates together loudly. She drops them on the counter above the

NONE OF THIS IS TRUE

dishwasher with a clatter and then goes into the hallway and yells, "Bedtime! Now!" to a startled-looking Leon.

When she comes back to the kitchen, Josie and Walter are collecting themselves together and the atmosphere between them is horrendous.

"Well," says Josie. "Thank you so much for a lovely evening. The food was delicious. But I think we'd best let you get on now."

Alix drops her head into her chest. She sighs loudly and says, "I am so sorry. So, so sorry. But yes. And thank you for coming."

Walter brings his empty beer bottle and places it gently on the counter. He looks like he's about to say something, but then the moment passes, and he turns to leave. She sees them to the door and Josie pats her arm and gives her a strange hug.

"Men," she whispers into Alix's ear. "Fucking *men*."

Alix cleans the kitchen after they leave. Then she sits and finishes the third of a bottle of wine that was left of the one she'd been sharing with Josie. When the kitchen is dark and the dishwasher is running and she feels drunk enough, she gets to her feet and goes to the living room, where Leon is still sitting in the dark, curled into the big sofa, the cat at his side, staring at the TV screen with wide, exhausted eyes.

She sits down next to him and gently pulls his headphones away from his head. "It's late, baby. We both need to go to bed now."

"Can I have five more minutes?" he asks sweetly.

The sofa feels nice. The cat is purring. She nods and says, "OK. I'll put my timer on." She sets the timer on her phone to go off in five minutes and leans back into the sofa, pulling her son's feet onto her lap.

"Why were those people here?" Leon asks after a moment.

"Oh," she replies, rubbing his toes absent-mindedly. "I'm interviewing them. For a podcast."

He nods. Then he turns to look at her and says, "Why was the lady standing outside your studio?"

"The lady who was here?"

"Yes. The lady who was here. She was standing outside your studio, when you were in there with that old man, like she was listening. I saw her. Through those doors. She looked really cross. Really, really cross."

10 P.M.

Josie and Walter walk home in silence. Josie feels sick. All the rich food (she'd expected something more sophisticated from Alix than stodgy pasta and can't help feeling a bit shortchanged) and all the wine. She's cross that her expensive champagne never made it out of the fridge, and cross with the way that Alix just dumped her roses in a cheap-looking vase and didn't trim the stems or fluff them out at all. They weren't the cheap ones; they cost twelve pounds. They deserved better.

And the whole night, of course, was completely ruined by Nathan doing what he'd done. Alix had been distracted and sharp. She had not been a good host and it had not been a good evening.

Once home, Josie opens the front door and calls out into the darkness of their flat, "Fred! Mummy's home!"

The dog comes hurtling toward her and jumps into her arms.

She takes the dog out for a wee and then brings him back in again.

She notices that Walter has discarded his new Primark outfit and is back in joggers and a baggy T-shirt, the smart shirt and trousers left pooled on the floor by the linen basket like a silent two fingers up at her.

She passes Erin's room and puts her ear to the door, listens to the sound of her gaming chair squeaking. She thinks of the little boy in the pajamas on the sofa at Alix's house, with the huge headphones on, staring blankly at the screen for hours and hours, totally ignored and neglected, and thinks, really, what's the difference? Is she really such a bad parent? Who's to know how he'll end up ten, twenty years from now?

She watches Walter take a beer from the fridge, open it, and go to the table in the bay window. He clears his throat and lifts the lid of his laptop. They have still not spoken to each other. The atmosphere between them is worse than it's ever been in all the time they've been together.

"You were an embarrassment tonight," she says to Walter.

He ignores her. She hears him sigh heavily through his nose.

"The whole thing, Walter. I wanted to die."

"Mm-*hm*," he intones, his gaze on his laptop, his fingertips clicking the keys.

"Walter," she shouts, "I'm talking to you."

"Yes. I can hear that."

"So talk to me!"

"Talk to you about what, exactly?"

"About tonight. About how you embarrassed me."

Finally, his fingertips stop clicking off the keys and he turns and looks at her. He looks so tired and so old that it startles her for a moment. "In what way," he says, "did I embarrass you?"

"Just—just by being *you*."

"That's nice, Jojo."

"I'm not trying to be nice. The whole evening was a disaster. I'd been so looking forward to it and it was horrible. And you, you just sat there with your stupid beer looking like everything was beneath you. You made no effort at all. I had to do all the work."

"All the work? What work? Listen, I really don't know what's going on between you and that woman, but I can tell you something for certain. She's no 'friend' of yours. She doesn't even like you."

Josie feels the breath inside her lungs freeze and stop. "Of course she does."

"No, Josie. She doesn't. She's just trying to get inside that tiny, weird brain of yours and work out what makes you tick."

For a moment it feels to Josie that she is in the eye of a storm, that the universe has fragmented into a million tiny pieces and is swirling and whirling around her, that she is all that is still in the world. She closes her eyes, but the feeling grows stronger.

"Stop. Calling. Me. Weird."

"Well, stop *being* weird."

"Stop it!"

"I'm not sure I can do this anymore."

"Do what?"

"You, Jojo. I can't do *you*."

"And what do you think it's like for me? Walter? Living with *you*. Living like *this*." She gestures around the room. "I can't do this anymore either. I'm at the end of my tether. I can't keep it all locked inside. It's killing me, Walter. It's killing me. I need someone to know. I have to tell Alix!"

Walter stares at her through tired, disappointed eyes, and he says, slowly and coldly, "You really are stupid, aren't you? Stupid as they get."

At the sound of these words, Josie feels the swirling fragments of the universe slow down and thicken and then clear and all that is left is red-hot fury that feels as if it's burning her from the inside out. She thinks of the things she heard Walter saying to Alix in the recording studio, poisoning her with his vile lies, and she knows that it is here, at last, the moment she has been waiting for; she feels certainty rip through her like a cyclone.

PART TWO

PART TWO

SATURDAY,
13 JULY

The familiar chime of the Ring doorbell slices into Alix's dream. At first she thinks that it is her alarm, that it is six thirty and she must get up and get the children ready for school. Then her eye catches the time, and she sees that it is 3:02 a.m. and she remembers that last night was Friday and that today is Saturday and then, and only then, does she register the fact that the other side of the bed is unslept in.

"Fuck's sake," she mutters to herself, pulling back the duvet and ripping herself from the warmth of her bed. "Fuck's *sake*."

She tiptoes down the stairs and hears the Ring bell chime again and her blood heats with rage. Fucking Nathan, waking up the fucking children. She wrenches open the door, ready to flounce silently, furiously back to bed, but then stops and gasps when she sees that it is not Nathan.

It is Josie.

Josie stands, defeated, her shoulders slumped and tears streaking through a mask of grazes and dried-up blood on her face. The dog peers over the top of his denim carrier.

"Oh my God, Josie! Oh my God. What happened?"

A choked sob emerges, but no words.

Alix opens the door wider and says, "God, come in!"

She helps Josie through the door and into the kitchen, where she sits her carefully on the sofa. "What happened, Josie? Please, you have to tell me."

"It was Walter," she says through juddering sobs. "He attacked me."

"Walter did this?"

"Yes! And it's not the first time. It's when he's been drinking. He just sees red."

"Here," says Alix. "Let me get a wet cloth, get this face cleaned up, see if there's any damage."

Josie nods defeatedly.

Alix takes a clean tea towel from a drawer and runs it under the tap. She dabs Josie's face gently with it, revealing a horribly swollen and split lip and scuff marks down both cheekbones.

"The back of my head too, I think?"

She turns her head and Alix sees that there is encrusted blood on her crown, beneath which is a small split in her scalp.

"Any dizziness?" Alix asks.

Josie shakes her head. "No. I feel OK. Just a bit shocked."

"Shall I call you an ambulance?"

"No! No, please don't. It will just set off a load of things happening that I really can't deal with right now. And I'm fine. Really."

Alix takes the bloodied tea towel, rinses it under the tap, squeezes it out, and hands it to Josie. Then she fills the kettle and switches it on. "What happened, Josie?" she asks. "I mean, everything seemed OK when you left?"

"Well. Yes and no. I mean, Walter was grumpy, obviously, because of Nathan not coming. I think he thought it was really rude, which it was. He wouldn't talk to me the whole walk home. And then he had another beer when we got home, and things sort of escalated.

He called me all sorts of horrible names. Told me I was stupid. And I saw red and went for him."

"You mean you attacked him?"

"Yes. Well, no. I intended to, and I know he might look like an old man, but he's very strong, still. He's big. And he overpowered me. Completely. Just kept pounding and pounding and pounding. And then—"

"Then what?" Alix catches her breath.

"Then Erin walked in. Erin came in and saw what he was doing and she tried to get him off me but he hit her too."

"Oh my God. That's just horrific. Is she OK?"

"Yes. She's fine. She's at a friend's house."

"And where's Walter?"

"I don't know! Still there, I suppose." Tears fall from Josie's eyes again and she dabs them away with the damp tea towel.

Alix breathes in and then places her hand over Josie's. "You know we should call the police?"

Josie glares at her. "No!" she says. "No. Please. Don't."

"But, Josie, look what he's done to you. He's committed a terrible crime. You say he's done it before. He hurt your child! I—"

"No! I'm not having the police getting involved. Absolutely not."

"But what are you going to do? I mean, are you going to go back there?"

"I'm not going back there."

"And what about your mum? Have you told her?"

Josie widens her eyes at Alix and groans; fresh tears start falling. "I can't tell my mum! She'll just say it's all my own fault. She'll take his side."

"Take his side? When he's done this to you! Of course she won't."

"You've met my mum. You've seen what she's like. She thinks I'm the lowest of the low."

"No, that's—"

"It *is*. It is true. I cannot tell my mum. I can't tell her any of it."

"But you have to tell someone. Surely."

"I'm telling you! For God's sake. I'm telling you!"

"Yes. And I'm glad you've told me. But—"

"But what?"

"I just think you need to tell someone in your inner sanctum?"

"*I haven't got an inner sanctum,*" Josie wails. "I've got Walter and I've got the girls and I've got Fred and I've got you."

Alix feels the contents of her stomach curdle slightly at Josie's intonation of the word "you." It sounds proprietorial and odd. No, she wants to say. No, you don't *have* me. But she puts her arm around Josie's shaking shoulders and squeezes her reassuringly. "Let me get you a cup of tea," she says. "Unless you'd prefer something stronger?"

Josie looks at Alix with red, glassy eyes and says, "Do you have brandy?"

Alix smiles and gets to her feet. "I certainly do."

Josie sighs deeply while Alix gets the brandy. "Any sign of Nathan?"

"No. Looks like he's decided to stay out."

Josie tuts softly. "Men," she says again. "Men."

Alix doesn't react with the words she wants to utter. She doesn't say, *Please do not ever compare your elderly, dead-eyed, pedophiliac gaslighter of a husband with mine, who has a drink problem but is fundamentally decent.* Instead, she gently pops the cork back in the brandy bottle and brings the glass to Josie, who takes it from her with a shaking hand.

"What are you going to do?" Alix asks, knowing even as she does so that Josie is assuming that she will stay here, but hoping, desperately, that she will respond otherwise.

"I don't know."

"I could talk to my friend Mari, she's very involved with a domestic violence charity. She could suggest a safe place for you to be. I can give her a call, right now."

"No. Don't disturb her. It's fine. I'm fine. If it's OK with you, Alix, I'd feel safest just staying here with you tonight?"

Alix feels her insides curl up in a knot. "Oh," she says. "I mean, I'm not sure, it's a bit . . ."

Josie's eyes widen and she draws her body in on itself, recoiling slightly from Alix's words. She looks as though she might be about to cry, and Alix says, "Sure. Of course. I'll make up the spare room for you. It'll be fine."

She sees Josie's body language soften immediately, her shoulders grow round. She hears a tremulous sigh come from her quivering mouth and then the words "Thank you. Thank you so much."

10 A.M.

I am literally the worst person in the world.
I can either come home now and prostrate myself
at your feet, or I can kill myself. Your choice.

After the weirdness of the previous night, Alix is too relieved to hear from Nathan to be angry anymore. She replies quickly.

Please don't kill yourself. I need you.
We have a problem. Get back soon!

He replies with a GIF of a man running and Alix smiles, despite herself.

Josie is in the guest bedroom on the top floor. Alix peered through a small gap in the door earlier and the dog, perched at the foot of the bed, lifted his top lip briefly and began growling, so she'd quietly retreated. But that was two hours ago and there's still no sign of her.

Alix tiptoes back up the stairs and peers once more through the gap in the door. A smell hits her, violently, a smell she recognizes all too well from her own dog-owning days. In the corner of the room, thankfully on wooden floorboards, is an arc of tiny dog droppings and a puddle of urine. Fred bares his teeth at her and this time she lets him bark.

The noise rouses Josie from her deep sleep and she sits up suddenly. Alix is taken aback by the state of her face, which looks worse this morning than it did last night, the bruises blooming into vivid pools of mustard and mauve. "Oh," she says, blinking blindly into the half-light. "Oh. God. Hi."

"Hi," says Alix. "How are you doing?"

"Oh. God," she says again. "Sorry. I was out cold. What time is it?"

"Just gone ten."

"I'm sorry. I had no idea." She turns her head to the side and sniffs the air. Her eyes find the pile of dog mess and she groans. "Oh no! I am so, so sorry. I slept through his toilet time. Poor baby. Just give me some cleaning stuff and I'll deal with it."

Josie climbs painfully from the bed. She is wearing Alix's Toast pajamas, which she lent her last night.

"It's fine. I'll do it. You get back into bed. I'll bring you some coffee."

Josie nods gratefully and swings her legs back into the bed. "Thank you so much, Alix. That would be amazing."

Alix passes Leon on the stairs on her way back down.

"Why is she still here?" he whispers.

"She had an accident," Alix replies. "On her way home. I'm just going to take care of her for the day."

"She looks really scary," he whispers.

"You saw her?"

He nods. "I peeped in. Her dog growled at me."

"Well, she'll be gone by bedtime tonight, so let's just be kind to her for now. Yes?"

Leon nods again.

Alix makes Josie a cappuccino and brings it up to the guest room, with a roll of kitchen towel and a spray cleaner. She places the coffee by the side of Josie's bed and collects Fred's droppings into a sheet of paper, puts them in the toilet in the en suite, then sprays and cleans the whole area. She pulls down the sash window, saying, "Let's get some fresh air in here, shall we? I can walk the dog for you, if you like?"

"Oh. Yes. I'm sure he'd love that. His harness is in the carrier. Over there."

Alix passes her the harness and Josie straps him into it and then clips on the lead. The moment he sees the lead his demeanor changes and he happily walks off with Alix without a backward glance at Josie.

Alix takes him to the park. It is a gray morning, but with the promise of better weather to come. She allows her head to clear as she walks. She thinks back to her encounter with Walter the previous night, when she'd taken him to look at her recording studio. She thinks of the things he'd said about Josie.

She's not who she makes out to be. Not at all. . . . Josie just likes to control things.

He'd described her as wanting to be seen as simple, as acting as though there was nothing in her head when really there was too much. He'd described her as having an elastic relationship with the truth. And as with everything that Walter had said last night, it could be taken more than one way. He was either painting her badly to make himself look better, or he was telling the truth. And if he was telling the truth, then what did that mean? What was in Josie's head? Good things, or bad things? From the very start of the project, Alix had been attracted by Josie's slight weirdness: the denim, the old husband, the clipped, detached way in which she spoke. It would be easy to assume that all her weirdness was a result of having spent her childhood with a narcissistic mother and her adult life with a man like Walter. But what if the weirdness was innate? What if the weirdness was what had led her into such a strange marriage in the first place? What, she wonders, if Josie was actually mad?

And as she thinks this, she pictures her baby boy, alone in the house with a stranger. She picks up the dog, tucks him into the denim carrier, and walks home as fast as she can.

10:30 A.M.

Josie hears the front door click open and then slam closed. She thinks it must be Alix back from the park with the dog, and peers down the stairs. But it's not Alix. It's him. Her stupid husband. He looks worse than she feels. His red hair is stuck together in clumps, his suit jacket is slung over his shoulder, and he's wearing sunglasses even though it's cloudy. She sees Leon run up the hallway and into his dad's arms.

"You smell bad," says Leon.

"Thanks, mate," says Nathan. And then his gaze heads up the staircase and he spots Josie. She sees him jump slightly, a look of horror passing over his face.

"Oh my God," he says, clutching his heart. "Sorry. You made me jump. It's Josie, yes?"

Josie nods.

"It was just the, er, the pajamas. They're Alix's, aren't they? Moment of, er, cognitive dissonance. How are you?"

"Well," says Josie, gesturing at her facial injuries. "Not the best."

"My God. I hope that didn't happen here?"

Josie grimaces. Does he really think this is something to be joked about? "No," she says. "Of course not."

Nathan blinks at her and then turns toward the living room. "Any idea where Alix is?" he asks.

"She's taken Fred out to the park. She should be back any minute."

"Fred?"

"My dog."

"Oh," he says. "Right. Well. I'll, er, see you."

Then he drops his jacket on the newel post at the bottom of the stairs and heads into the kitchen.

Josie goes back to her room and changes into the clothes that Alix gave her this morning: a white T-shirt and some loose blue trousers. She unbraids her hair and brushes it through with her fingers, watches the flakes of dried blood drift to the floor, pushes it back into a ponytail, and ties it with a band. She brushes her teeth in the en suite, admiring the lovely tiles that have been arranged in a herringbone style: so simple, yet so effective.

After she's brushed her teeth, she examines her appearance in the mirror. She looks terrible. The bruises have spread and changed color overnight. Her bottom lip looks like a split tomato and the blood has dried to a black crust. She smiles and the scab breaks open a little, releasing a tiny droplet of scarlet blood. She dabs it away with the tip of her tongue and then heads downstairs.

"So," says Nathan as she walks into the kitchen. "What happened to your, er . . . ?" He describes her face with his hands.

"An angry man," she says.

"Seriously?" He looks up at her through his pale eyelashes, his lips pulled back into a letter box of disquiet.

"Yes. My husband did it."

"Oh my God. That's awful."

"Yes. It's terrible. Only slightly more terrible than a husband who doesn't come home for a dinner that his wife has cooked for him and spends the whole night out somewhere in his work clothes."

Josie relishes the symphony of expressions that plays across Nathan's doughy, booze-wrecked face. She stares at him and waits for him to find a response.

"Well, yeah," he says. "That was pretty shit. It's, er . . ."

"It's an issue."

His left eyebrow scoots up his face. "Yes," he says tersely. "But rather an issue between me and Alix, I'd say."

"Well, not last night it wasn't. It was painful for all three of us. And look what it led to."

Nathan looks aghast. "I'm sorry, what?"

Josie sighs. "The only way I could persuade my husband to come here last night was by telling him that *you* were going to be here; i.e., another man. Because he's a man's man, Walter. And he came under duress. And you didn't show up, so he felt like a prize idiot. It was a horrible evening, and he took it out on me."

Nathan's face is a picture.

"Well, I'm really sorry to hear that," he says, flushing slightly. "Really sorry."

Josie purses her mouth. "You should be a better husband."

Nathan blinks at her. "Wow," he says after a moment. "Wow."

The front door clicks again, and they both turn to see Alix walk in, looking slightly breathless and stressed. Her face softens when she sees Nathan, which makes Josie feel bizarrely furious.

"Hi," says Nathan.

"Hi," says Alix, taking the dog from the carrier and passing him over to Josie. "I see you and Josie have found each other?"

"We certainly have," Nathan replies drily.

Josie sees him throw a meaningful look at Alix, trying to send her a message with his eyes. She sees Alix frown slightly, trying to work out what the message might be.

"Anyway," Josie says. "I might just go and have another lie-down, if that's OK with you, Alix? I'm still feeling completely shattered."

"Yes," says Alix. "Of course. Can I get you anything? Some breakfast?"

"Oh. No. Thank you. I don't have much of an appetite."

"No. Of course. Well, just message me or shout down if you need anything, won't you?"

Josie smiles wanly and nods.

She passes close to Nathan as she leaves the kitchen, sees him recoil slightly, smells the fumes coming from him, and feels a surge of dark fury. At the top of the stairs, she stops and waits, listens to the conversation coming from the kitchen. There's a long, telling silence, which she knows consists of Alix and Nathan exchanging looks. Then she hears muted, urgent whispering, whispering that grows louder and louder, until she is able to make out the words "Well, what was I supposed to do?" from Alix and the words "Fucking ridiculous" from Nathan. And then she hears Leon come into the kitchen and ask for something to eat and the conversation changes and moves on.

She goes back to the spare bedroom and closes the door. She opens her handbag on the bed and roots around one of the interior pockets, until she feels the hard edges of the key that she'd taken from the flat last night. As her fingers find it, she experiences a sequence of flashbacks: the heft of flesh and bone, the splash and spatter of blood, electric light strobing in and out between splayed fingers, the metal taste of blood, the salt taste of sweaty hands, the sounds of muffled crying. She sees herself, as if from above, curled on the floor, the dog snuffling at her head, and then she hears the silence that followed, broken only by the hiss of a bus opening its doors at the stop outside the window, the whimper of the dog, the rumble of the bus leaving again.

She takes the key, and she slides it under the mattress.

SUNDAY,
14 JULY

"Have you spoken to Erin?" Alix asks Josie in the kitchen the following morning.

Josie nods. "Just messaged her. She's fine."

"And, dare I ask, Walter? Have you spoken to him at all?"

"No. No I have not. And I don't intend to."

"So—how are you going to move forward?"

Alix hears a small catch in her voice as she words her last question. Josie has been here for only a day or so, but Nathan hates her, the kids are weirded out about her face, and the cat is not happy about having a dog in the house who keeps growling at her.

"I really don't know, Alix. I feel like I have a lot to process."

"Maybe your mum could—"

"No!" Josie breaks in before Alix has got even halfway through the sentence. "I am not involving my mum. No. I am just going to work this out for myself."

"Yes, but, Josie, you have to work this out with Walter. Don't you see? You're going to need to see him."

Alix sees a dark shadow pass across Josie's face, accompanied by a slight shake of her head. "Not yet. I'm not ready to talk to him yet."

"Do you want me to talk to him?"

"No. God. Definitely not. I just want to . . . I just need to . . . Alix, I need to be here. Just for a while. Is that OK?"

Alix feels her insides curdle. "I . . . Well, yes. Of course. For a while. But I have my sister coming to stay next week. I'm afraid we'll need the guest room back then."

"Oh." Josie blinks. "Right. When is she coming?"

"Saturday."

"Oh. I see. OK. Well, I'll be out of your hair by then. I promise."

Alix swallows down a bilious realization of what she has just allowed to happen—Josie thinks she is welcome to be here all week—and smiles. "Thank you. And I'm sorry."

"You have nothing to be sorry for, Alix. Honestly. You're amazing."

Alix waits a beat before she asks her next question. "Listen, Josie. I know people who can help you—women who can help you. My friend Mari le Jeune who I told you about. I interviewed her for my podcast. She's the cofounder of a domestic abuse charity, the biggest in the country. She'd be able to help. I can put you in touch with her if you want. If you're feeling unsafe?"

She draws in her breath as she waits for Josie's reaction, but Josie merely nods and says, "OK. Thank you. But I feel safe. I promise."

"Oh," says Alix. "Good."

"What are you doing today, Alix?" Josie asks.

"Oh. Nothing much really. Nathan's working today so I was going to take the kids out for lunch."

"I . . . Never mind, then."

"No. Go on."

"I was just thinking, since I'm here, maybe we could spend

some time on the podcast. I really feel like I want to talk about the girls."

Alix nods, containing her response. "Sure," she says, "yes. Let me just tell the kids where I'll be and we can get going."

Hi! I'm Your Birthday Twin!
A NETFLIX ORIGINAL SERIES

A woman sits in a café next to a large steamed-up plate-glass window.
Behind her and out of focus, a man is cleaning a big chrome coffee machine with a white tea towel.
The woman smiles uncertainly at the interviewer and clears her throat.
Below, the text reads:

Mandy Redwood, School Administrator, Parkside Primary School, 1998–present day

"Alix Summer's kids were both at Parkside. Lovely kids. Some families just light up a school like ours, you know, and the Summers are one of those families. And so it was surprising when Alix came to me that day, back in 2019, asking after the Fairs. You couldn't imagine two more different families, two more different mothers. Obviously, at the time I had no idea that Alix was making a podcast about the Fairs. So I told her what I remembered. But it was only after everything happened, later on, that I went through the records, and that's when I remembered other things too. Like the day that Roxy broke a child's finger in the reading corner. Trod on it. Just stood there, crushing it under the sole of her shoe. The kid screaming."

Mandy shudders and smiles drily.

"Of course we had to bring the parents in after that and they were just . . ."

Mandy looks down at the tabletop while she searches for the right word.

"Emotionless. Completely emotionless. It was the strangest thing. I put it down to shock at the time, but now . . . now I know what was really going on in that house. Well, it all makes more sense."

She shudders again.

Then she shakes her head slightly and sighs.

The screen fades to black and changes to footage of an empty recording studio.

The camera pans around the room.

Below, the text reads:

Recording from Alix Summer's podcast, 14 July, 2019

Alix: "What did Walter do, when you told him about the child with the broken finger?"

Josie: "Well, I didn't tell him. He went off to work early back then, out of the house by seven o'clock most mornings, not back until five or six; the school day was a total mystery to him. I think he set foot on school premises about five times over the years the girls were there. So, I just didn't say anything."

"And Roxy didn't tell him?"

"No. Roxy didn't tell him. It was just . . . well, his temper. You know. We were all a bit scared of him."

"Was he violent? With the girls?"

"Not then. No. But he was rough. He'd push them about. Especially Roxy. But not violent. That came later."

Josie sighs loudly.

"I have not been a good parent. I have not been a good parent."

"What do you mean?"

"I just mean . . ."

She sighs again.

"I let bad things happen. I didn't stop them. I just let it all happen."

2 P.M.

Alix's phone buzzes for the third time in a row. She puts her finger in the air and presses pause on the recording, removes her headphones, and says, "Sorry, Josie. I should get this. It's Eliza. Hi, baby."

"Mum. Can you come back inside now? Leon's being really annoying and I'm hungry."

Alix glances at the time. It's nearly two o'clock. "Yes. I'm really sorry. Yes, I'm coming in now."

She throws Josie an apologetic look. "I'm so sorry. But I've really left them alone for long enough now."

Josie nods. "Yes," she says. "Of course. Sorry. I'm being selfish. It's just I've kept this stuff all locked up for so long now and I'm scared that if I don't get it all out in one go, it might go back in again."

Alix smiles. "We won't let that happen, Josie. OK? Let's take a break for today and then we have all day tomorrow. I assume you won't be going into work tomorrow?"

Josie nods.

"All day tomorrow, then. OK?"

"Yes," says Josie. "OK."

MONDAY,
15 JULY

Josie awakes to the sounds of Alix's family getting ready for school. For a moment the sound is reassuring, like an echo of a happy day at the beach or a childhood Christmas. For a moment she is back in the early days of parenting, when her babies were adorable and her husband was handsome and strong. It occurs to her that maybe this was never actually the case, that she is looking back through an out-of-focus lens. But it had been better, at first—it had to have been better. Otherwise, what on earth was it all for?

She gets out of bed and throws on the linen gown that Alix left for her. She picks up the dog and puts on her slip-on shoes and heads downstairs. "Morning," she says as she walks into the kitchen.

She sees the children turn and gawp at her. The sight of them in their Parkside uniforms is unnerving and she gawps back. The dog growls when he sees the cloud-cat sitting on the kitchen counter.

"Morning, Josie!" says Alix, who is wearing a white embroidered tunic top over yoga pants and has pulled her hair from her face with a fabric headband. She is barefoot and cutting a banana into slices directly over a toasted bagel and looks like one of her Instagram posts come to life. "Come in. Can I get you anything to eat?"

Josie shakes her head. "No. Thank you. I'll just have a coffee. Is it OK if I use your machine?"

"Oh, don't worry about that. Nathan will make you one. Nathan!"

Nathan appears from the terrace clutching an empty cereal bowl and a mug.

"Can you make Josie a cappuccino?"

Josie sees a look of antipathy pass across his face, masked with a grim smile. "Sure," he says. "Sugar?"

Josie nods. "One please. Thank you."

She takes a seat on one of the mismatched chairs at the table, opposite Leon, who eyes her suspiciously. "My children went to your school," she says. "When they were small. But they're big now."

"Where are they now?"

"Oh," she says, "Erin is staying at her friend's house and Roxy is off traveling the world."

"So they're adults?"

"Yes. They're adults." Josie feels her voice crack dangerously on the last syllable and clears her throat. "I hear you still have Mandy, in the office?"

Leon nods seriously. Josie lets her eyes linger on his hands, still plumped up with whatever it is that lives under the skin of young children. There's a scab on the knuckle of his thumb and she remembers scabs. She remembers verrucas and nits and ingrown toenails and baby teeth hanging on by threads and all the other tiny, perfect defects of small children. She resists the urge to touch the scab, to give it a magic kiss. She resists the urge to say, "Oh no, you have an owee." She feels the loss of her children so viscerally and horribly that she could scream with the agony of it.

She manages a smile and says, "Mandy was there when my children were there."

Leon runs his hands back and forth along the edge of the table and then looks up at Josie and says, "How come you're the same age as my mum, but your children are already adults and we're only small?"

"Well. That's maths really, isn't it?"

Leon looks at her questioningly.

"So. If I'm forty-five and my oldest daughter is twenty-three, then how old was I when I had her?"

Leon screws up his face and says, "Is that forty-five take away twenty-three?"

"Yes! Yes, that's exactly what it is. Clever boy!"

"So that's . . ." He unpeels his fingers from his fist, one by one on the tabletop, like an unfurling blossom, as he counts it out. "Twenty-two?"

"Oh my goodness! And how old are you?"

"I'm six."

"Six! And you can do such complicated maths! That's amazing. Yes. Forty-five take away twenty-three is twenty-two. And that's how old I was when I had my first child. And what is forty-five take away six?"

"That's easy. It's thirty-nine."

"Yes! So your mum was thirty-nine when she had you. And that's why my children are grown-ups, and you are still only six. Because everyone does things at different times."

Josie turns and looks at Alix. Alix is smiling. "He's very good at maths, your boy."

"Yes," says Alix. "Yes. He is. Leon's good at everything, aren't you, baby? Apart from being ready to walk out the door when it's time to go to school. So—come on. Let's get those shoes on, shall we?"

———————

Soon the house is empty. Nathan has gone to work, and Alix is walking the children to school and will be gone for at least half an hour.

Josie is alone. She crosses the kitchen and looks at the artwork on the special board that has been installed for the children. She looks, in particular, for any signs of stress or darkness, remembering the unsettling drawings that Erin and Roxy used to produce, the concerned looks on teachers' faces at parent-teacher meetings as they passed across pieces of artwork that displayed what they described as "signs of emotional stress." But here there are only yellow suns and orange flowers and happy mummies and smiling daddies. Here is the art of healthy children living in a happy home. She unpins a tiny scrap of a sketch; it's a girl, drawn in minute detail, with a giant bow in her hair and a small dog on a lead that looks a bit like Fred. Underneath is the word "Teeny."

Josie doesn't know who the girl is meant to be or whose dog it is meant to be, but the image is so pure and perfect that she knows she needs it. She slips it into the pocket of the linen dressing gown and rearranges the other drawings a little to hide the space.

Then she notices a calendar. It is printed with family photographs. Her eyes go to this Saturday. There it is: "Zoe and Petal." Zoe is Alix's sister's name. She feels a reassuring sense of calm. Alix had not been lying to her. Her sister really is coming to stay on Saturday. She smiles a small smile and traces the calendar entry with her fingertips.

She opens the fridge then, lets her eyes roam over the contents, is surprised to see Cheese Strings and mini Peperamis, not surprised to see something in a tub called skyr and something else in a tub called baba ghanoush.

She feels she should be showered and dressed by the time Alix returns from dropping the children, so she heads upstairs. There are three rooms on this floor. One bedroom for Alix and Nathan. One bedroom for Leon. And at the back of the house, overlooking the garden, is a small study. Josie goes to the study door and peers inside. A desk in the window, a wall of bookshelves, and there, against the back wall, what looks like a sofa-bed. She hitches up the bottom cushion and sees the metal mechanism, then lets the cushion drop again. So. There is another spare room in the house. She does not have to leave on Saturday. She smiles and heads up the next flight of stairs to her room next to Eliza's on the top floor.

She's not ready to leave. Not even slightly.

Hi! I'm Your Birthday Twin!
A NETFLIX ORIGINAL SERIES

The screen shows three young people sitting on high stools in a dimly lit bar. Two young women, one young man.
They're casually dressed in jeans and T-shirts; they all have tattoos and one of them wears a beanie hat.
The text below reads:

Ari, Juno, and Dan,
subscribers to gaming platform Glitch

The man speaks first. He has an American accent:

"So, yeah, I think we were all just kind of messing around that night. We had a couple friends over, we'd had a few beers, it was a hot July night. All the windows were open. So we weren't paying as much attention as we normally would. We weren't, you know, like *rapt.*"

Interviewer, off-mic: "So you were normally rapt?"

"Yeah. I guess. I mean—she was amazing. We just knew her as her player name. Erased."

Interviewer, off-mic: "Her player name was Erased?"

"Yeah. I can see now that was sort of a play on words, sort of a combination of her real name and a comment on her real life. But we didn't know anything about her real life. She was just Erased to us. She played with a, like, green screen backdrop—so we couldn't see her actual room; it looked like she was in an empty warehouse. She was really quiet. She virtually whispered. That's unusual in this world. But that was part of what made her cool. So it was the noise that alerted us that something weird was happening."

"From your computer?"

"Yeah. We saw her getting off her chair and she never did that. She never moved. And she disappeared and it was all kind of a blur, because of the green screen. You know how it messes with movement? Screaming. Shouting. Banging. And then it went dead. Literally, just dead. Her chair sat there, empty. We watched and we watched and we watched and she did not come back. And we all started messaging each other. Like, all over the world. But nobody knew where she lived. Nobody knew her real name. Nobody knew anything about her."

The girl in the beanie hat speaks.

"We had footage of the whole thing. I called the police. They were like, what do you want us to do about it? She's on the other side of the world. We sent the footage to Glitch. They didn't have a physical address for her. Just an IP address and email details. They told us she was in, like, North London? So we started messaging anyone we knew in North London. We just became obsessed with this thing. It went viral. In the community. It was all anyone was talking about. And then suddenly, just as we were getting close to finding out who she was and where she lived, the story broke. And then holy crap, our minds blew. Our minds just totally and utterly *blew*."

9:30 A.M.

Josie is ready and dressed and sitting at the kitchen table when Alix gets back from dropping the children at school. The dog is in the back garden, sniffing around the flower beds. Alix sees that Josie has attempted to cover up some of the damage to her face with makeup and wonders for a moment where she had found it. She had arrived here on Saturday morning with only her tiny handbag and the dog.

"You look better," she says, indicating Josie's face.

"Yes. I was sick of seeing that horror show in the mirror. I found a tube of something in the bathroom cabinet. I hope you don't mind?"

Alix shakes her head distractedly. She's 99 percent sure there was no foundation or makeup in the bathroom cabinet in the en suite to the spare room, but maybe a guest left it there without her noticing.

"I just have a couple of jobs I need to do around the house, and then we can get going. Is that OK?"

"Absolutely," says Josie. "I'm happy just sitting here, in your lovely kitchen."

Alix throws her the warmest smile she can manage and then heads up to the bedrooms. She wrenches dirty bedclothes off Leon's bed and bundles them together. Then she redresses it with fresh sheets and empties his wastepaper bin into a black bag. She does the same in her bedroom and in the bathroom. As she moves from job to job, she is followed by a sense of unease. She tries to unhitch it from her psyche, but she can't. Everything feels wrong; everything feels off-kilter. She hears the dog yapping in the back garden and peers out to see him staring longingly at a squirrel up a tree. She pictures Josie sitting at the kitchen table, the strange benignancy of her, the placid smile. She doesn't seem like someone whose husband assaulted her on Friday night and who had to escape in the early hours and hasn't been home since. She doesn't seem like she's in the eye of a terrible personal trauma. She seems . . . happy?

She brings the dirty laundry and the black bin bag downstairs and there she is, just as she'd left her. "I'll be two more minutes," she calls out to Josie before taking the laundry into the utility room.

"No rush!"

And there it is. That strange, unnerving note of jollity.

A moment later they are in the recording studio, each with a coffee in front of them and headphones on. The time is almost 10 a.m. and Alix presses record.

Hi! I'm Your Birthday Twin!
A NETFLIX ORIGINAL SERIES

The screen shows a dramatic reenactment of a young girl sitting at a stool by the open-plan kitchen in Josie's apartment.

She is laughing out loud at something that another young woman, an actress playing Josie's younger daughter, Roxy, has just said.

An actress playing Josie sits on the sofa, looking at a magazine and smiling quietly.

The text beneath reads:

Recording of Josie Fair from
Alix Summer's podcast, 14 July, 2019

"I have to tell you about Brooke."

"Brooke?"

"Yes. She was Roxy's friend. From school. Roxy never had a friend until Brooke. But she turned up at the beginning of year ten, and they were inseparable immediately."

The screen shows the two girls sitting on a bed, cross-legged, playing with phones and laughing together.

"Brooke was difficult, like Roxy, and potty-mouthed. And she was fearless too. Scared of nothing and nobody. But I liked her because she was a good influence on Roxy. She got Roxy studying that year. She persuaded Roxy that GCSEs were useful, and she was fun. We weren't a fun family. Not in that way. But Brooke was fun and she made us fun too, became almost a part of the family. She lived in a tiny flat with two small half siblings, didn't get on with her step-father, had lots of issues at home, so I think she saw our place as a kind of refuge? It was a lovely time, in retrospect. And then we got toward the end of their year eleven, the GCSEs were coming up, Brooke was over a lot, revising with Roxy."

The screen shows the two girls sitting on the floor, poring over exercise books.

"But suddenly one day, just before the exams started, it was all over. Roxy came home from school, said they'd had a big fight. Said she'd punched Brooke. Given her a fat lip. We got a call from the school, asking us to come in. But then Roxy disappeared. Right in the middle of her exams. Just gone, for three whole days. Finally she reappeared, looking grubby, shell-shocked, said she'd been sleeping rough, been taken into a hostel, hadn't slept for three nights. I ran her a bath; she was in there for over an hour."

Screen shows the actor playing Roxy lying in a bath in a darkened bathroom.

"Then she came out and told me what had happened. Told me about Brooke . . . and Walter."

There is a prolonged silence.

The screen shows Roxy disappearing under the bathwater, her hair spreading out around her.

"Walter?"

"He'd been grooming her. All along. Just like he did with me. All those times she was here, when it felt like she was part of the family, it had been more than that. And then, just like he did with me, he bought her a necklace, he took her to the pub, he slipped a shot of vodka into her lemonade, and then, on her sixteenth birthday, he slept with her."

The screen goes black and slowly changes to a young girl, sitting in shadow on a chair in a studio.

Josie's voice continues in the background:

"While I was at work and Roxy was at school doing an exam, he invited her into our home and he slept with her in my bed. *In my bed.*"

"How did Roxy find out?"

"Erin told her. They thought Erin wouldn't notice because of the way Erin is with her gaming and everything. But she did. She heard them and then she saw through the crack in her bedroom door Brooke leaving and she told Roxy when she got back from her exam and the next day Roxy went into school and she beat Brooke. Beat her bloody."

The screen oscillates between dramatized scenes of two girls fighting in a school playground and the girl sitting on the stool in shadow.

"Shortly after Roxy came back from the homeless shelter, she left for good. We haven't seen her since."

A light flashes very briefly onto the face of the girl sitting on the stool, illuminating a small portion of her face.

The closing credits roll.

11 A.M.

Josie stares into Alix's eyes. Alix looks mind-blown. Horrified.

"I know," says Josie. "I'm sorry, it's gross. But there it is. There is the truth about the man I married."

"Did you confront him?"

"No," she says. "No. Not then. I pretended I didn't know."

There it is again, across the smooth surface of Alix's face, that flinch, that pinch.

Josie can hear Alix gulping drily. She comes in for the kill. "That night," she says, "on Friday. When we got home from having dinner here with you. That was the first time. The very first time I ever confronted Walter about what had happened with Brooke."

"And that was why . . . ?" Alix gestures at the damage to Josie's face.

Josie nods. "Yes. That was why. Exactly."

They stop for lunch. Alix toasts some sourdough for them and serves it with hummus and baba ghanoush.

She glances across the kitchen table at Josie and says, "Any word from Walter?"

"None. No."

"Would he normally be in touch after an episode like this?"

"I've never walked out on him before."

"So, you normally just sit it out?"

"Mm-hmm. Yeah."

"So, what was different this time?"

"Everything, I guess. Ever since I turned forty-five, even before we started making this podcast, I've been feeling different about everything. I mean, that was why I was in that pub in the first place that night. We never normally go out to eat. At least, not to places like that. And then I met you and . . ."

Alix stares fixedly at Josie, not wanting to give away any of her interior disquiets through a twitch or a blink.

"It felt like fate, like destiny. It was a turning point for me, my moment to take control of my narrative, unburden myself, share my truth—change. And so on Friday night, the minute he first raised his hand to me, I already knew it felt different. I already knew I would go and that I wouldn't come back."

Alix swallows drily. "When did he first hit you?"

"Oh, you know. I mean, it would be hard to say exactly. It was a thing that happened slowly. You know. A little push here and there. Around the same time he started to be physical with the girls. I preferred it in a way. Preferred it if he pushed me around than them.

Shocking, when you think about it. A man like that. A big man. Touching girls, women—hurting them. I mean, it's impossible even to fathom. Like the sort of people who hurt animals." Her gaze drops to Fred, who sits at her feet staring at her meaningfully. She tears off a corner of sourdough dipped into the baba ghanoush and passes it to him. He chews it excitedly.

"Has he ever hurt Fred?"

"No. Not yet. Probably only a matter of time though, I guess." She passes another piece of bread and dip to the dog and then glances up at Alix. "What about you?" she asks. "Has Nathan ever hurt you?"

"Oh. God. No." And Alix realizes as she says it how it sounds. It sounds smug and entitled, as if her life is lived on a different plane to Josie's, as if only a woman like Josie would have a husband who hit her, only people who were brought up on estates and married to electricians experienced domestic violence, when, of course, nothing was further from the truth. "No," she says again, toning down her incredulity. "Never."

"And the kids?"

"No. Neither of us has ever hit the kids."

Josie pushes her plate away from her and stares directly into Alix's eyes. "But obviously, you have other problems. You have the drinking thing."

"Yes," says Alix. "I do. Although I am hoping after Friday night that that might be the end of it."

"Well, we'll see, won't we?"

And there's an edge to her voice which makes Alix think that Josie actively wants Nathan to go on another bender, to commit another cardinal sin, to blow it somehow. That she actively wants Nathan to be as bad as Walter.

TUESDAY, 16 JULY

"When is she leaving?" Nathan whispers sharply into Alix's ear the next morning.

They're standing side by side in their en-suite bathroom, over their respective washbasins. Nathan is buttoning his work shirt. Alix is smoothing in her face cream.

"Fuck. I don't know. I've told her that Zoe's coming to stay on Saturday, so she knows that at least she has to be gone by then."

"Wait. Hold on. Zoe's coming? Did I know about that?"

Alix sighs and rolls her eyes. "Yes, Nathan. You did know about that. It's been in the diary for a month. We've talked about it. Zoe and Petal sleeping over. And Maxine and the boys are coming over too and we're having pizza and margaritas."

"So, a kind of girls' night? No men?"

She sighs again. "No, you don't have to stick around. But, Nathan, please just come home at a proper time. I can't have my sisters judging you too. It's bad enough having *her*"—she points at the ceiling, indicating Josie in the room above them—"judging you. Please just have a normal night out and come home and come to bed and be here when my sister wakes up on Sunday morning."

Nathan makes a face at her reflection in the mirror. It's his sweetest face. She can't help but soften to him. "Good," she says, smiling slightly. "Good."

"But all bets are off if that woman is still here come Saturday night."

"She won't be," Alix replies. "I promise you. She'll be gone."

———————

Josie is clutching a pile of bedding when she walks into the kitchen at eight thirty.

"Alix," she says. "I am so sorry. Fred had an accident in the night. In fact, a few accidents. I think maybe it was that stuff we had yesterday. That brown stuff. The baba—?"

"Ghanoush?"

"Yes. I think it's not agreed with his stomach. I'm really sorry, but there's some mess on the floor too. But let me sort it all out. Just tell me where the cleaning stuff is, and I'll do it all."

As she speaks, Alix watches in horror as Fred dribbles diarrhea across the kitchen floor. "Oh," she says, taking the bedding from Josie's hands. "Oh dear. Listen. You take him out in the garden. I'll clean this up."

"I'm so sorry, Alix. I really am. He's never done this before."

"No. No. Of course. Please don't worry about it."

Josie throws her an apologetic look and picks up the dog and heads into the garden, where he immediately squats and empties more liquid from within himself. Nathan, who is drinking his coffee on the terrace, looks from the dog to Josie and then turns to catch Alix's eye through the bifold doors, throwing her a horrified look. Alix shrugs and gathers cleaning stuff from under the sink. She thinks of Saturday. She thinks of saying goodbye to Josie, and then the arrival of her sisters and the opening of tequila bottles and squeezing of limes and the calls and shouts of pizza preference to whoever is accessing the Deliveroo app and the children buzzing from room to room, and she wants it so badly she can almost taste it. But for now, she has liquid Pomchi shit to clean up and soiled bedsheets to wash and, of course, a bed to redress. She retches slightly as she lifts Fred's mess with superabsorbent kitchen towels and antibacterial kitchen spray and throws them in the bin.

"Kids," she says, through gritted teeth. "Chop-chop. We're going to be late."

She leaves the house five minutes later, her nostrils still thick with the smell of dog shit.

———————

Harry, her next-door neighbor's son, is just turning toward his house when Alix gets home half an hour later.

"Hi!" she says.

He turns at the sound of her voice and looks at her benignly. "Hi," he says.

"How are you?"

"Oh. Yeah. I'm good, thanks. How about you?"

"Yes. I'm good too." She glances at her front door and then joins Harry at the turning to his garden path. "Roxy Fair," she begins quietly. "Do you remember a friend of hers called Brooke?"

"Er, yeah. I remember her. She was a bit . . ."

She watches his face as he struggles to find the words he's looking for.

"A bit of a . . . a player?" he says eventually.

Alix throws him a disapproving look. "An opinion based on . . . ?"

"Yes. Sorry. I mean nothing really. She was just quite mature for her age. Quite heavy-handed around boys. I have no idea if she was actually sleeping around, but that was the impression she gave."

"And what happened to her? After you all left school? Do you have any idea?"

He blows air from his cheeks and says, "She went missing, as far as I recall. Ran away, maybe? I can't quite remember. But I do know there was some kind of falling-out between Roxy and Brooke, toward the end?"

"Oh. Right. And what was that about?"

"I don't know. But it was toxic for a while. Really toxic. There was a fight. Like, a cat fight? One of them got a split lip. Can't remember which one."

"And Brooke. Can you remember her surname?"

"Yeah, I can. It was Ripley."

"And Brooke spelt . . . ?"

"B-R-O-O-K-E. I think."

"Amazing!" Alix flashes him a smile. "Great. Thanks. Say hello to your mum and dad for me, won't you?"

———————————

Josie is gone when Alix gets back inside. The kitchen still smells faintly of disinfectant and shit, and she opens up the sliding doors to let fresh air in. Then she makes herself a coffee and opens her laptop and googles "Brooke Ripley."

There are many, most of them too old to be Roxy's Brooke. She opens Instagram and searches for her there. There are five. None of them looks quite right, but she clicks on each in turn. They live in places that someone who'd been brought up in Kilburn would not end up living, at least not at the age of twenty-one. None of them looks quite right either. Then she goes onto Facebook and searches for her there. She clicks first on *People* but runs once more into a seam of unlikely candidates, before clicking on *Posts*. And there—her heart stops and then races—there is her name, *Brooke Ripley*, highlighted, in a sequence of posts about a missing girl.

Alix clicks on the first post. She reads the first few words: "Please help! Anyone in Kilburn/Paddington/Queen's Park/Cricklewood areas. My beautiful niece Brooke . . ."

And then she starts.

Josie is standing in front of her, clutching Fred.

"Oh!" says Alix. "You made me jump!"

"I've cleaned the floor upstairs," she says. "And opened the window to let some air in. If you want to give me some fresh bedding, I'll pop it on."

"Great. I'll get some out for you next time I go up."

"Again, I am so sorry. He seems fine now. I think he just needed to pass it through his system. I've never fed him anything like that before. He clearly wasn't built for it."

"Bless him," says Alix. "Poor little thing. Are you up for some more recording this morning?"

Josie nods. "Absolutely. Yes. Let me just get myself a coffee."

"Great. I'll just pop to the bathroom. See you soon."

Alix shuts her laptop and heads upstairs to grab some fresh bed-clothes for Josie from the cupboard on the landing. She leaves them at the foot of the stairs, intending to let Josie do it herself, but something makes her carry them up the stairs to the top floor. The door to the spare room is ajar. A breeze ruffles the curtains through the open window. The clothes that Josie was wearing when she arrived in the early hours of Saturday morning are hanging, laundered and fresh, from the freestanding rail. The pajamas that Alix lent Josie are folded neatly on the stripped bed. In the en suite a damp towel hangs from the rail, and on the glass shelf above the sink is a tube of Alix's foundation that she has no recollection of having ever put there, and also a tube of her mascara. She picks them up and looks at them curiously, as if they might offer her an explanation.

Then she sets about remaking the bed in the fresh clothes. She stuffs the pillows into their cases, shakes the duvet into its cover, and tucks the sheet under the mattress, and it is as she is doing so that she feels something hard and cold. She locates it and pulls it out.

It's a key. It's attached to a fob with the number 6 written on the internal paper label. The fob is streaked with dried-on blood. Alix drops it, as if it is white-hot, then slides it, quickly, urgently, back under the mattress and closes the bedroom door behind her.

Josie is waiting for her in the kitchen. She smiles. "Ready?" she says.

Alix nods.

Hi! I'm Your Birthday Twin!
A NETFLIX ORIGINAL SERIES

The screen shows a woman walking through a park with a chocolate Labrador. The sun is setting in the sky behind her and is a deep bloodred.
The next shot shows her sitting in a small armchair, next to a blazing wood fire in a grate, the dog at her feet sleeping. The woman has a glass of red wine in front of her and her legs curled up beneath her. The text underneath says:

Ffion Roberts, Brooke Ripley's aunt

The woman called Ffion opens up her laptop, which is briefly shown on-screen.

It shows a Facebook post.

The camera returns to Ffion and shows her reading the post:

"'Please help! Anyone in Kilburn/Paddington/Queen's Park/ Cricklewood areas. My beautiful niece Brooke went to her school prom on Wednesday. She told friends that she was going to meet "a friend" afterward and her school friends said goodbye to her at the bus stop outside the prom venue, on Shoot Up Hill in Cricklewood, at just after nine p.m. We have CCTV footage of her getting on the number twenty-eight bus at nine eleven and getting off again near the top of Maida Vale at nine twenty-two. After that, we don't know where she went, but she is not answering her phone and her mum and all her family are worried sick. If you have any idea who she might have been going to meet on Wednesday at nine thirty, please, please let us know. And please share this as far as it will go. The police have been informed but there's only so much they can do.'"

She closes the laptop and looks up at the interviewer. Her eyes are filled with tears. Her face crumples and it is clear she is about to cry.

"I'm sorry."

She turns away from the camera.

"I'm really sorry. Could I just have a minute?"

WEDNESDAY, 17 JULY

The Facebook post shows Brooke Ripley in a white, fitted ankle-length dress and silver trainers. She looks pensive in the photo, fragile and unsure. It's only because Alix knows that a mere six weeks beforehand this girl was being groomed and abused by Walter Fair that she can see so deeply into her soul, read so much into the uncertain tilt of her head, the slimness of her smile. She is amazed, in fact, that Brooke Ripley went to her school prom at all, given the horrific backdrop to it all.

The Facebook post, which has been shared around twenty times, is a plea from Brooke's aunt Ffion, writing on behalf of Brooke's mum.

Alix reads the comments. They're all of the "thoughts and prayers" variety. Nobody has a clue. A girl called Mia who was in the edges of the prom photograph with Brooke replies: "That's me in the photo. Like literally saw her just a few minutes before she disappeared. She said she was going home. Wish I knew where she was," accompanied by a sad-face emoji and a heart.

Alix clicks on Mia's profile and finds that it has maximum security settings, all the way down to blocking access to her friends list. She clicks on *Message* and stares for a moment at the empty space in Messenger. What would she say? And how?

She switches screens at the sound of footsteps down the stairs. It's Josie, still wearing the same outfit that Alix had lent to her on Saturday. It's now Wednesday. She has her own clothes hanging in her room, cleaned and ready to be worn. Yet she is still wearing Alix's.

"I was thinking," Alix says. "If you're going to be here for a couple more days, would you like me to go over to yours and pick up some clothes for you?"

She sees a flash of something pass across Josie's face. "No," she says, her mouth set firm. "No, thank you."

"The weather's turning though—it's going to be really hot the next couple of days. Pushing thirty. I could pick you up some more of those summer dresses?"

"Honestly." Josie's mouth softens. "Honestly. It's fine."

"Well, let me know if you change your mind."

"Yes," says Josie. "I will."

"And what will you do? On Saturday? Where will you go?"

She tries not to stare too hard at Josie as she finds her answer to this question, as she already knows that she will be struggling, already knows that Josie has no plan beyond the end of each day.

"I suppose I'll . . ." She trails off momentarily. "I'm not sure. I mean, how would you feel . . . ?"

Alix feels herself stiffen.

"I noticed that there's a fold-out bed. In the study. I mean, I could always sleep there, while your sister's here? I don't suppose anyone will be using the study on a Saturday night? And I'd absolutely stay out of your way so that you and your sister can do sister things?"

Alix's mouth has turned dry. This is it. This is the line that she had put metaphorically inside her relationship with Josie from day one, and each day they have been stepping a little closer and a little closer and right now they are touching it with their outstretched toes and once that line has been breached Alix no longer has any idea how she will regain control of the situation. She knows, with a sickening certainty, that she has to have Josie gone from her house by Saturday afternoon. But she also knows, with a sickening certainty, that Josie is currently controlling her and that making her leave the house before she's ready to do so would spell the end of the podcast just as it was gearing up toward being something riveting and unmissable. She thinks all of this in the two seconds it takes for her to say, "Well, let me ask Nathan. I'm kicking him out of the girls' space on Saturday night so he might well end up in the study, working."

She glances quickly at Josie, long enough to observe a slightly menacing back-tip of her head, a cool refinding of her bearings.

"Well," she says, "OK. But let me know as soon as you can."

"Yes," Alix replies warmly. "Yes! Of course."

When Josie mentions that she won't be going into work that afternoon, Alix invents a reason to leave the house. Everything has been so intense since the moment that Josie and Walter walked into her house on Friday night. Every minute of every day has been overshadowed by the existence of these people and their horrible, messy lives and by the physical presence of Josie and her dog in Alix's home. Time has lost its form and its meaning. Another weekend is approaching and on the other side of that weekend is the end of the school term and then there will be six long weeks of unstructured time and loose-limbed days and she needs something which feels normal and just for her. She tells Josie she is going to return some library books and then she heads into the park to have her lunch at the café.

The café in Queen's Park has formed the basis of huge swaths of Alix's life since she and Nathan moved into the area ten years ago.

She sees ghosts and hears echoes of herself at all the different stages of herself; pregnant with Leon, with a newborn and a five-year-old, with mums from nursery, mums from school, with Nathan and the kids at the weekends. The ice-cream kiosk makes her think of Leon and Eliza with bright blue mouths after eating the bubble-gum flavor. The beers in the chilled cabinet make her think of the slightly woozy sensation of daytime drinking on hot summer afternoons. She's sat at each table at various points, lived different versions of herself in multiple light-refracting fragments. So today she will sit in the café, and she will eat a panini and she will live another fragment of her life and she will try to feel normal, to feel like the Alix of six weeks ago, the Alix who hadn't met Josie Fair.

She orders her panini, the one she always has, goat's cheese and ham, and she orders an iced tea, and she sits with her numbered wooden paddle on the table in front of her and waits for her food to arrive and waits to feel normal. But the normal doesn't come. Maybe normal is over there, she ponders, on the other side of the park somewhere; maybe it's in the sand pit, where she still takes the children sometimes when they're feeling little. Or maybe it's on the zip wire in the adventure playground. Or in the petting zoo, which she and Nathan had walked past drunkenly on the night of her forty-fifth birthday, the dark night air still warm on their bare skin.

Her panini arrives and it is the same panini she always has but it doesn't bring her normal. It feels like Josie has taken Alix's normal and swallowed it deep down somewhere inside her darkness. Alix thinks of the blood-smeared key under the mattress with the number 6 scrawled on it. She thinks of Josie rooting through her recycling bin while she was out with her family. She thinks of Josie in her home, right now, wearing Alix's clothes, Alix's makeup, scattering her hair, her dead skin cells, everywhere she goes. She pictures Josie going into their study, spotting the sofa-bed, going into Alix's bathroom, taking her foundation. Then she sees Walter having sex with Brooke, Erin with her ear to the wall, Josie pretending it hadn't happened, getting on with her life.

Alix pushes the panini away and gets to her feet. She needs to get this podcast finished. Get it done, immerse herself in this filth, get to the end of this miserable story, get Josie out of her house, and reclaim her life. But first, she needs to walk past Josie's flat, peer through the window, see if she can get a sense of what Walter might be doing or thinking.

12:30 P.M.

Alix said she'd be gone for an hour. She said they'd do some recording when she returned, if Josie was up for it. An hour is a long time, Josie thinks. A long time to be alone in someone's house. Alix told Josie to help herself to lunch. "Whatever's in the fridge, just help yourself."

So Josie peers into the fridge. She sees the rest of the baba whatever it is, the brown stuff that made Fred sick. She shudders. Then she sees a block of cheddar and thinks that a piece of that and a slice of bread and butter will be all she needs. She eats the tiny lunch at the kitchen table, staring blankly into space. Fred snuffles around the kitchen, looking for crumbs. The floor is surprisingly messy. There has been the plastic twist from the top of a loaf of bread on the floor for three days now. Nobody seems to see it. It's not commensurate with the image that Alix likes to present on Instagram. None of it is, really, not when you look up close. But that doesn't matter. Josie is not naturally tidy herself, she's only tidy because Walter likes it that way, and so she feels happy for Alix that she's allowed to have a plastic bread-bag tag on her floor for three days without it causing an argument.

A moment later she finds herself striding across the kitchen, picking up the tag, and putting it in the pocket of her trousers.

She opens and closes the silky-smooth drawers in the kitchen until she gets to the messy one with all the things in it. She leafs through takeaway menus and ballpoint pens and packets of tissues and bulldog clips and books of postage stamps and bottle stoppers and rubber bands. Everything has been thrown in—there is no order to any of it. Her fingers feel the sheen of a photograph and she pulls out a column of passport shots. They're of Leon looking somber and serious, the pale-blue collar of his school shirt just visible. She slides it into her pocket too.

She thinks of her underwear drawer, at home, of the trophies and trinkets tucked away behind her socks and bras. Not just Alix's. The others too. She feels an itch to go home, just for a moment, to tuck the child's drawing and the bread tag and the photos of Leon into the drawer. She could do that, she's sure. She'd be in and out in seconds. Nobody would see her. She'll go tomorrow, she decides, after work.

And then she pulls out a shiny black business card with Nathan's details on it. The name of his company—"Condor and Bright, Commercial Property Consultants, EC1"—and his mobile phone number beneath his office number is printed on it. She puts it in her pocket.

Hi! I'm Your Birthday Twin!
A NETFLIX ORIGINAL SERIES

The screen shows a young, very bubbly woman. She has a mass of blond curls tied back into a ponytail and wears large gold hoop earrings and a fitted black cardigan.
She sits on a small red sofa in a dimly lit bar and is shown rearranging herself a few times and trying to find the perfect pose.

"Can you see down my top at this angle?" she asks the interviewer.
The interviewer is heard saying, "No, you're fine," off-mic.
She laughs and says, "Good. Well, then. Let's go."
The text beneath reads:

Katelyn Rand

"Well, I wouldn't say I was a friend of Josie's. I knew of her. She knew of me. I lived on her estate when I was small and I remember her and her mum. Particularly her mum. Everyone knew Pat O'Neill. She was larger than life. You didn't want to get on the wrong side of her."

Katelyn laughs wryly.

"And I remember my mum telling me about Josie suddenly leaving home at eighteen and the gossip that went round at the time, that she'd gone off with an older man. Last time I saw her I guess I was about ten? And I didn't see her again for years and years. Until I brought some stuff into that shop where she worked. Stitch, the alterations place in Kilburn, and I recognized her immediately. She hadn't changed at all, weirdly. Pretty sure she was still wearing the same clothes she used to wear when she was a teenager! So I got chatting with her and she asked me what I did and I told her about the acting. Told her I was struggling. You know. As actors do. Made light of it. And she said—and these were her exact words—'I might have a gig for you. Give me your number.' So I gave her my number and then, yeah, a few days later she called me. And that was that. Up to my neck in it. Up to my fucking neck."

12:40 P.M.

It's a twelve-minute walk from the lush greenness of Queen's Park to the stained gray of Josie's street. Even on a sunny day the stucco houses look humiliated by their poor condition. Alix stares first from across the street and then from outside, directly into the windows. She sees a table in the bay. It's a dark wood, the sort that is unfashionable these days. There are three dark wooden chairs around it with barley-twist spindles. She can make out a sofa facing toward an older-looking television. Blank walls. A kitchen open to the living room is built into an alcove at the back. The cabinets are pine clad with white plastic handles. She can make out a dark passageway leading to a door. Denim curtains are half-drawn over the smaller window. Through the gap she can see a bed, freshly made with a pale floral duvet and two floral pillows, a pair of denim cushions, some white Formica-clad drawers.

It looks like a rental that's just been vacated by its previous owners, spruced and tidied and dressed for its next occupants. It does not look like a flat that is currently being lived in. She goes back to the big bay window, casts her eyes around the room again. It is hard to believe that a domestic incident occurred here in the early hours of Saturday, that a big man beat his small wife until she was bloodied and bruised.

And where is that big man? she wonders. There is a laptop closed on the dining table. But nothing else. Josie described him as never going out. As always being home. But he is not home now. So where is he?

She looks, one more time, at the sofa. She pictures Walter and Josie sitting side by side in the aftermath of his atrocity with Brooke, silently watching TV. Then she pictures Walter, five years later, slamming his wife's head against the wall in rage at her belated accusations.

As she turns back, she looks slightly to her left. She sees a double-decker bus rumbling down Kilburn High Road a few hundred feet away, heading south toward Maida Vale. And as she sees it, she thinks of Brooke Ripley climbing off a bus in her white column dress five years ago, just there.

Just there, in fact, at the point where Kilburn High Road meets Maida Vale.

Just there, a two-minute walk from Josie and Walter's flat.

2 P.M.

Alix stares hard at Josie. She tries to make her face look soft, but it's difficult because inside she feels all hard edges and spikes and darkness. Josie has her headphones on and is drinking tea out of Alix's favorite mug. (Alix suspects that Josie knows it is Alix's favorite mug and that is why she always uses it.) Alix adjusts the volume on the controls and then clears her throat, watching the lines jumping on the screen of her laptop. Her next question feels solid on her tongue, like something that she might accidentally swallow and choke on. She clears her throat again and says, "So. What happened to Brooke?"

"Brooke?"

Alix smiles and nods. "Yes. Brooke."

"I have no idea. Never heard from her again."

"Never heard from her again?"

"No."

"Did you never try to find her?"

Josie narrows her eyes at Alix and throws her a questioning look. "No. Why would I? After what she did?"

"Well, maybe she might have had some sort of an idea about where Roxy was."

Alix watches Josie's face as she reaches for a reply.

"No," she says after a pause. "No. She wouldn't have known. They had that big fallout. It was all over between them. Completely."

Alix raises an eyebrow coolly, finding it virtually impossible to cover her feelings.

"How would you feel," she says, "about me getting in touch with Brooke? Getting her side of things? For the podcast?"

"No."

It's as immediate and definite as a slammed door.

"Why not?"

"Because . . . just, no. It's too much. I'm telling you what I want to tell you. What I *need* to tell you. I have to live my life on the other side of this podcast. You know? Show my face in the world. And if you get her involved . . ." She stops and inhales.

Alix waits.

"I just don't trust her. That's all."

"You must wonder, though? What happened to her?"

"Of course I do. I wonder all the time. About Roxy. And about Brooke. All the time. It's like my life . . . it's like it ended that day. You know. Like all the good things stopped."

"But Erin," Alix says. "What about Erin?"

"What about Erin?"

"I mean, she must bring you happiness. Surely? What was it like for her when Roxy left? You barely talk about Erin."

Josie shrugs. "There's not much to say."

"Well, shall we just try?"

Josie nods.

Hi! I'm Your Birthday Twin!
A NETFLIX ORIGINAL SERIES

The screen shows a dramatic reenactment of a woman sitting on a sofa in an apartment, staring through the window as a bus goes past.

The text below reads:

Recording from Alix Summer's podcast, 17 July, 2019

"After the Brooke thing, my relationship with Walter became a game of chess. It was like I was a pawn, being pushed about by some huge invisible finger from square to square with no thought of my needs and wants. Walter was the king, of course, and everything in the home was done to protect him. I'd created a kind of invisible barrier around my family, behind the door of our flat. I'd been doing it for years, of course, all throughout the fourteen years of the children being at school, with the mums and the teachers and the social workers and my work colleagues and the next-door and upstairs neighbors; I kept people away. But that was when nobody had really done anything wrong. When all I was worried about was being judged for having badly behaved children, a violent husband. But now I was in danger of being judged for having a husband who seduced teenage girls and slept with them in his own home, and yes, I did go onto his laptop, and yes, he had been looking at things that were illegal and disgusting and actually very upsetting, and yes, Walter is a pervert and a criminal, disgusting, repellent, a man who I would never touch again, not in that way. And I told him as much. Told him that that side of our marriage was over. So I cooked and cleaned and worked and smiled at people I trusted, kept my head down around people I didn't, and then two years ago I told Walter I wanted a dog because I was sick of not having anything to love and he said if we were going to get a dog, then he wanted an Akita or a Doberman or something he could feel proud of walking down the road and I said, "'*No*, this dog is for me and I want a dog I can carry like a baby, because you ruined my babies, you ruined them.'"

"Because, by then, not only had Roxy gone, but Walter had started abusing Erin."

The screen fades and the credits roll.

2:30 P.M.

"Abusing? What do you mean?"

Josie tips her head back slightly and rolls her eyes to the ceiling. Alix waits with her breath caught painfully at the back of her throat. She feels as if she'd known this all along, somehow, like this had been a terrible hum in the background of everything right from the very start.

"I mean that nearly every night, when I fall asleep, Walter gets out of bed and goes into Erin's room. And then, when I get up, he's sitting at the table in the living room acting like nothing happened."

"And? I mean—how do you know?"

"I just do. That man thinks he's the king, you see. He lets me have my way here and there, like with the dog. Like coming here for dinner. But he does it in the way that a king would do it. A thrown treat." She gestures with her arm. "You have to run for it. You know. But as far as he's concerned, everything in that flat is his. It all belongs to him, and so the minute I told him I wasn't his anymore, that he was no longer allowed to touch me, he took the next nearest thing. He took Erin."

"Have you ever seen anything? Heard anything?"

Josie shakes her head. "I put in my earplugs. I stay in my room until the morning comes."

"Fuck! Josie!" Alix can't help it. She cannot contain the shock and dismay. She's meant to be impartial. Her job is not to judge or react, but simply to ask and listen. But this—she'll edit out her reaction, she knows that—this is too animal and raw to remain circumspect about, especially, and yes, she knows it's the most awful cliché, but especially as a mother.

"What was I meant to do?" Josie snaps. "It was so gradual. I didn't realize at first, what was happening. I just happened to wake up a couple of times and see the empty bed. I'd ask him where he'd been, and he'd say he'd been chatting online with his kids in Canada. And I thought: Why does it have to be in the middle of the night? What's wrong with the evening? And once I'd worked out what was happening, well, I thought she'd come and tell me. Erin. I kept waiting. But instead, she just went more and more into herself. Stopped eating anything I gave her. She'd always been fussy, but she got fussier and fussier and then started asking for baby food."

"Baby food?"

"Yes. She said, 'I want that stuff I used to have when I was little. The stuff you gave me out of a jar. When you used to feed me with a spoon.' I mean, I assumed it was some kind of—what do they call it?—regression, I suppose. She wanted to be a baby again. To be safe."

"But, Josie, sorry," Alix interjects, sensing that Josie is skimming over vast swaths of important backstory. "What did Walter say? I mean, you must have said something to him, surely?"

Josie shakes her head and Alix sighs so loudly it makes the audio display on her laptop oscillate wildly. "I'm really sorry, Josie. Really, I am. But I need to get this straight. You are telling me that in the aftermath of what happened with Walter and Brooke, your youngest daughter ran away from home and you withdrew conjugal favors from your husband, and that as a result of that, your husband started to visit your older teenage daughter in her bedroom every night, to, you assume, sexually abuse her. Your daughter began to regress to the point of wanting to eat only baby food and stopped leaving her room entirely. And this has been going on for the past five years?"

"Around about. Yes."

Josie's voice is clipped. Her mouth is pursed.

"And you have not spoken to either your daughter or your husband about it?"

She nods. "That's correct."

"It just . . . happens?"

"It just happens."

"And your daughter. Erin. Was she restrained in any way? I mean, was she free to leave?"

"Yes. She was free to leave."

"But she didn't?"

"No. She didn't."

"And why do you think that is?"

"He probably got inside her head. He probably made her think it was OK. The way he does. You know?"

Alix leaves a moment of silence. Her listeners will need it at this point. But she needs it too. Then she asks the question that she fears the answer to.

"Before Friday night, Josie, when you and Walter had your fight, the night Walter beat you, when was the last time you'd seen Erin?"

She shrugs. She sniffs and wriggles slightly in her chair. "About six months? Maybe a year? About that."

"Not at all? Not once? Not even going to the bathroom?"

"She waits until I'm not in the house. She doesn't want to see me."

"But how do you know that?"

"Well, she'd come and see me if she did, wouldn't she? She knows when I'm there. I feed her. I leave her the food and then she puts the empties outside her room. And don't think, don't think for a minute, that I didn't want to see her, because I wanted to see her more than anything, but when something goes on for that long it, well, you know, it just gets harder and harder, doesn't it? Harder to turn back and do the right thing. I stopped at her door, every day, twice, three times a day. I stopped. And I touched the door and I made my hand like this." She forms it into a fist with knuckles. "Like I was going to knock. And I never did, Alix. I just never did. And don't think I don't hate myself because I hate myself so much. So much. Hate that it took so long for me to break this. To stop it."

"And it took a dinner at my house . . . ?"

"Yes. Like I told you when we first met up, it was all about breaking patterns. Going to the fancy pub that night. Getting rid of the denim. Getting to know you. Doing this." She gestures at the space between them. "It was as if I had to break small patterns before I would be ready to break big ones."

Alix nods, slowly, and peers at Josie through narrowed eyes. "I see," she says. Although she really doesn't. "I see. But you say that Erin has been a virtual recluse for the past few months, hasn't left her room, or the house. So, where did she go, exactly, on Friday night? Which friend has she gone to stay with?"

Josie repositions herself. "I have no idea."

"Someone she went to school with?"

"Oh. I doubt that. No, probably just someone she knows from gaming. An online friend."

"You must be so worried about her."

"Yes. I am. I'm horribly worried about her. I'm worried about her, and I'm worried about Roxy."

"And what about Walter? Are you worried about Walter?"

"God. No. Why would I be worried about him? He's a pervert and a wife beater. He's a monster. I despise him. I absolutely despise him. I'm glad—"

She stops herself short.

"Glad what?"

"I'm glad he hit me. I'm glad he hurt me. It got me out of there.

Got me out of that sick prison. I'd take the beating all over again to be free."

Her face sets hard, and Alix wishes this were a documentary, not a podcast. She wishes her listeners could see the way Josie's face has frozen into a mask, and the single, glycerin tear that appears in those black eyes of hers and spills down her cheek in a straight line.

"What will become of him? Of Walter? Will you tell the police about what he did to Erin?"

She wipes the tear away with the back of her hand and sniffs. "No," she says. "That's not my move to make. That's up to Erin."

"Have you talked to her about it?"

"No. I haven't spoken to her at all. She won't take my calls. Or reply to my messages."

Alix makes a circle of her mouth and exhales. None of this makes any sense. None of it. "Have you thought about going to the flat and going through Erin's computer? Seeing what you can find?"

"I don't know anything about computers."

"Well, yes, but I do. I could come with you?"

"No. No, thank you. Erin will come to me when she's ready."

"But, Josie, think about it. Erin has been abused under your roof for years. You've done nothing to protect her. She waits until you're out of the house before she uses the bathroom. What on earth makes you think she's going to get in touch with you?"

Josie sighs and shrugs. "You're probably right," she says. "I'm sure you're right. But whatever happens, it's better for her than being in that flat with that man. Whatever happens, at least she's free."

3:30 P.M.

Alix stands outside the school gates. She has brought the dog, who has not been taken for a walk yet today. She wanted an excuse to leave a little early, to be out a little late. Her head is bursting. She feels sick. Mothers chat with her and she chats back, glad of the opportunity to take herself completely out of the place she's spent the past few hours. The dog sees another dog and yaps at it and Alix apologizes to the dog's owner. Children fuss around the tiny dog and Alix says, "Be careful, he can be a bit snappy." Someone asks if the dog is hers and she says, "No, he belongs to a friend," then corrects herself and says, "To someone I know."

She takes the children to the park and watches them on the swings, the dog tucked under her arm. She wishes the dog could talk. The dog would know, she thinks, the dog would know everything. She wants to talk to Josie's mum, but she has promised Josie that she won't.

She can't stop thinking about Walter, about the way he'd been on Friday night when he came for dinner. The brand-new clothes with the creases still in. The moderate drinking (he had only two beers, all night). The quiet way he'd talked to her in her recording studio about his "Jojo," about her lying and her making up stories to suit her own narrative. She'd put it down to the behavior of a gaslighter; she'd assumed that it was all part of his act. And maybe it was. But she can't shift the discomfiting sense that there's something else. Something behind this dark, yet somehow typical, story of a family blighted by the dysfunction of a controlling and dominant man.

She's not who she makes out to be. Not at all.

That's what he'd said. And as much as her gut tells her to believe a woman who says she has been abused, it also tells her that Josie is not to be trusted.

THURSDAY,
18 JULY

Alix and the children have left for school, but Nathan is running late for work. Josie had heard him say something to Alix about a meeting in Bishopsgate at 10 a.m., not worth him heading to the office beforehand.

Just as Alix had predicted, the weather has turned from pleasant-for-mid-July to unbearably hot. Nathan sits in the garden with his laptop and a cup of coffee and, even from here, Josie can see the sheen of sweat on his forehead. It occurs to her that he sits in the garden in the mornings deliberately to avoid having to share space with her indoors. She forces a smile and slips through the gap between the sliding glass doors. She's still wearing the clothes that Alix gave her on Saturday. She has her own clothes hanging in her room, but she no longer wants to wear them, even though they are clean. She had hoped that Alix might take pity on her seeing her descend the stairs every morning wearing the same top and trousers, that she might offer to lend her something new. But she hasn't.

"God," she says, standing a few feet from Nathan. "It's boiling, and it's not even nine o'clock!"

"They're saying thirty-two by lunchtime."

"Bloody hell."

She allows a silence to pass before turning to him and saying, "Oh. By the way. Alix said you might be using the study on Saturday night? When her sister is here?"

"Oh," he says, looking slightly flustered, and Josie knows immediately that he and Alix have been talking about this, secretly, privately, behind her back. "Well, yeah. That was the plan. But no. Apparently, they're all sleeping over now. I think Alix was going to tell you. Both sisters and all three kids. They're going to be using the fold-out. So . . ." He clears his throat and trails off.

Lies. All of it.

"Oh," says Josie. "That's fine. I'll find something. But what about you? Where will you be hiding out?"

"Oh, I'll probably hang out here for a bit and then head off for a couple of drinks with some mates."

"The same mates you were with when you didn't show up for dinner last Friday?" She tries to inject a hint of playfulness into her words, but she fails. She's so cross she could scream.

He throws her an uncertain look and shrugs. "I'm not sure yet," he says. "I'm not sure." Then he necks the dregs of his coffee, slaps his hands against his legs, and says, "Well, time for me to head into work. What are you up to today?"

"Nothing really. We'll do some more of the podcast, then I'll go to work. That's it really."

"And what are your plans, Josie? Generally? I mean, obviously from Saturday you'll need a plan. Won't you?"

Josie eyes him coolly. He has gone off-script, she can tell. This is not what Alix told him to say. This is, she thinks furiously, none of his bloody business. But she manages to sound civil when she says,

"Yes. I'll need a plan. But what I've found, Nathan, is that life shows you the way when you forget to make one. So, you know, let's wait and see." She shrugs and heads back into the kitchen, scoops up the dog, and takes him to her room, where she waits until she hears the sound of Nathan slamming the front door behind him a few minutes later. She watches him through the small window in her bedroom, slinging his suit jacket over his shoulder, sliding his stupid sunglasses onto his stupid nose, walking down the street as if he were the king of the universe.

Alix said she was going to the shops after the school run, she said she'd be home about nine thirty. It's 9:10 a.m. now and Josie shuts the dog in her room and tiptoes down to the next floor. Alix and Nathan's bedroom door is wide open, which she feels is a sign of some sort that Alix isn't precious about people seeing inside. She hasn't properly investigated their room yet. It feels too much. Much too much. But Nathan has put her in a bad mood with all his talk of "plans."

If Nathan thinks she should have a plan, she decides, then a plan she will have.

Alix and Nathan's bed is very big. It has a bedhead made out of rattan and pale green velvet. It is unmade; huge voluminous clouds of creamy duvet are bunched up at the foot of the bed, kicked off no doubt during the encroaching heat of the previous night, with two fat pillows squashed into fortune cookies at the top end and two more kicked onto the floor on either side. The walls are hung with a mishmash of prints and paintings and photographs. A pair of milky-white lights hangs from the ceiling, one on each side of the bed, instead of table lamps, Josie supposes. There's a square bay window with a little seat built into it, overlooking the back garden. It's scattered with discarded clothes, mostly Nathan's, including a nasty-looking pair of threadbare socks (you'd think he could afford new ones).

Between the bedroom and the en-suite bathroom is a kind of anteroom, or dressing area, with clothes hanging on either side: Alix's on one, Nathan's on the other. She spends a minute or two leafing through Alix's clothes. She rubs the fabrics between her fingers, the silks and linens and soft bamboo cottons. She pulls open the shoe drawers beneath and looks at the neat rows of golden strappy sandals and suede heeled boots and silken heels with ankle straps. She wants to take them out and try them on, admire herself in the full-length mirror. But the minutes are ticking by, so she turns to Nathan's rail and starts feeling through his pockets. She doesn't know what she's looking for precisely, but she has a very strong feeling that Nathan is stupid enough and Alix is trusting enough for her to find something she will need.

She pulls out crumpled paper receipts and business cards and empty chewing-gum packages. She pulls out paper clips and sugar packets and the wrinkled paper tubes from drinking straws; boarding passes for flights to Brussels and Dublin; a comb; half a Polo mint. And then, yes. There. Right there. In the inside pocket of a blue business jacket, exactly what she was looking for. A tiny clear bag with a residue of white powder clinging to its insides. She pictures him now, in a bar, his tie slung over his shoulder, surrounded by tequila shots and baying men, snorting cocaine off a glass-topped table. Despicable, she thinks. Just despicable. With a wife and children at home. In another pocket she finds a scrap of paper napkin with an illegible number written on it. And in another a cardboard sleeve for a hotel key card—the Railings—with the room number 23 written on it.

She takes all three items and puts them in her pocket, goes back to her room, and waits for Alix to come home.

Nathan wants her to have a plan.

Well, now she's got one.

Alix returns a few minutes later. She is laden with bags from the supermarket and Josie watches her unload them onto the island in the kitchen. Melon-and-strawberry fruit bowl. Crunchy Nut cornflakes. A huge steak. A bag of onions. Pouches of cat food with pictures on them of a cat that looks exactly like the cloud-cat, as if Alix's cat has had her very own personalized dinner designed for her.

"I'll go to my mum's," Josie says to Alix. "On Saturday. When your sisters come."

Alix stops what she's doing, a cylinder of chocolate biscuits held aloft in her hand. "Oh!" she says. "OK. That's great. What changed your mind about getting in touch with her?"

Josie shrugs and pulls out a tiny loose hair from Fred's fur, lets it float lazily to the floor. "I didn't really have a choice, I suppose. I mean, Nathan told me about your other sister coming to stay. So I know the fold-out bed will be taken. Though I thought your other sister lived in London?"

"Yes. Yes, she does. But her kids didn't want to miss out on the fun. They wanted to sleep over too. So yes. I'm sorry about that. A bit of a, er, last-minute thing. But I'm so glad you're going to see your mum! I really think it's time."

Josie nods, as though she has given Alix's words serious thought and now agrees with her. "It is what it is," she says. "But while I'm still here, we've got two more days, we should make the most of them."

"You mean, the podcast?"

"Yes. We should try and get as much down on tape as we can."

Josie feels her heart pick up under the cotton of Alix's expensive T-shirt at the thought of next week. She feels the heat in the air, the sun burning already as it starts its arc across the empty sky and blazes through the glass roof of Alix's kitchen extension, and it's only going to get hotter.

By Sunday it will be pushing thirty-five.

She'd thought she'd have longer. She's running out of time.

She glances up to see Alix staring thoughtfully at her. "I'm not sure what else there is to chat about now? I mean, we got to the end, I think? We're up-to-date. Apart from the events of Friday night, of course. Would you like to talk about that?"

Josie nods, her mouth tightly pursed.

"Shall we . . . ?" Alix gestures to the studio.

"Yes," says Josie. "Let's."

Hi! I'm Your Birthday Twin!
A NETFLIX ORIGINAL SERIES

The screen shows a dramatic reconstruction of a couple walking down a dark street.
The text reads:

Recording from Alix Summer's podcast,
18 July, 2019

"*He* hadn't wanted to go in the first place. Made such a fuss. I bought him some nice new clothes, but he refused to wear them, insisted on wearing cheap stuff from Primark, deliberately got a terrible haircut, just to spite me. And then of course, when Nathan didn't make an appearance . . ."

Josie sighs.

"Well, you could see how annoyed he was. And then he seethed the whole walk home. I could feel it coming off him. The dark rage building and building. By the time we got home . . ."

The screen shows a couple letting themselves into the Fairs' building.

"... the atmosphere was putrid. I couldn't control my anger by that point. I felt it all, all of it, rolling and churning through me like a storm, and finally, after all these years, I found the strength to hurl it out of my gut and into the air, to hit Walter with it, right between the eyes. I just screamed at him. 'Pedophile! You're a pedophile! You groomed me and you took me when I was too young to know what I wanted. And then you groomed Brooke and you took her when she was too young to know what she wanted. And then you abused your own daughter. The only daughter you have left after what you did to Roxy. You have abused your daughter over and over again and I have let you do that because I have been programmed by you to believe that you are God and that you can have anything you want. But you are not God, Walter, and you cannot have anything you want. You cannot. And it stops tonight. What you're doing to Erin. It stops *tonight*. No more. No more.'

"And then I ran to Erin's door and I pushed it open and there was my baby, my Erin, staring at me from wide, dead eyes. I said, 'Pack a bag, baby. Quickly. I'm getting you out of here. We're leaving.' I said, 'I know what Dad's been doing and I'm so, so sorry, baby. So sorry that I abandoned you.' And that was when I felt it, a blow to the back of my head, then a kind of deep radiating heat and pain and wetness. I turned and saw Walter's arm coming back toward me, with the remote control he'd just used to hit me held in his hand, coming toward my face, and then he beat me with it, all over my face and head. Erin just stood there; so thin, she was. So thin. And I threw myself toward Walter and shoved him in his chest with both my hands outstretched and said, '*Enough. That is enough.*' And I saw him raise his hand to hit my child and I just *flung* myself between them, and then, as quickly as it had started, it stopped."

The screen shows an actor playing the part of Walter, breathing heavily in the doorway, the remote control hanging from his hand, the actors playing Erin and Josie, standing in Erin's room, their arms around each other. Then Walter turns and leaves.

"A moment later I peered into the living room. Walter was sitting at his laptop. The remote control was sitting on the coffee table. It was like he was trying to give the impression that none of it had ever happened, like I didn't have a split lip and blood seeping down the back of my neck. It was as if he thought we were all just going to carry on. Normally. Like we always did. But he was wrong. I grabbed my handbag, I grabbed the dog, I grabbed Erin, and we left. Neither of us said goodbye."

The screen shows Erin and Josie closing the front door of their building behind them; the actor playing Josie turns, slightly, to look at Walter in the bay window.

The screen fades to darkness.

11 A.M.

Alix exhales. She has not breathed for what feels like minutes. The scenario that Josie has painted inside her head is making her feel claustrophobic, as if she is trapped in that dark, shabby flat with all three of them. She can smell it inside her nostrils: the fear and the blood. She pictures them on the street, Josie and Erin, carrying just what they grabbed as they left, the blood congealing on Josie's face. Walter, still and unrepentant in the bay window.

But that is where the picture starts to fragment. Josie walked from her home near Kilburn the sixteen minutes to Alix's house in Queen's Park. But it was 3 a.m. when she appeared on Alix's doorstep. It was cold. What happened between ten o'clock, when they would have returned home, and 3 a.m., when Josie arrived here?

She glances up at Josie and says, "Where did you go? When you left the flat?"

Josie issues a small laugh. "Well, here, obviously."

"But in between?"

"Nowhere."

"But—you said that the argument started when you got home. And it only lasted a few minutes. I just—"

Josie interjects. "No. It didn't happen when we got home. I didn't say that. It happened when Walter got out of bed. Like he does nearly every night. Like I told you. We went to bed and then I couldn't sleep. It took me ages. And then I finally dropped off and I felt him, I felt him peel back the covers. I knew. I knew what he was doing. Where he was going. And that was when I confronted him."

"So, you were in bed. In your pajamas?"

"Yes."

"And then you got up and followed him?"

"Yes. I saw him going to Erin's door. And that was when I screamed at him."

"But you weren't wearing your pajamas when you came to me. You were wearing the dress. The lovely dress."

"I put it back on. I wasn't going to walk halfway across Kilburn in my pajamas."

"But the dress had blood on it. How did the dress have blood on it if you weren't wearing it during the attack?"

"Alix. I don't understand what you're trying to say. Are you saying that you don't believe me?"

"No! Not at all. Of course not. But listeners are going to be hearing this like it's a novel, they'll notice plot holes. You and I have been having this conversation for a month, but listeners will be gobbling this down in a day once it's out there and edited down. It needs to make sense. For the listener. Do you see?"

Josie sighs deeply. "Well, yes. I suppose. But you'd think that the sort of people who listen to your stuff would have some sympathy, some empathy. You'd think they'd understand that when something like that happens, like what's happened to me, when someone has been the victim of abuse and violence and gaslighting, that maybe they might get a bit confused."

"Yes. Josie, yes, of course. That's absolutely true. So I just want to help you to unpick it all a bit and then put it back together. So that it makes sense. That's all. So Walter got out of bed in the early hours. You accosted him. He attacked you. He tried to attack Erin. Then you and Erin collected a few things—you got redressed—and then you both left together?"

Josie nods firmly. "Yes."

"And you walked here—and Erin? Where did Erin walk?"

"The opposite direction."

"At three in the morning?"

"Yes."

"Did she have things with her?"

"I suppose so, yes. A small bag."

Alix smiles glassily at Josie. She wants to push through. She wants to understand how Josie could have left her vulnerable daughter to walk somewhere, God knows where, all alone in the middle of the night. She wants to know. But she can tell that Josie is shutting down now, pulling up her drawbridge. She sighs. "I hope Erin is OK. It's very scary thinking of her all alone in the night."

"Yes," Josie replies firmly. "But she's safer out there than she ever was in her own home. Wherever she is, she's safe."

She says this with a strange certainty, as if the world were not full

NONE OF THIS IS TRUE

of dangerous people who prey on the vulnerable, as if nothing bad could possibly have happened to her daughter between three o'clock on Saturday morning and now.

"I really think we should try to track her down, Josie. It's been nearly six days. No messages. No calls. I know she's safe from Walter now. But is it possible she might have found herself somewhere worse? That maybe her online friend wasn't who they claimed to be? I mean, you hear that sort of thing a lot, don't you? People with fake online identities. It's just—"

"She's *fine*, Alix. She's fine. She can take care of herself."

"But you said she can't. You said you've been feeding her baby food. You said—"

Alix flinches as Josie pulls off her headphones and slams them on the tabletop. "I'm trying to tell you my story, Alix. *My truth.* And you seem to be trying to make it into something it isn't. You either want my story or you don't. You can't have it both ways. You just can't."

And then she picks up her dog from her lap and storms out of the recording studio, leaving Alix reeling in her wake.

SATURDAY,
20 JULY

J osie wakes early. It's her last morning waking up in Alix's house. Her last morning opening up the curtains and seeing the view of Queen's Park from the small window, instead of the gray staring faces of people on the bus from her old bedroom. It's the last morning of wearing Alix's pajamas and showering in Alix's designer bathroom and drinking coffee from Alix's shiny coffee machine. There had been a takeaway curry the night before. Josie had attempted to contribute some money toward it, but Alix had refused to accept it. "It's your last night," she said, her hand gently touching the top of Josie's hand. "It's our treat." There'd been wine from a huge glass and a TV show with surround-sound audio booming through the house and Leon curled so that his toes were gently buried under Josie's leg. Then the creak and bang and babble of a family putting itself to bed: hushed whispers, the click of light switches, the cloud-cat meowing gently from the darkened hallway as if to ask where everyone had gone.

It was, in some ways, the most perfect night of Josie's life.

Josie sighs heavily. The air is limpid and sticky. Her phone tells her that it is already twenty-one degrees, and it is only seven thirty. The one time, Josie thinks, that she could really do with a disappointing English summer, and the weather gods deliver an almighty heat wave.

She glances at the dress and cardigan that she was wearing when she arrived here a week ago. She pulls the dress to her nose and sniffs it. It smells of Alix's detergent. It smells of Alix's house. She showers, using Alix's spicy-smelling shower gel, and washes her hair using Alix's herby-smelling shampoo, and she wraps herself in Alix's thick, thick towels and sits on the side of Alix's squashy bed and for a moment she feels a wash of sadness pass through her. But then she thinks of what she has planned next, and the sadness quickly fades.

"Oh!" says Alix when Josie walks into the kitchen a few minutes later. "You're back in your own clothes!"

"Yes. Well, of course." She holds the worn clothes and the pajamas in one hand, the dog in the other. "Where shall I put these?" she asks about the clothes.

"Oh, just give them to me. Here."

She hands them to Alix, who takes them through to the laundry room.

"Thank you!" Josie calls after her. "Thank you so much." Then she asks, "What time are your sisters arriving?"

"Oh, five-ish, I think. So you don't need to rush. Just take your time." She throws Josie one of her golden smiles and then tears open a packet of croissants. "Want one?" she asks, and Josie nods.

Nathan comes downstairs an hour later, Leon trailing behind him in his pajamas. Nathan eyes Josie up and down and says, "Pretty dress, Josie."

"Thank you," she says, feeling simultaneously flattered and repulsed.

Eliza comes in a few minutes later and starts to cry about something mean someone had said to her on Snapchat and that is when Josie knows that it is time for her to go. She puts Fred into his carrier and slings her handbag over her shoulder.

She sees Alix eyeing her worriedly. "I can drive you?" she says. "It's quite a long walk, especially in this heat?"

Josie shakes her head. "It's fine," she says. "I'll walk in the shade. I'm not in any rush."

"And your mum knows you're coming?"

"Yes. She knows."

Alix brings Josie into her arms then, and for once Josie lets herself be held.

When they come apart, Alix is looking directly into Josie's eyes. "Please stay in touch, Josie. Won't you? Get the help you need and stay in touch."

And then the milky-blue door is between them, Alix and her world on one side, Josie on the other.

Around the corner, Josie opens her handbag to check that it is there, the money she has been collecting all week from the various cashpoint machines between Alix's house and her job, the thick reassuring weight and shape of it, held together with one of Eliza's pink glitter hairbands she'd found on the staircase earlier. Then she takes out the sunglasses she found under a chair in the garden this morning—a large pair with forest-green frames—places them on her face, and starts walking.

The sun beats down from a heartless sky as she heads toward the next place.

PART THREE

SATURDAY,
20 JULY

The house feels different immediately. It feels lighter and softer, and it feels, at long last, normal again. Alix stands for a moment in the hallway and absorbs the change in the energy. The cat sashays down the hall toward her and throws itself around Alix's legs celebratorily, as if she too knows that her territory is returned to her. Alix gathers her into her arms, carries her into the kitchen, and puts her up on the work surface near her food bowl.

"Gone?" says Nathan, peering up at her over his reading glasses.

"Gone."

"Are you sure? Have you checked?"

"No, I haven't checked. But I know she has."

"Will she be OK?" asks Leon.

Alix smiles at him. "She'll be fine. Her mum will get her the care she needs."

But the words sound hollow somehow, meaningless. Not because she doesn't think Josie's mum would help her, but because she's not entirely sure that that is where Josie is going. It's an unsettling feeling, but she puts it to one side, because today is the day she's been looking forward to all week and she has things to do, not least to sort out the spare bedroom for Maxine and the boys and the study for Zoe and Petal.

Her tread feels light up the stairs knowing that there is nobody up there on the top floor, knowing that her part in Josie's drama is over. But a small shadow remains.

Josie has not stripped her bed, but has left it neatly made, the pillows plumped and fat, the surface of the duvet slick. Alix unmakes it and strips it.

Josie has left the shower room sparkling clean, her towels hung straight and symmetrical from the heated rail. Alix yanks them down and adds them to the laundry pile.

She pushes open the window and closes the curtains against the burning sun, which will be shining directly into this room by lunchtime.

She surveys the room, and it feels almost as if Josie was never here, as if none of it really happened. She drops to her hands and knees and looks under the bed. Some dust bunnies, but that's all. And then she straightens up and runs her fingertips underneath the mattress.

The key is still there. The one with the number 6 on the tag. For a moment she considers jumping to her feet, running to the front door, seeing if she can catch up with Josie to hand it back to her. But immediately she knows she mustn't. She knows that this key means something. That maybe it has been left for a reason. She pulls it out gingerly by the metal hoop and stares at it for a moment, before putting it in her pocket.

She redresses the bed, replaces the towels, and closes the door behind her.

———————

Zoe arrives first. She is the older of Alix's sisters. The smallest. The quietest. Petal is the youngest of the cousins, Zoe's long-awaited only child, conceived and born when she was forty-one via donor insemination. Maxine arrives half an hour after Zoe. She is the younger of Alix's sisters and has two boys, Billy and Jonny, one the same age as Leon and Petal, the other the same age as Eliza. Maxine is the tallest and the loudest and her boys are horribly behaved but theirs is not the sort of family to care, and frankly, after weeks of listening to Josie describing the behaviors of her two children, they now seem like angels in comparison.

Alix has set up two paddling pools in the garden and has a huge bucket of ice in the shade for chilling the wine and the children's drinks. All three sisters are wearing billowy cotton dresses and the air smells of the sun cream that they have rubbed into each other's necks and shoulder blades. Nathan gets back from a trip to the local garden-supplies center at about six with a new water sprinkler after discovering that the old one is dead. He sets it up and the children run through it screaming with delight. He sits with the sisters for a while and drinks a beer, slowly, almost unnaturally so, pacing himself, Alix assumes, for the real drinking which will commence when he's with his friends later. She swallows back the feeling of discomfort that hits her when she thinks about Nathan's plans for the night and remembers his promise to her. She is 99 percent certain that he will not let her down. He loves her sisters and has always been eager to have their approval and he knows that if he lets Alix down tonight, they will both judge him very harshly. Not only that, but she has promised him sex if he's home before midnight. She reaches out her hand at one point and squeezes his wrist with it, both affectionately and warningly. He smiles down at her and she can see it there, his resolve, to do better and be better. She squeezes his wrist again and turns her attention back to her sisters.

At seven o'clock they order their pizzas and start making the margaritas. Maxine is responsible for this undertaking as she spent three years working in a cocktail bar in her twenties. At seven thirty Nathan leaves. Alix follows him to the front door and puts her lips to his neck and brushes her leg against his groin. "Be good," she says. "Please."

"I swear," he says. "I swear."

He kisses her softly on the lips and then on her neck and it is so unusual for them to behave like this these days, to be playful, to be sexual, that Alix feels a flush go all the way through her. She watches him from the window in the hallway, in his navy shorts, his floral-print shirt, his red hair pushed back from his face by black sunglasses, and she thinks that she has missed him. That she wants him. That she is already looking forward to him coming home. And then she turns back to the chaos of her sisters and their children and the calls of "Who wants a salty rim?" and the hot, hot sun beating down through the roof of her kitchen and onto the tiled floor.

7:30 P.M.

Nathan has his phone to his ear as he heads through the back streets toward Kilburn tube station. He's talking loudly in that way that some people do, as if he thinks everyone in the world wants to hear his business. His voice grates through Josie's head, even from a distance. There's been a change of plan, according to the one side of the conversation that Josie can hear. They're not meeting at the place they'd arranged to meet; they're meeting at the Lamb & Flag. "Yeah, and I'm not getting shit-faced, remember. I told Alix I'd be home before midnight. I'm on a promise. Yeah!" He laughs. "Exactly!"

He hangs up and Josie stares at the back of his head in disgust. How could Alix even contemplate it? she wonders. How could she think she needed to promise him anything, simply for him to behave like a civilized human being? She is out of this man's league in every way. Josie feels her respect for Alix wane, records another tiny degradation in her feelings for her, but then remembers what she is doing and why and feels restored again.

She follows Nathan into the tube station. She's wearing a new dress that she bought from Sainsbury's this morning. It's not as nice as the things she bought when she was with Alix, but it's good for the heat and it's also unfamiliar to Nathan. Her hair is tucked inside a straw hat, also from Sainsbury's, and she's wearing red lipstick for the first time in her life, which makes her look even less like herself.

She has googled the pub where Nathan is meeting his friends, just in case she loses him on the tube. It's in a side street off Oxford Street, near the back end of Selfridges; the nearest tube station is Bond Street, six stops away.

Kilburn is an overground tube station, and she is glad not to be underground in this heat. A breeze comes from nowhere and ruffles the hem of her skirt and cools the sweat on her neck. Nathan, at the other end of the platform, is fiddling with his phone. He's wearing shorts and his legs are skinny and pale, like a child's. Once again, she wonders what on earth Alix has ever seen in this man. At least, she thinks, at least Walter was good-looking when he was young. Strong. Tall. Handsome.

The tube arrives and twenty minutes later Josie is following Nathan across the chaos of Saturday-night Oxford Street, where the shops are all still open and the pavements are heavy with shoppers and early diners. What a strange people we are, she thinks of her countrymen: where other people take to the shade, to the air-con, stay indoors and close their curtains in the heat, the English hurl themselves at it, like pigs into a furnace.

At a table outside the pub are three men, who all get to their feet and make baying, animal noises when they see Nathan approaching. They bang him on the back and force a pint into his hand and then squeeze up along the bench so that he can sit down and they all look like him, or at least different versions of him. One is Asian, one is Black, one is white with dark hair, but they are all dressed the same, they sound the same, laugh the same. They are a pack, she thinks, a pack of men. Men who should be home with their families, not sitting here acting like a bunch of overgrown schoolboys.

There is an Italian restaurant next to the pub, with tables on the pavement. She sits down and orders a Coke and a pasta dish with fresh tomato and basil. Nathan and his friends break out into deafening laughter roughly every forty-five seconds. More pints are brought to the table and a round of shots. She hears Nathan telling his friends that he is celebrating because they have just got rid of the "houseguest from hell."

"Oh yeah. Who was that, then?" says the Asian one.

"Friend of my wife's. Or maybe not quite a friend, but this woman she's been doing a podcast about. She got in a fight with her husband and turned up on our front step last weekend with a bashed-up face. Alix let her in, *of course*. She's so bloody soft, my wife. And this woman refused to go home, refused to go to the police, refused to go to her mum's, just sat in our house all week wearing Alix's clothes with a face like someone just farted. And today, she finally left! So, cheers! Cheers to having my house back!"

Josie turns and watches them sourly as they bang their beer glasses together and say "cheers."

"Where did she go?" asks the dark-haired guy.

"No fucking idea and I do not care. I have never felt less comfortable in my own home, that's all I know. The woman was a freak."

Someone makes another of the animal noises, and they bang their glasses together again.

Josie pushes her half-eaten pasta away from her. The things that Nathan is saying are not nice, but she's not surprised. She knows that Nathan didn't like her being there. But that's fine. It all just strengthens her resolve.

She picks up her phone and finds the message thread she started earlier. She types another message.

> He's at a table outside the Lamb and Flag.
> The one in the flowery shirt and red hair with
> three other men. Can you be here in ten minutes?

The reply comes immediately.

> I'm just getting off the tube.
> I'll be there soon.

Josie sends a thumbs-up emoji and puts down her phone, a small smile playing at the corners of her mouth.

9 P.M.

Josie watches Nathan's face register a small shock of pleasant surprise when the young woman stands over him and says, "Can I sit here while I wait for my friend?"

"Oh, yeah. Sure. Of course." Nathan squashes along the bench closer to his friend and the woman squeezes herself on the end, so that her arm presses against his. She places a drink on the table in front of her and rummages through her tiny handbag, pulls out a packet of tobacco and some Rizlas, and makes herself a roll-up. Josie watches her turn to Nathan and say, "Want one?"

"Oh," says Nathan. "No. No, thank you. I never have . . ."

"Do you mind if I do?"

"Not at all. Go ahead. Not a problem."

Josie can see color rising through Nathan's face. The woman is wearing a floaty black halter-neck top and tight white jeans and her curly blond hair is tied back from her exquisite face, which is makeup free in the way that requires a lot of very expertly applied makeup.

Nathan manages to find his way back into his conversation with the three friends, but Josie can see that he is struggling now, that he is hyperaware of the stunningly beautiful young woman sitting right next to him, her bare arm brushing against his bare arm every few seconds. The woman plays with her phone for a few minutes and then she swears under her breath and bangs her phone down on the table. Nathan turns to her and says, "Are you OK?"

The woman sighs. "Just been blown out," she says. "By my friend. She's always doing this. Every single time. Seriously. This is the third time in a row. God."

"That sucks," says Nathan. "I hate it when people do that to me."

"Yeah. It's just disrespectful, isn't it?"

They don't say anything for a moment. The woman takes a drag of her roll-up and blows it out of the side of her mouth. Nathan picks up his pint glass and takes a sip. "I don't suppose I could stay with you guys for a bit?" the woman says. "Just while I finish my drink? Seems a shame to waste it."

"God. Yeah. Of course. Please."

"Oh, thank you so much. You're a savior. I'm Katelyn, by the way."

She offers him her hand to shake, and he takes it. "Nathan," he says. "Nice to meet you, Katelyn."

Then he introduces her to the rest of the group, she shakes their hands, they smile, she smiles, they are all delighted that a beautiful young woman has joined their group, they are holding in their soft stomachs and bringing their best games to the table. Josie watches in satisfaction and then sends Katelyn another text message.

> *Bloody brilliant. Let me know when you've done it. I'll be waiting for you.*

Then she pays for her unfinished pasta and her flat Coca-Cola and heads away from the pub and into the maelstrom of the hot summer night.

10:30 P.M.

Alix sends Nathan a text message.

> *Hi! We're being very bad. You having fun?*

She watches the ticks on the message for a while, but they stay gray. She swallows down the sense of discomfort and puts her phone away. She'd been secretly hoping that he might have been home by now. The later he's out, the higher the chance of him losing himself to the night.

Zoe is making herself a mint tea. She has a natural cut-off point for drinking; she's always the first to stop. Maxine and Alix are drinking the warm dregs of a bottle of Prosecco they opened earlier that had been found bobbing around darkly in the ice bucket in the garden. Petal is in bed as Zoe is very firm about bedtimes. The other children are playing a computer game in the living room incredibly loudly and Alix is about to go in and tell them to be quiet as there is a bedroom on the other side of the living-room wall where the house next door is converted into flats, and she doesn't want to disturb the neighbors, but for now, she is enjoying the soft edges of the night, the night air cooling down the intense heat of the day but still warm enough for bare arms. She's enjoying the conversation; they're discussing their upcoming summer holiday, a big villa in Croatia, all three of them, their children, the husbands, their mother, a pool, ten days of happiness. It was booked back in January and felt at first close enough to touch and then, as the winter passed slowly into spring, impossibly distant and now it is only twenty-two days away and Zoe shows them the new bikini she just ordered from John Lewis on her phone and they discuss their boobs and their bellies and their hormones and their moods and then, suddenly, it is nearly half eleven and Zoe is yawning and making moves toward bed.

Alix checks her phone to see if Nathan has sent her any suggestion that he might be on his way home. But there is nothing. She smiles tightly at something that her sister has just said. She doesn't want to have to answer questions about it. Her sisters are aware that Nathan has started binge drinking again, but Alix hasn't told them quite how bad it's been and what hangs in the balance here, the slender fulcrum that her marriage is currently resting upon.

By the time all the children have been corralled into their beds and the sisters are getting ready to get into theirs, it is midnight. Alix sits straight-backed and tense on the edge of the bed. She will wait until five past midnight and then she will call him. For now she walks toward the bathroom, discarding her clothes in the walkthrough wardrobe as she goes. And as she kicks off her sandals and leans down to put them away, she notices something in her shoe rack. A small clear plastic bag. A scrap of napkin with a number scrawled on it illegibly, and the name "Daisy." A cardboard holder for a hotel key card. The name of the hotel is the Railings. She knows it, it's near Nathan's office in Farringdon: a hip boutique place with all the window frames and brickwork painted chalky black. The guys at Nathan's office often use it for after-work drinks and client entertaining. Nathan has taken Alix there on a few occasions too, where they've had drinks but certainly never taken a room. She holds the small plastic bag to the light and sees a residue of white powder clinging to its insides.

She feels a dark cloud of nausea pass through her from the bottom of her gut to the back of her throat. She looks at the items again. There are no dates on any of them. They could have come from anywhere at any time. But she knows they didn't. She knows they are from one of the number of nights that he has recently spent away from his home, away from his bed, in a black hole he claims not to remember.

She brushes her teeth furiously in the bathroom, staring at the warped face of a wronged wife that looks back at her from the mirror. She has never been a wronged wife before. She has never, not in all their years together, suspected that her husband might have been the type of husband to pick up women in pubs and take them to hotels, then come home twenty-four hours later and pretend not to remember anything. She has never had to confront this feeling before, and it is sickening.

She thinks of her sisters, who are already cross with Nathan for not being home by midnight, imagines what they would think if they saw the things she'd just found on the base of her shoe drawer, imagines the things they would tell her she should do, the punishments she should mete out, the actions she should take, and she thinks no, she wants to deal with this her way. Calmly. Rationally. Alix is not a dramatic or a reactive person. She is a person who likes to step away from situations that make her feel bad, to look at them objectively as if they were happening to somebody else, and then make a decision based on how best to keep the peace and maintain the status quo, because Alix, as much as it pains her to admit it to herself, needs to maintain the status quo—for the sake of the children, for the sake of her lifestyle, for the sake of all of them. She has too much to lose by acting in rage, far too much. She needs to give Nathan a chance to prove that her fears are unfounded, and then they can carry on.

At seven minutes past midnight, she returns to sitting on the edge of the bed and she taps his number.

The call rings out.

12:30 A.M.

It is after midnight, and Josie pictures Alix in her bedroom, wondering why her stupid husband hasn't come home yet. She pictures her leaning down in the dressing area and finding the pieces of evidence she'd left in her shoe rack this morning before she left, the key-card holder, the little bag, the illegible phone number with a girl's name she'd added to it. *Daisy.* She'd been pleased with that. The sort of ultra-feminine, young-sounding name that would set alarm bells ringing.

She pictures Alix calling her stupid husband and the call ringing out.

She pictures Alix's stupid husband in a loud bar in Soho doing shots and lines with lovely Katelyn.

Her phone buzzes and she picks it up. It's Katelyn.

We're goin in. When u comin?

Right now, she replies. *I'm leaving right now.*

SUNDAY,
21 JULY

Alix cannot sleep. It is nearly 3 a.m. and she lies wide awake, on her back, staring up at the ceiling. The air is hot and sticky, and an electric fan rustles the pages of the paperback book on the bedside table. She is simultaneously shocked and entirely unsurprised that she has been let down by Nathan. And she is humiliated that she had thought that an offer of sex might have been enough to tempt him home by midnight when, it now seems, he does not need to come home to find someone who wants to have sex with him.

In her mind she replays all the times he has expressed his disappointment in men who cheat. His friends are all "good guys," he says, guys who would never do that. He has said he couldn't comfortably be friends with men who treated their wives like that. But yet . . . Daisy; cocaine; room number 23.

She'd messaged Giovanni at about 1 a.m., who claimed they left Nathan at a bar in Soho just before midnight.

Alone? she asked.

As far as I know, he replied, and she knew he was lying.

She wishes she were the sort of woman who keeps a stash of sleeping pills in her bathroom cabinet, like in American TV shows. She wishes there were something she could do to switch her brain off. Eventually she gives up on bed and heads downstairs. The cat is happy to have an unexpected nocturnal visitor and Alix crouches down to stroke her. Through the glass roof of the kitchen extension, she sees a fat, orange moon overhead. She imagines the same orange moon hanging over Nathan, wherever he is, whatever he is doing, possibly glowing off the soft skin in the dip at the small of his back as he moves in and out of some faceless woman called Daisy in a boutique hotel room somewhere.

Alix wakes at five o'clock. The first thing she does is reach for her phone and check it for anything, absolutely anything that might suggest the possibility that her husband is coming home. But there is nothing. She rests her phone on her bedside table and lies back down. The sun is coming up and her curtains glow peachy red while the house creaks and sighs as it expands back to size. She feeds the cat and drinks a huge glass of water and a moment later she hears footsteps down the hallway and there is Petal.

The shock of her niece, fresh and tiny in a blue cotton nightdress, contrasted against the dark griminess of Alix's thoughts all night, almost takes her breath away. "Good morning, sweetie," she says. "You're up bright and early."

"I always like to get up early," she says. "I like it being just me."

Alix nods at her and smiles and then offers her food to eat

and juice to drink. She heaves open the back doors to let out the stale night air. She empties the dishwasher and glances at Petal, every now and then, as she slowly eats a bowl of Special K at the kitchen table. She doesn't talk to her, leaves her to enjoy her early-morning solitude. She calls Nathan. She makes a coffee. Calls Nathan again. She has no idea, none whatsoever, what she should be doing.

Alix did not know it was possible for time to pass as slowly as it passes that day. She goes back to bed at 7 a.m. and sleeps for an hour or so, but is soon wide awake again, the morning sun burning through the curtains and across her body, her head full of needles of sharp anxiety and shards of fragmented thoughts. She forces herself to eat some toast and necks three espressos in a row, none of them touching the sides of her exhaustion. How long, she wonders, how long can she merely sit and wait?

At nine o'clock she feels it is polite to call Giovanni. He picks up immediately. "Gio," she says. "Nathan is still not home. Please, if there's something you're not telling me, tell me now!"

The thick, putrid silence on the other end of the line tells Alix all she needs to know. "No," he says stiffly. "No. We just left him in a bar. Like we always do. There was nothing."

"Well," Zoe says when Alix relays this back to her a moment later. "Bro code. He would say that, wouldn't he?"

Alix sighs. She knows that Zoe is right.

"What time does he normally get back after a bender?" Zoe asks.

"The afternoon?"

"Well then, let's not worry until the afternoon," says Zoe and Alix nods but then something occurs to her and she pulls out her phone and opens up her banking app. She and Nathan have a joint bank account. They always have done, ever since it became clear that Alix was never going to be a big earner and that Nathan already was. Nathan never looks at it. He never looks at bank statements or restaurant bills or keeps receipts. He spends money on the assumption that he is roughly balancing his outgoings with his income and, for the most part, he is correct.

She scrolls through the pending payments section of her online statement, looking for anything to explain where he might be, but there is nothing. Nothing since a payment to the bar in the West End that Giovanni said they'd left him in, of £25.60. No Uber payments. No hotel charges. Nothing. He has disappeared without a trace.

The afternoon arrives. Dark clouds appear overhead, and the temperature finally drops a degree or two. Zoe and Maxine have stayed longer than planned and there is a weird unsettledness in the air, as if they are in a waiting room expecting an announcement of some kind.

Alix spends an hour in her walk-in wardrobe ransacking the pockets of Nathan's clothes, looking for more clues to his behavior, but there's nothing. Her sisters offer her food, but she can't eat. She can't think. She can barely breathe.

The dark clouds gather momentum and then, at just after four o'clock, the rumbling begins, and by four thirty the rain lashes down, the air fills with petrichor, and the heat finally drops. They run around closing windows all over the house. Alix calls Giovanni again, but he doesn't take her call. Her sisters tell her they have to leave in an hour, their children have homework to do, their cats need feeding, it's a school night, and Alix realizes that the moment her sisters leave, she will be trapped in the house, unable to leave without the children, and she quickly changes out of her summer dress and into leggings and trainers and walks as fast as she can toward Giovanni's house, half a mile away. He's lying; she knows he's lying. She needs to see him face-to-face, to look into his eyes, look into his partner's eyes, get the truth about what happened last night.

He looks shocked when he sees her at the door. He opens it a crack and then fully open with a sigh of surrender. "Still no sign of him?" he asks meekly.

"No. Still no sign. And, Gio, please, don't treat me like an idiot. I know something happened last night. Look." She empties her pockets of the things she'd found in her shoe rack. "Look," she says again. "These are Nathan's. I found them last night. He makes out he's purer than pure, and then I find girls' phone numbers scrawled on napkins, bags of cocaine. I mean, seriously, just be honest with me. Was there a girl involved last night? Just tell me!"

And then all the remaining puff goes out of Giovanni, and he invites her in and sits her at his kitchen table, which is covered with the debris of a family lunch, plates and dishes brought in from the sudden rain still with splashes of rainwater on their rims. She sees Giovanni and his partner exchange a look and then he turns to her and says, "There was a girl. But seriously, honestly, Alix, it wasn't anything. And I swear, Nathan has never gone off with a girl before. I don't know who that Daisy is on the napkin. Maybe someone who wanted a job or office space or something. We talk to randoms all the time when we go out. But he has never, ever gone off with someone. I swear. But last night this woman came and sat with us. Her name was Katelyn. Said she'd been stood up by her mate, was it OK if she hung out with us for a while. And she ended up staying and drinking with us and then we left the pub to go to the bar in Soho and she came with us. But I swear, Alix, there was nothing going on with them. Nathan kept talking about you. Kept saying he was married. How beautiful you were."

Alix blinks slowly. She glances at her wedding ring and turns it once around her finger before looking up at Giovanni again. "And then what happened?"

"What do you mean?"

"I mean, you said you left Nathan in the bar at midnight. Did she leave too?"

Giovanni drops his gaze to the tabletop. He shakes his head slowly. But then he looks up at her quickly and says, "She was saying she was going to get him home. She was saying that Nathan told her he was on a promise and she was going to make sure he got home to . . . well, you know?"

Alix exhales heavily and lets her head roll backward. "He told a complete stranger about our sex life?"

Giovanni nods again. "But, honestly, it was just fun. Just banter. She just seemed like one of the boys, you know. She didn't seem like she was . . ."

"Like she was what?"

"I don't know. Like she was going to lead him astray, I guess. It just felt like one of those nights, you know, when Nathan wasn't going to stop. One of those nights when he was going to get lost to the night, and—honestly? I think we were glad he had someone with him, so that we could, you know, just go home."

He glances up at her sheepishly. "I'm sure he'll be home soon," he says. "You know what he's like. He's probably home right now. Just walked in through the door." He smiles at her, but she doesn't return it.

"What did she look like? This Katelyn?"

"Pretty?" he says, his voice racked with apology.

"How old?"

"Youngish? Maybe late twenties? Early thirties?"

She sighs and rolls her eyes. "I wish you'd told me this earlier," she says. "I wish you hadn't lied."

"I'm sorry, Alix," he says, picking at a bit of paper with his fingernails. "I'm really sorry."

MONDAY, 22 JULY

Walking the children to school the next morning feels surreal. The air is cool and green, and she has thrown on a jacket over her summer clothes. The streets teem with children in sky blue and navy. Alix stares at them keenly. None of them has a father who went missing this weekend.

Ten minutes after she gets home, she notices she has a missed call from a number she doesn't recognize. She googles the number and feels a jolt of nervous energy surge all the way through her when she sees that it is the number for a hotel just off Tottenham Court Road, and then a wave of relief passes through her. She pictures Nathan waking up after the biggest bender yet, rubbing his eyes, looking at the time, realizing that he's been out cold for forty-eight hours, looking for his phone, discovering it was out of charge, using the hotel's landline to call her, and everything falls into place. She calls the number back immediately with slightly shaking hands.

"Hi!" she says briskly to the young-sounding woman who answers the phone. "I think it's possible that my husband just called from this number. Nathan Summer? Is he staying there?"

There's a tiny pert silence and then the young woman says, "Oh, hi. Is this Alix Summer?"

"Yes," she says. "Yes. I, er—how did you know my name?"

"Well, actually, it was me who just called you, Mrs. Summer. I'm really sorry. I didn't know what else to do. But Mr. Summer was here this weekend and unfortunately, after he failed to check out this morning, we used the master key to let ourselves into his room and found quite a lot of damage? We found his business card in the room and we tried calling him a few times on his mobile but it kept going to voicemail and so I called his office number just now to see if I could get hold of him that way, but they said he hadn't come into work today and they gave me your number and I hope you don't mind me calling you like this?"

Alix freezes while scenarios spool wildly through her head. Finally, she says, "No. Of course not."

"But we will have to charge Mr. Summer for the damage to his room, I'm afraid."

"Sorry, can you just explain what happened? Blow by blow. Because I'm afraid I don't really understand."

"Oh! Yes! Sure!" the young woman responds brightly. "Mr. Summer checked in here on Saturday night. Quite late. His companion told us that she'd paid online for two nights."

"Companion?"

"Yes. The person he was with."

"And who was that?"

"I'm afraid I don't know. I wasn't working on Saturday night. But the room had been prepaid for two nights. Mr. Summer seems to have left at some point on Sunday without checking out, nobody saw him leave and we have no record of it, and when we went to his room this morning to request that he vacate it, it was empty. No sign of Mr. Summer or his companion. And the room, I'm afraid, was trashed."

"Trashed?"

"Yes. And we are going to need to take some sort of payment to cover the costs, I'm afraid. And since his companion's card is being declined and we are unable to contact Mr. Summer, we'd be very grateful if you could help us to sort out this issue."

"The room," says Alix. "My husband's room. Has it been tidied yet? Has it been cleaned?"

"No, we're waiting for management to send over a specialist cleaning team. It hasn't been touched."

"OK. Well, I'd like to see it, please. Because my husband hasn't come home, he's disappeared, and maybe there might be something in the room that explains where he is. Where he's gone. Please? I can be there in half an hour."

There is a short silence while the young woman goes to ask her manager and then she comes back on the line. "Sure. That'll be fine. We'll see you in half an hour."

The receptionist hands Alix the key. "It's room eighteen," she says. "On the second floor. Down there and up the stairs."

Alix heads down the corridor and up a narrow staircase. Room 18 is the second door on the left. She touches the card to the panel, and it clicks open.

The curtains are drawn and her eyes take a moment to adjust to the dark before she finds the slot for the key card and activates the lighting and it all comes to full and shocking life.

The room has been ransacked. The bedding has been pulled virtually completely off the bed so that the mattress is visible, and the duvet is hanging half on the floor. The minibar has been drunk dry; there are empties all over the floor. The remains of a McDonald's takeaway are scattered everywhere: ketchup-smeared paper packaging and greasy bags of cold fries. Alix picks her way gingerly across the chaos and toward the bathroom. Here there are wet towels on the floor, empty mixer cans in the sink, and there—Alix's stomach turns, violently—women's underwear, a thong made of cheap lace, removed and left discarded on the floor, blond curly hairs in the sink, a smear of tinted lip gloss on the rim of a glass, and the smell, just the sheer unmistakable smell of a woman everywhere in the air.

Alix sits on the side of the bath and stares about herself. She stands up slowly and peers into the bin, looking for clues. Back in the bedroom she starts to see more than a drunken, sexual interlude playing out in this room. She sees a picture hanging crooked on the wall, a crack in its glass. She sees a table lamp knocked onto its side. The bedside table is turned at a ninety-degree angle to the wall. And there, she sees, as she crouches lower and lower to the wooden floor, is a small smudge of what looks at first like marmite, maybe, or ketchup from the McDonald's, but comes away on the tip of her finger as bright scarlet blood.

She winces at the sight of it and stands up so quickly that blood rushes to her head. She turns in a circle, trying to find more answers to the thousand questions that flood her mind from the detail of the room, but there is nothing. A fight. A girl. Food. Drink. A discarded thong.

Alix sits on the edge of the pillaged bed and gets out her phone. She calls Nathan and it goes to voicemail. She goes back down to reception and when she talks to the young woman on reception, she realizes she is crying. "Please," she says, "please. I need to see your records. I need to see your CCTV footage. My husband has disappeared, and I don't know where he is and I can't take another day like this. I can't take another day of this *not knowing*. Please."

The receptionist smiles nervously and says, "Let me ask my manager. Give me a minute."

A moment later a glamorous woman with dyed black hair appears from the office behind the front desk. Her name badge says "Astrid Pagano" and she has intricate black tattoos up both her forearms.

"Please," she says in a soft accent, "come with me." She beckons her into the back office and Alix follows.

It's a tiny room and they are squashed together in front of the security monitors elbow to elbow. "I am sorry," says Astrid. "So sorry that you are having a difficult time. Let's see if we can find you some answers."

It takes a few minutes to find what they're looking for. The date stamp on the screen says "Sunday 1:41 a.m." First of all she sees Nathan and a pretty blond woman approaching the hotel. This must be Katelyn, she assumes, the girl Giovanni told her about. She looks older than Alix had imagined; she has a mass of blond curly hair tied away from her face in a ponytail, and very soft features. She wears white jeans and white trainers and a loose black halter-neck top and big gold earrings and looks like a goddess. Nathan, bringing up her rear, looks ridiculous in comparison. He can barely put one foot in front of the other and has to clutch the wall as he reaches the front door, to stop himself from falling over. The footage moves to another screen and here Alix watches Nathan stumbling around behind Katelyn as she checks them in. She has seen Nathan drunk many, many times, but never as drunk as he appears to be in this footage. Then they disappear from the screen, heading darkly toward the staircase at the back of the hotel. Astrid forwards through the next couple of hours and then pauses and slows the footage again at around 3 a.m. There is Nathan. He's dressed and still stumbling. He bangs into the console table opposite the front desk and then pauses for a moment and takes his phone out of his pocket. He switches it on and frowns at it, swaying slightly on the spot as he tries to focus on the screen. Then he puts the phone back in his pocket and heads out of the front door. Now they move to the second monitor and there he is, there's

Nathan out in the dark street, glowing briefly under the direct light of a streetlamp and then turning into shadows again as he moves away. He is lit up by the approaching headlights of a car and he turns, almost losing his footing as he does so. He shields his eyes briefly with the back of his hand and then smiles and waves.

The car pulls up to the left of the hotel, just visible in shot. Nathan weaves his way from the hotel entrance, down the pavement, and then gets to the passenger door of the car. Alix watches him as he goes to open the door and then he stops and stares at the driver, appears to change his mind about getting in the car, but turns back, maybe as the driver says something to him, and a moment later he climbs in. Then the car slowly pulls away, and the street is cast in darkness once more.

"Recognize the car?" asks Astrid.

Alix shakes her head. "Can we rewind a little bit, to just as it arrives? There," she says. "Pause it just there."

Astrid hits the pause button on the screen and there is the registration plate, fully legible. Astrid hands Alix a piece of paper and a pen and Alix writes it down.

"Maybe it's an Uber?" Astrid suggests.

Alix shakes her head. "No," she says. "Nathan would never get in the front seat of an Uber. He always gets in the back. It looked like he was expecting to know the driver. And then he didn't. But he got in anyway . . ." Her voice trails away. None of it makes any sense. Whose car did he think he was getting into? Who was he expecting to see at three in the morning? Whose message had he seen on his phone before he left?

Astrid is about to shut down the footage but Alix stops her. "Can I see her leaving, please? The woman? Is that OK?"

"Yes, of course."

And there is Katelyn, a few seconds later, looking cool and put together, no visible sign of whatever had happened between her and

Nathan in the trashed hotel room, not a hair out of place, her jeans still a pristine white. But just as she passes the front desk, Alix sees it—a red, raw scratch all down the side of her cheek. Katelyn turns again and it's gone, but Alix doesn't ask Astrid to pause it this time. She doesn't want to see it again. She doesn't want to know.

"The name of the woman who made the booking. Do you know who it was? Was it her? Katelyn?"

Astrid flicks screens to the hotel's booking system and clicks some buttons. "OK," she says, "so. The booking was made via a booking engine, earlier in the day. And no. The booking wasn't made in the name of Katelyn." She stops and inhales audibly. "And I really shouldn't be telling you this, as I'm sure you know. But I'm the boss today and I can see that this is important. So . . ." She turns back to the screen and clicks another button. "I can see that the booking was made in your husband's name but paid for with a card in someone else's name. The name on the card"—she turns to Alix and nods, just once, as if she already knows something—"was Miss Erin Jade Fair."

Hi! I'm Your Birthday Twin!
A NETFLIX ORIGINAL SERIES

The screen shows Katelyn Rand again, sitting on the red sofa. She sighs and says:

"So, Josie called me, shortly after us chatting at Stitch, after I gave her my number and she told me she had a gig. And the gist, apparently, was to catch out her friend's husband in the act of infidelity. Apparently, this guy had been sleeping around for years—yeah, *men*, right?—and this woman refused to believe the evidence of her own eyes and ears. And Josie just wanted her friend to know, to see, to start believing what her husband was capable of. I said, 'Er, no, I don't think so, I am not actually a call girl, you know. I'm an actor.'"

Katelyn laughs and shakes her head.

"She said, 'You don't have to sleep with him. You just have to get him into a hotel room. Just get it to look like you slept with him. And then leave the rest to me.' I mean, obviously, I thought it sounded batshit. I thought it sounded insane. But then she said . . . well, she said she'd give me a thousand pounds. And I thought, yeah. Why not? A thousand pounds, for one night's work, not even that. So I said yes. Awaited further instruction."

The interviewer interjects off-mic. "What was that?"

"She told me to get chatting to him outside this pub off Oxford Street. It was that really, really hot weekend in mid-July, remember? When it was like thirty-five degrees? And I got there and got talking to him and he was like, yeah, a really nice guy. Him and his mates. Sweeties. And he kept talking about how he needed to go home because his wife had promised him a shag, it was like this running joke, and I felt terrible, you know, really bad. I thought, well, I'll do my best, but really, there's only so much I can do. I thought my thousand pounds were hanging in the balance to be honest. But then I just saw him go, after his, like, fifth tequila shot, I saw his eyes go, I saw him just sort of go to a different place, and that was when I knew he wasn't going home to shag his wife. Poor woman."

She looks up at the interviewer and smiles sadly.

"Yeah. Poor both of them."

MIDDAY

Alix stands outside Pat's apartment for nearly ten minutes, ringing and ringing her doorbell over and over again until a neighbor appears at the door of the next flat along and tells her that Pat's not there, that Pat left for Stansted Airport on Saturday morning, that Pat was going on holiday, and that no, he had no idea where to. Spain somewhere, maybe?

"But did she go with her daughter?"

"Josie?"

"Yes. She was staying here with her. Or at least she told me she was."

"Didn't see Josie leaving with her," says the neighbor. "Haven't seen Josie for months. When Pat left the house on Saturday, she was on her own. But if I see Josie around, I'll tell her you were looking for her, shall I?"

"Yes," she replies vaguely. "Yes please."

Alix heads straight from Pat's estate to Josie's building on Manor Park Road. She peers through the window but sees no sign of life. It looks exactly as it had looked the last time she was here. The closed laptop still sits on the brown table in the bay. The bed is still neatly made in the bedroom. She notices that there is a side return to the left of Josie's building, blocked by a phalanx of wheelie bins. She moves a couple out of the way and then stands on her tiptoes to peer into the small, dirty window that overlooks the return. The curtains are drawn, but there is a small crack through which Alix can see the suggestion of mess and squalor, piles of clothes and boxes and the corner of an unmade bed, one leg of a scruffy black-and-red gaming chair.

This must be Erin's room, she assumes.

The return stinks. The bins are full and it's the tail end of a heat wave. She covers her mouth with her hand and heads back to the pavement. She rings on the doorbell, although she already knows there's nobody there. And then, when nobody comes, she heads home.

One very good thing about the vast range of women that Alix has interviewed over the years is the access it gives her to various forms of expertise. She has on occasion taken advantage of having certain email addresses in her address book and now she sits at her laptop and searches for Joanna Dafoe, the deputy commissioner of the London Metropolitan Police force, whom she'd had on her podcast a few years earlier and with whom she had bonded over Siberian cats and a habit of eating four Weetabix at a time.

> Joanna, I'm sorry, this is so cheeky of me, but my husband has disappeared and I'm pretty sure he's just sleeping off the mother of all benders somewhere, but I have seen CCTV footage of him being collected by a random car in the middle of the night, didn't look like an Uber, I have the plates. How easy would it be to find out who the car is registered to?

A little later, she goes to collect Leon and Eliza from school. The sun is shining and there's a cool breeze and the atmosphere is soft with the fading days of the school year, the promise of the long summer holidays to come, just three days from now. For a moment Alix feels as though everything could be normal, that she could go home and see Nathan waiting for her sheepishly in the kitchen, but then a few minutes later she checks her email and there is a reply from Joanna Dafoe, the deputy Met commissioner.

Hi Alix

Good to hear from you. Sorry you're having a tough time with things. Those plates came back registered to a hire company. The car was rented from them by an Erin Jade Fair on Saturday. Hope that helps! And please give Skye a snuggle from me.

Alix reads the email twice, three times. Then she pushes her laptop away from her and gasps, her hands over her mouth. Her thoughts jump and crash into each other, violently, and then clarity descends and she picks up her phone and calls the police.

"I know this might sound insane," she begins, "but I think my husband has been kidnapped."

Hi! I'm Your Birthday Twin!
A NETFLIX ORIGINAL SERIES

The screen shows a serious-looking woman sitting on a long leather sofa in front of a tall window with velvet curtains. She wears a trouser suit and heeled ankle boots.
The text underneath reads:

DC Sabrina Albright

"At first we didn't take it seriously. An estate agent from Queen's Park with a history of disappearing overnight on benders being kidnapped by a housewife in a hire car in the middle of the night. It just sounded like domestic nonsense, you know, an affair of some kind. Messy people's messy lives. We put it on the back burner. But then, a few hours later, we got the call."

Interviewer, off-mic: "The call?"

"Yes. An anonymous call, from a pay phone in Bristol."

The audio plays a recorded police call.

"Er, hi. I need to report a missing person. It's my . . . friend. Erin Fair. And her father. Walter Fair. They live at 43A Manor Park Road, NW6. I haven't heard from them for a long time. Not since, like, over a week ago. And Erin has special needs, and her father is quite elderly, and they usually never leave the house and I wondered if someone could go and check on them for me. Please. I'm really worried about them."

The camera goes back to DC Albright.

"It took a few hours for us to put the two reports together, the two mentions of the same name in the same day. *Erin Fair.* And then when we did it was like *pow.*"

DC Albright makes a head explosion gesture with her hands and arms.

"We sent a patrol car down to Manor Park Road and, well, you know exactly what happened after that."

Evening Standard, Tuesday, 23 July

A gruesome discovery was made on Monday night in a Kilburn back street. Police and detectives from Kentish Town Police Station went to a flat on the ground floor of a house in Manor Park Road after receiving an anonymous phone call from a woman in Bristol who was worried about not having heard from her friend for a while. Unable to establish the whereabouts of Erin Fair and her father, and after talking to neighbors, who told of loud screams and shouting late on a Friday night more than a week before, police entered the property by force. Immediately they were aware of a terrible smell emanating from somewhere in the flat, and a few minutes later the decomposing remains of Walter Fair, 72, were discovered in the bathtub. He had been badly beaten and left with his arms and legs tied together. Police then found Mr. Fair's daughter Erin Fair, 23, tied to a wooden child's chair in a storage cupboard in the hallway. The chair had been customized with leather straps and leg ties. She too had been beaten and was at first assumed to be dead but, after showing signs of life, was rushed to hospital, where she is now in intensive care in a coma.

According to neighbors, the Fair family had not been seen for a while, and Josie Fair, Walter's wife, has not been traced since the discovery was made. Police are currently investigating her disappearance, and also the disappearance of local man Nathan Summer, who was loosely acquainted with the Fair family and who was last seen outside a hotel in central London in the early hours of Sunday morning getting into a car hired using a card held by Mrs. Fair's daughter Erin. Mr. Summer's wife, the popular podcaster Alix Summer, had recently been recording a podcast with Josie Fair, and Mrs. Fair had been a houseguest with the Summers for a week prior to Mr. Summer's disappearance, claiming to have been a victim of domestic abuse at the hands of her husband.

Neighbors say that the Fair family kept to themselves and were generally "very quiet."

WEDNESDAY, 24 JULY

Alix collects the children from school. It's the last day of term tomorrow and they appear outside the playground weighed down with old projects, exercise books, and pieces of art, which Alix takes from them while they chatter and play fight each other. Mothers approach and touch her arm gently, ask her if she's OK. She smiles tightly and nods. She's not OK. She really is not OK.

There has been no helpful response to the press reports. No sightings of the hire car. No sightings of Nathan. No sightings of Josie. Erin's card has not been used again. Katelyn has not come forward. Nobody who knows Katelyn has come forward, even though the image of her taken from the hotel's CCTV with the large scratch down her cheek has been widely disseminated. The drops of blood found on the floor of the hotel off Tottenham Court Road have been sent for testing and the police are currently trying to trace the sender of some messages found on Erin's laptop. They are targeting dog owners and dog shelters, asking them to keep their eyes peeled for Pomchis. They are looking at CCTV footage from the cashpoint machines used by whoever has been using Erin's debit card to empty her account of nearly ten thousand pounds in cash since last week. They are looking at CCTV of Manor Park Road to see if Josie has been seen in the area since she left in the middle of the night almost two weeks ago, and they have traced the passengers of the six buses that passed the Fairs' home between 11 p.m. and 3 a.m. on the night that Josie claims to have been beaten by Walter to see if any of them saw anything through the window. They have traced people who Erin had been messaging in the days and weeks before her disappearance. They have been in touch with Walter's two sons from his first marriage, who are in Canada, and they have been in touch with Josie's employers and colleagues.

But it has now been nearly four days since Josie stole Nathan from outside the hotel off Tottenham Court Road and there is nothing. Not one thing.

Until now. As Alix puts the key into the lock of her front door, her phone rings. It is DC Sabrina Albright. "I wonder if we might be able to get you along to the station at some point? To see me and my colleague DC Bryant. At your convenience. We have found some objects in the Fairs' property. A strange selection of things. Including the edition of the interiors magazine you mentioned you'd seen Mrs. Fair remove from your recycling box while you were out. And something else, something that, well . . . if you were able to come along and cast your eye, see if you recognize anything else . . . ?"

"I can be there now. Just"—she glances around at her two children, still in their school uniforms, kicking off their shoes in the hallway, and thinks how long it would take for her mother to drive there from Harrow and says—"give me an hour. I'll be there in an hour."

On the table in front of Alix lies a Nespresso pod, a bottle of the expensive hand soap that she uses in her guest WC, her bracelet with the little hanging crystals that Nathan had given her for her birthday, a receipt from the organic supermarket dated Alix's birthday, the interiors magazine, a shiny teaspoon, a card from Alix's kitchen wall that Eliza had made for her three years ago after Teeny the dog died, and a strip of passport photographs of Leon. She feels her mouth turn sour at the sight of these tiny, vital, intensely personal parts of her family ephemera on the cold institutional tabletop.

But there are other things too, on the table in front of Alix. There is a photograph of two tiny children sitting one on each knee of a young girl, all three children beaming into the camera. There is a hair scrunchie made of pink satin. There is a rubberized phone case with gems arranged into flowers glued to the back. There is an empty Hubba Bubba container. There is a single silver earring with a crucifix hanging from it. There is a scrunched-up paper napkin with pink smudges on it, and a large silk flower attached to a cir-cle of elastic. She shakes her head and says, "These aren't mine. I don't know, I mean, I assume they belong to her girls? But this . . ." Her eyes go to the photo of the young girl with the toddlers on her knees. "This isn't Erin or Roxy. But the girl . . . she looks familiar. She looks . . ." Alix trawls her mind for the place in her life where she has seen this face before. And then she gets it and she points at the photo as her heart gallops under her ribs and says, "Brooke Ripley. That's Brooke Ripley, isn't it? Look! And I remember Josie said Brooke had two small siblings, her half brother and sister? And that . . . hold on . . ." She grabs her phone from her bag and runs a search for Brooke Ripley on Facebook. "There." She shows it to Chris Bryant and Sabrina. "Look. It's her. And . . ." Her eye goes to a detail on the prom-night photo of Brooke that she had not noticed before—a large white flower attached to her wrist. Her throat burns dry, and she clutches her stomach unthinkingly with her left hand. "Look," she says, her eyes going from the photo to the flower and then to the two detectives. "Look."

The detectives stare at the items and the photo on Alix's phone, and a chill permeates the warm office.

"There's a key," she finds herself telling Sabrina. "Josie left it under the mattress in my spare room. It has blood on it."

"Describe this key?" Sabrina says to Alix.

"It's small. Gold, I think, or brass. A single key. There's a plastic tag attached, one of those that comes as part of a multipack, with the clear plastic window, with the number six on it. Just that. I have it at home. I can give it to you. I'm sorry. I should have given it to you before. I didn't think."

"Please, don't worry. You're being incredibly helpful. And this"— Sabrina gestures at the silk wrist corsage, the photograph of Brooke Ripley with her two young siblings—"this could be very important. We will be doubling up our attempts to find Brooke's family. And in the meanwhile, please just take care of yourself and your family. We'll call you when we have anything more to share." Alix gets up to leave and then stops when she remembers something that has been nagging at her for days.

"Was that all?" she asks the detective. "There wasn't a necklace? With a golden bumblebee pendant?"

"No," says Sabrina. "Not that I'm aware of. But if it turns up, I'll let you know."

"Thank you," says Alix, her fingers going instinctively to her clavicle where the pendant used to hang. "That would be great."

Alix's mother looks up from the kitchen table, where she is sitting with Leon when she hears Alix close the front door behind her half an hour later. She throws her a look that says, "Well?"

Alix shakes her head, just perceptibly, and busies herself for a moment, putting things in the dishwasher, plugging in her phone to charge, wiping cat hair off the hob. When she's done, she gestures at her mother to join her in the garden. They sit side by side, staring down the garden toward the back wall. The bright evening light glints gold off the windows of Alix's recording studio and for a moment she wonders if she will ever again sit behind the sound desk, ever again take pure, focused interest in somebody else's life.

"So?" her mother says after a short moment.

"Nothing," says Alix. "They have nothing. But . . ." She shivers slightly as she recalls the unpleasantness of seeing those tiny pieces of her life, her home, her family, laid out in front of her, pulled from the depths of, apparently, Josie's underwear drawer. The thought of Eliza's precious drawing of her with Teeny, Alix's just departed dog, and Leon's slightly startled-looking four-year-old face nestling in amongst Josie's sad, faded underwear makes her feel nauseous.

"They found some items in one of her drawers: some stuff belonging to me. Things she'd stolen from the house. Nothing valuable. Just bits." Her voice cracks and she clutches her mother's hand inside hers and feels her mother's squeeze back hard.

She doesn't tell her mother about the corsage, about Brooke Ripley, about the blood-smeared key hidden under Josie's mattress. She just holds her hand and stares into the middle distance, holding back the tears that threaten to overwhelm her.

"He'll show up," her mother says softly. "I know he will. I can feel him. He's out there. I reckon he'll be home by the weekend."

And it's just what Alix wants to hear. She wants to think that she too can feel him out there; she wants to feel certain that he will walk in through the door this weekend, that he will have a tale to tell her over wine, that they will curl up together in bed, his body maybe smaller, thinner, his arms around her desperate with the relief of being home, that they will wait, wait to talk about Katelyn, wait to talk about the hotel room, they will heal, come together, love, and then they will fix whatever was so broken that Nathan ended up in a hotel room with a girl called Katelyn in the first place. She wants that ending to this story and she kisses her mother gently on her cheek and says, "Thank you. Yes. Thank you."

Hi! I'm Your Birthday Twin!
A NETFLIX ORIGINAL SERIES

The screen shows Katelyn Rand sitting on the small red velvet sofa.

"So, Nathan was still going on and on about wanting to go home and have sex with his wife, even though he could hardly put one foot in front of the other. We ended up in a bar in Soho and I could tell his mates were fading a bit, getting restless. It was so hot that night and, I mean, they weren't young, you know? But he kept wanting *one more drink*. So I said, 'Listen. Why don't you guys go? Leave him with me. I can get him home.' And then they left and I told Nathan I would get him home, but first we should have something to eat to sober him up, and I took him to the hotel that Josie had told me to get him to. She said there was a room there, booked under Nathan's name, all paid for. Just had to check him in. Easier said than done. Could barely keep him upright. Had to sort of prop him up while I did all the business. He kept saying, 'Where's Alix? Is she here? Is she here?'"

"And I said, 'Yeah. She's upstairs, waiting for you. Come on, sweetie, let's get you up there.' And then we got into the room, and he said he was hungry, so I got us a McDonald's delivery; we ate that; he drank all the miniatures. All the time he just kept saying, 'Where's Alix? Is she coming? Is she coming?'"

"I said yeah. She's coming. She's in an Uber. She'll be here soon. And then . . . Well, he tried to leave. Yeah."

She brings her hand to the back of her neck and rubs at it, smiles apologetically at the interviewer off-screen.

"That was bad. And I was just like watching my phone for a message from Josie, telling me that she was coming, and I was calling her and calling her, and I'd locked the door and was standing in front of it. He was going *nuts*. 'Let me go. Just let me go!' And then he started throwing stuff about, knocking stuff over. Didn't touch me, though, but he accidentally caught me on my cheek with the edge of something sharp. And I was like trapped in this room with this total nutter, losing his shit big-time, and Josie was not answering, not answering, and then finally at about three o'clock in the morning she called. She said send him out. Tell him Alix is out there, in a black Kia, reg plate blah, whatever it was. So I unlocked the door, let him go. Dropped some underwear on the floor in the bathroom. Sprayed my perfume all about the place. Messed up the bed. Left. Ten minutes later a thousand pounds landed in my PayPal. And that, I assumed, was that. Jesus Christ."

She sighs, runs her hand around the back of her neck again.

"I couldn't have been more wrong about that, could I?"

THURSDAY, 25 JULY

Alix's mother spends the night. She comes with Alix the following day to the end-of-term assembly in the overwarm school hall, where the doors are standing open but no cool air is getting in. They sit side by side on a bench, their knees bent up into sharp angles, and Alix knows that her mother, though young for her age, will be glad when it is over and she can stretch her legs again. It is the end of primary school for Eliza. In the world in which she lived before Saturday night, this had been the day that Alix had been feeling most anxious about. The end of an era. The end of the safety net of a kind, nurturing primary school. No more sky-blue polo shirts for Eliza. No more Velcro-fastening book bag. No more assemblies for Alix to join in, no more museum trips for her to accompany.

And then it is over, the school spills out, the sun is shining, the summer has begun, six weeks of innocence and freedom and the beginning of a new stage of her daughter's life and she feels none of it. They go to the park and queue for ice creams. The children play with their friends. Alix sits with her mother, away from the other parents. They head home and Alix puts the children's uniforms in the washing machine for the last time until September. She waits as long as she can, which turns out to be 4:58 p.m., and then she pours wine for herself and her mother.

And then, as she glances at her empty glass and considers the possibility of pouring herself another one, even though it's not yet five thirty, her phone rings, and it's Sabrina Albright.

"Guess who's just walked into the station, Alix? And wants to see you?"

Hi! I'm Your Birthday Twin!
A NETFLIX ORIGINAL SERIES

The screen shows a young woman sitting in a vintage armchair placed in the middle of an empty, softly lit room.
She has blond hair, shaved short on one side and grown to shoulder length on the other. She wears a buttoned-up pale blue shirt and black jeans.
She has many earrings in both ears and smiles nervously.
On the screen below are the words:

Roxy Fair, daughter of Josie and Walter Fair

The screen cuts to the title graphics and the episode ends.

2:50 P.M.

Roxy picks at the skin around her fingernails and stares at the clock on the wall. She is about to find out what the hell is going on, if anyone would ever actually come and see her. A few minutes later the door opens and a pair of feds walk in, a man and a woman, Chris and Sabrina they're called, and they smile and say how sorry they are about Roxy's dad and then they clear their throats and open notepads and the woman says, "Do you know where your mother is, Roxy?"

Roxy shakes her head. "I haven't seen her since I was sixteen."

"We've managed to get hold of your grandmother Pat O'Neill?"

Roxy nods.

"She's in Menorca, but she's heading back tomorrow. She says you'll be able to stay with her, if you want?"

"I can't stay. I have work. I need to get back."

"OK. That's fine. But you should know, if you haven't already seen it in the news, that we are actively searching for your mother in relation to your father's murder and the attempted murder of Erin."

Roxy flicks a gaze at the female police detective and then at the male. "Seriously?"

"Yes. There's a lot going on at the moment, Roxy. And I think it might be best to talk you through it a step at a time, so it doesn't get too confusing. Is that OK?"

Roxy nods tightly.

"It sounds as if your mum and dad had a row on the night of Friday, the twelfth of July. They'd been for dinner at a friend's house—"

Roxy interjects with a snort of laughter. "Yeah, right."

"A woman called Alix Summer had recently befriended your mother. They'd been working on some kind of project together for a few weeks. This culminated in a dinner invitation on that Friday night. A few hours after your mother and father left Mrs. Summer's house, your mother reappeared on Mrs. Summer's doorstep badly injured, claiming to have been beaten by your father."

"My father?"

"Yes. That is what she told Mrs. Summer. She told Mrs. Summer that she and Erin had left the flat together in the early hours of the morning and implied that your father was alive and well. She then spent a week living at Mrs. Summer's house, before leaving on Saturday morning, telling Mrs. Summer that she was going to her mother's flat, your grandma Pat. The same night, Mrs. Summer's husband disappeared after a night out in town drinking with friends. The two events would seem to be entirely unrelated, apart from the fact that the hotel room that Mrs. Summer's husband was staying in when he disappeared, and the car that was filmed collecting him from the hotel he was staying at, were both paid for by a debit card in the name of . . ."

The woman pauses, and Roxy stares at her as if to say: "Well, go on then."

"Erin Fair."

"What, sorry, my sister, who is currently in a coma, paid for a hotel room for some random guy?"

"We don't think it was your sister, Roxy. We think your mother has been using your sister's card. And here's the thing, we've been investigating your sister's bank account and, well, there had been a remarkable amount of money in there. Over forty thousand pounds. And in the last two weeks, over ten thousand of those pounds have been taken out from cashpoint machines in Queen's Park. And according to what your mother told Mrs. Summer, your sister, Erin, had special needs. She ate baby food and didn't leave the house and yet she had money coming into her bank account on a daily basis. All from a live-streaming company called Glitch. Do you know anything about this aspect of your sister's life?"

"Yeah, she's famous."

"Famous for what?"

"Gaming. People pay a subscription fee to Glitch and then they get to watch players online. And my sister is one of the best."

"So, she earns money playing video games?"

Roxy can't believe how old some people sound, like they live in a different world than her, but she controls the urge to roll her eyes and she says, "Yeah. That's right."

"So, erm . . ." Both detectives adjust their sitting positions. The man stares at his paperwork; the woman glances up at Roxy: "Where do you think your mother might be?"

Roxy lets out a rasp of laughter. "You're asking me that?"

"Well, yes."

"Not going to be able to help you, I'm afraid. My mother . . ." Roxy stops, her spiky facade slipping for just a moment. "My mother hated me. My mother hated my father. My mother hates my sister. She's obviously taken Erin's money to start a new life without any of us in it."

"But is there anywhere in particular? A place that meant something to her? Mrs. Summer suggests that your mother was very nostalgic about the early days of family life. Overly so, maybe? So was there somewhere you went as a family, maybe?"

Roxy shrugs. She doesn't see her childhood in that way. There's no golden glow emanating from any area of it. "We used to go to the Lake District every summer. For a week. I hated it, all of us stuck in a caravan, or some hairy cabin with, like, spiders everywhere. But she loved it. She used to drink wine every night and go on and on about the views."

"Can you remember whereabouts in the Lake District you used to go?"

"Yes. Ambleside. Right by the water."

Roxy watches them write this down. She narrows her eyes at them and says, "You know there's no way my dad ever laid a finger on my mum, don't you?"

"Well, we do have photographic evidence that shows your mum's injuries."

"How?"

"Mrs. Summer took them, last week."

Roxy sighs and tuts. "Sorry, *Mrs. Summer . . . Mrs. Summer*. Who the hell is this Mrs. Summer?"

"She's your mother's friend."

"But my mother doesn't have any friends."

"She's a friend, but she's also been making a podcast with her."

"A podcast? What sort of podcast?"

"She was interviewing your mother about her life."

Roxy can't help but laugh. "Seriously?"

"Yes. We've listened to the recordings. They're quite . . . harrowing."

"In what way?"

"Your childhood. The abuse. What happened to your friend Brooke."

"Brooke?" Her heart turns black for a moment; her stomach churns.

The detectives exchange a look. "Yes. Brooke Ripley. She was your friend, from school. She had a relationship with your father?"

"Had a relationship with my—?"

"She went missing, you know, about the same time you left home, and we're investigating the possibility that her disappearance might have been related to your parents."

"You're joking, right?"

"No. We're not joking. We're acting on the testimony left by your mother on Mrs. Summer's podcast recording."

Roxy shakes her head and closes her eyes. "Listen. I can't deal with this, OK? What else did my mum say to this woman?"

"She shared hours of testimony with her. All of which pointed toward a very toxic domestic situation in your home, toward the possibility of spousal and child abuse, including the alleged sexual abuse of your sister." The woman stops, licks her lips, touches the paperwork with her peach fingertips. "By your father."

"My—?" Roxy slams her hands down on the tabletop and the two detectives jump slightly. "Seriously? My dad? That's what my mum told her, is it?"

"She said that your father left the marital bed every night and went into Erin's bedroom, then didn't come back."

"Yes. He was gaming with her."

"Gaming?"

"Yes. He was part of the thing, part of the act, you know. The subscribers loved my dad being there. He would just sit behind her and make wisecracks. He had a nickname. Pops. Erased and Pops. That was part of why her stream was so popular, because of him."

"So why do you think he didn't tell your mother about it?"

"She just couldn't—could not deal with anything he had to do with either of us. She was so jealous of him, of the fact that we loved him. She was sick with it. You know. Sick in the head. So tell me, please, I can take it. Tell me what she did to him. Tell me what my mum did to my dad."

———

Roxy sits outside the chichi coffee shop on Salusbury Road. Her brain is on fire. It's hot with things, with thoughts rolling and jostling and images flashing and pounding, and she acts like she doesn't care, she acts like she's seen it all before, but she hasn't and her dad is fucking dead and Erin is attached to a thousand wires in a hospital room, her life still hanging in the balance. She shreds a paper napkin with tense fingers, then realizes what she's done and balls the shreds together tightly. She glances up through the plate glass and sees a woman walking hurriedly toward the shop. She's tall, and her hair is very blond, it looks natural, but Roxy can see the roots starting to grow back in her side parting. She is wearing flared jeans and a sweatshirt, stack-heeled trainers, and no makeup. She looks like she hasn't slept

for days. She sees Roxy as she enters the café and looks at her questioningly. Roxy nods.

"Hi, Roxy." She sits down. "God. This is . . ." She seems lost for
words and her eyes scan Roxy's face as though she's trying to remember it for later. "I can't believe it's you. I just feel like . . ." Her hands
go up in the air and flutter around vaguely before landing in her lap.
"Are you OK?"

Roxy nods. Roxy is always OK and would never want anyone to
think otherwise.

"I'm really sorry about your father."

Roxy nods again. Then she looks at Alix and says, "What did my
mum tell you about my dad?"

Alix eyes her uncertainly and then says, "I'm not sure how true a
lot of it was?"

"Just tell me."

So Alix does.

3 P.M.

"Is that comfortable?"

Alix looks across the desk in her recording studio at Roxy, who
is adjusting her headphones. Roxy nods and gives her a thumbs-up.

"Great."

Roxy is five foot tall and terrifying. Her jaw juts defiantly, even
when she's being pleasant.

"This is all bullshit," she'd said in the café just now, loud enough
for the two young mums sitting behind to pause their conversation
and turn slightly in their seats. "I can't believe she told you that stuff.
It's—" And she'd been about to launch into her own telling of her
childhood when Alix put her hand up to stop her.

"How would you feel," she said, "about contributing to the podcast? Telling your side?"

"When?" Roxy asked.

"Now? I live just up there. Two minutes away. Less."

She'd expected Roxy to say no, to be cagey and private and prickly, but Roxy had immediately picked up her small rucksack and started to stand up. "Is this going to be like a true crime podcast, then?" she asked, and Alix had felt a shiver run through her at the realization that somehow, through the stultifying fug of fear and dread, it had escaped her that that's exactly what she was now doing. She was making a true crime podcast, out of the events of her own life.

Now she plays Roxy a small part of one of Josie's recordings. It's from the day that Josie told her about Brooke. She watches Roxy's face as she listens, the looks of confusion and incredulity that pass across her fine features. She shakes her head occasionally, as if trying to dislodge something from her ear. Alix presses pause and waits for Roxy to speak.

Hi! I'm Your Birthday Twin!
A NETFLIX ORIGINAL SERIES

The screen changes to a close-up reenactment of someone pressing record on a mixer desk.
Underneath the text reads:

Over the next twenty-four hours, Alix Summer recorded nearly four hours of testimony from Roxy Fair.

Roxy's voice plays over a blurred visual re-creation of the Fairs' apartment interior.

A teenage girl can be seen from behind, chatting to an older man in the kitchen.

"Brooke Ripley started late at my school. Everyone hated her. I remember being glad because it took the spotlight off me for a moment. She was kind of pretty, looked older than fourteen, big boobs. And we sort of paired off just because everyone hated us. And yeah, she and I got quite close. Really close. In fact, Brooke and I ended up being, like, together, you know? I'd always known I was gay, from a really young age. But Brooke was my first girlfriend, and it was seriously intense for a while. We were really in love. Didn't tell anyone about it, only Erin. But not Mum, not Dad. And I remember this time, it was Christmas, my dad was home. I remember that now. He was baking cookies, in his Christmas apron. We were listening to Christmas music. It was kind of nice, felt like a normal family for once."

Alix interjects: "Were you not a normal family?"

"No. We were not a normal family. Not by any stretch. But right then, in that moment, it felt normal. And my dad was laughing and joking and I looked at Brooke and I thought: I bet you wish your dad was like mine. I remember thinking that. I remember it really clearly. I felt proud. You know? And yes, of course my mum hated it. Hated seeing us all having a laugh. All being happy. Afterward Brooke said something like, 'I think your mum hates me.' I said, 'Why do you say that?' She said, 'I dunno. The vibes I was getting off her.' I think Mum just really resented her, because she could tell how much I liked her. How much we *all* liked her. She could tell that Brooke was more important to me than her, that I loved her, you know, and she couldn't deal with it. She couldn't deal with anything that wasn't about her. She was sick with envy."

The background scene changes to a school playground filled with teenagers in uniform.

Alix asks: "And then there was a fight? According to witnesses, you and Brooke had a physical fight on school premises toward the end of your last term of school."

"Yeah. She, er, or at least I *thought* she'd said something about Erin. Someone told me she'd used a derogatory word about her. So I just went in, like I do, stupid, no fact-checking, lamped her. School suspended me, even though I was about to start my exams."

The screen changes to Roxy sitting on a stool in an empty bar.

She is smiling coolly.

On the recording, she can be heard sighing.

"I was kind of impetuous, when I was young. I was kind of a nightmare, to be honest. And that was it for me and school. I was done with it. I was done with all of it. But mainly I was done with my mother. So I ran away from home. I wanted Brooke to come with me. She said she wasn't ready. She wanted to do her GCSEs. She wanted to go to the stupid fucking prom. She wanted to do it all properly. So I just went without her. Hoped she'd come to her senses. Hoped she'd come and find me. But instead, she just went and disappeared. Into thin air. And that was that."

Alix asks: "So you running away from home—it was nothing to do with your father and Brooke? There was nothing going on? Erin didn't tell you she'd heard them having sex? None of that actually happened?"

Roxy raises her gaze to the camera and shakes her head.

"I've never heard so much bullshit in my life."

11 P.M.

Roxy sleeps in Alix's spare bedroom that night. Despite her coarse bravado, Alix senses the soft child beneath, the sixteen-year-old girl living in a toxic environment who just needed someone to nurture her. As Alix shows her to her room, she explains that this is where her mother had slept for a week, just before she disappeared. "She had this key, hidden under her mattress. It had the number six written on it. I gave it to the police, but they couldn't match it with any of the locks in your parents' house. Do you know anything about it?"

Roxy shrugs. "No."

"You don't have access to an outhouse or a shed or, I don't know, some kind of storage unit?"

"I don't think so. Although my dad had a garage, I think. His dad kept some old banger in it, I think. I do remember going in there once or twice, when we were small. It was all, like, dusty and cobwebby."

"Do you remember where it was?"

"Yeah. Round the back."

"Round the back of what?"

"The house. There's this sort of—what's it called? A mews? Like two sets of garages, facing each other, about seven or eight of them, I guess?"

"And how did you get to this mews from your house?"

"Like out the front and then round the corner and through a gate. But we also had a window in the bathroom that opened up onto it too."

Alix and Roxy exchange a look, but neither of them gives voice to their thoughts.

Hi! I'm Your Birthday Twin!
A NETFLIX ORIGINAL SERIES

Screen shows a mother and teenage daughter sitting on a sofa in a sixteenth-century pub, with a small brown dog sleeping between them.
The mother has cropped white hair and red-framed reading glasses.
The daughter has long blond hair that hangs in heavy, tonged curls to her waist. The text beneath reads:

Clare and Georgie Small, holidaymakers at Ambleside Manor Lodge Park

The daughter, Georgie, speaks first.

"We were there in July 2019. Me, my mam, my dad, my brothers. We'd just arrived two days before. It was during that heat wave we had back then. It was so hot, even up there by the lakes. We didn't see her come. Just woke up the next morning and she was there. Sort of waved at her across the park, didn't we? She had a little dog with her, and she sort of waved back but I could see she wasn't friendly. But that was OK. We weren't there to make friends."

Clare, the mother, speaks.

"The lodges are built for privacy, you see. It's not like an average holiday park where you're all rammed in. The lodges are new, only built a couple of years ago, and they

all face out over the lake and have space around them so
you can't see into other people's properties. So yeah, we
knew she was there, but we didn't see much of her. She
just sat out on her deck at night with a glass of wine staring
across the lake at sunset. I raised a glass to her once. She
raised hers back at me. But that was as far as any interaction
went. Then one day, about three or four days after she
arrived, she wasn't there anymore. She'd just up and left.
But the car was still there. Thought that was strange. But
didn't think a lot about it after that. We stayed for ten days
all told. And it was on our last day that the police arrived
in Ambleside."

Georgie interjects: "Just unbelievable that we'd been there
all those days. Just hanging out, drinking, doing water sports,
admiring the views, having fun, living our best lives, when
all along . . ."

Clare touches Georgie's arm and Georgie wipes away a tear.

"I mean, what's the matter with people? Seriously. What the
hell is the matter with some people?"

SUNDAY,
28 JULY

The house feels quiet without Roxy, without Nathan, without her mother. Just her and the children on a long, overcast Sunday. Roxy had messaged her earlier from the hospital to say that Erin was still unconscious, still wired up, still in a critical condition. And all around her the news is breaking like a slow, shocking tsunami. The awfulness of it is too big for Alix to fully process. Her sisters message her constantly. They should be WhatsApping now about their upcoming holiday. They should be sharing pictures of new dresses bought and asking for reading recommendations, asking if the villa has hair dryers, making reservations for dinner as it's impossible to seat that many people in a restaurant without advance planning. Alix should be trying on swimwear in the mirror in her room that has a rear view and wondering if she could still get away with a bikini at forty-five and then thinking that God, yes, *of course* she could and if she couldn't now, then when could she? And she would suck in her stomach and turn this way and that and think, not bad, not bad at all for a middle-aged mother of two.

That's what she should be doing now.

Instead, she is trapped in a Gothic, tick-tocking, slow-burn night-mare. So she is quite glad of the distraction at around two o'clock that long, never-ending Sunday, when Pat O'Neill calls her from the hospital and says, "Roxy's been telling me about your podcast. About the things that Josie told you. I just think, Alix, for the sake of balance and the truth, that I should come in and talk to you. Tell you my side of the story. Be-cause I know you think I was probably a bad mother and in many ways I was. But honestly, you need to understand Josie properly, what she's really like, before you can even hope to make any sense of what's been going on."

"Can you come now?" Alix says, and then she gives Pat her ad-dress and sits in the kitchen and waits for her to arrive.

Hi! I'm Your Birthday Twin!
A NETFLIX ORIGINAL SERIES

The screen shows a blurred dramatic reenactment of a young girl sitting in a bright, modern flat.
She has brown hair cut into a bob shape and is playing with a toy on the floor.
An actor playing a young Pat O'Neill stands in the kitchen of the flat, talking to a man. She is laughing at something he has just said.
The actor playing young Josie watches them curiously.
The text underneath says:

This is the voice of Pat O'Neill,
talking to Alix Summer on 28 July, 2019.

"It's true that I was not ready to be Josie's mother. Not ready at all. I was coming to the end of the second year of my degree in social anthropology. I was at my peak. I felt so alive. So vibrant. I just wanted to keep going. Keep plowing on, see how far I could get. And then I got pregnant and because I didn't show, I had no idea until it was too late to do anything about it. Josie's father was long gone by then. I can't even remember his surname to this day. Isn't that awful? I think it began with a *K*. Kelly, maybe? Anyway. Josie arrived and I was not ready. No. I wasn't ready to be a mother. But mainly, I was not ready for Josie."

The actor playing young Josie in the reenactment turns and looks at the camera.

"She was a dark child. And yes, maybe that was partly to do with me, with my style of mothering. I wanted her to be independent. I wanted her to be strong and impressive. I probably left her to her own devices too much. It's important, though, for children to make their own mistakes and learn from them. It's not good to never let your kids fuck up. But she was so needy. So needy. I gave her as much as I could, but it was never enough. And it wasn't just me. She did it with her friends; I saw it happen, time after time. She was a brooding presence in social situations; it was almost as if she spent her whole life just waiting for someone to show her that they didn't want her. She pushed so many friends away over the smallest thing. And as for me ever having a boyfriend—forget it. Seriously, forget it. She turned psycho whenever she thought a man might encroach on our lives. She would play cruel tricks on them. Insult them. Pretend to be ill if I was going out on a date. She even made a voodoo doll once, I kid you not. I mean, where did she even get the idea from? But yes, she made one of a man I was seeing and left it lying around the flat, with pins sticking out of it when he came round to see me. So all of them upped and left, of course they did. And then I started seeing Walter—"

Alix's voice cuts in. "I'm sorry?"

"I started dating Walter. When Josie was about thirteen?"

There is a prolonged silence.

"Josie didn't tell me that."

"Well, no, of course she didn't, because she only told you what she wanted you to know, what suited her weird narrative. And that's exactly why I'm here talking to you, you see. Because Josie didn't tell you lots of things and Josie's run off letting the whole world think that her husband was a monster, that he groomed her, that he abused his children, and the world needs to know that's rubbish. *You* need to know that's rubbish. Walter Fair was far from perfect. He was quite controlling. Liked things done his way. He was quite full of himself, yes. And obviously I knew it was wrong that we were having an affair behind his wife's back. Of course I knew that. But he was a loving man, a real man, he just wanted to love and to be loved. He just wanted a quiet life. And what we had was very real, very intense, and I was prepared to wait it out until he found the right time to leave his wife. At first Josie was very resistant to him, as she was with all my boyfriends. But then as she got older she seemed to become fixated on him. She would try to divert his attention away from me and onto herself. She would put makeup on when he came over and say disparaging things about me, about how old

I was, how fat I was. At first Walter and I used to joke about it together, but then the jokes stopped, around the time Josie turned sixteen, and then, just after she turned eighteen, they told me."

There is prolonged silence. Then Alix speaks.

"So you didn't know? You didn't know that they were together before that?"

Pat sighs. "Obviously I should have known. As Josie's mother, *I should have known*. And I take full responsibility for the fact that I dropped the ball. I was so desperate for Josie to be independent, to have her own life. I just wanted—and I know how bad this sounds—but I wanted her to be somewhere else. Not at home. I hated it when she was at home; she cast this mood, this atmosphere. I didn't want to talk to her. I didn't . . . God save my soul, I didn't *like* her. So I never asked her where she'd been, what she'd been doing. I didn't want to know. I was just happy that I didn't have to deal with her. But God. The shock, when I found out. The pure horror of it. And you know, when Walter and I were together, Josie used to tell me I was disgusting for being with a married man. And then she went right in there and snatched him away from his wife, and from me."

"So, in your opinion, Walter didn't groom Josie?"

"Groom her? You mean manipulate her into a relationship with him? No. I don't think so. I think she saw him, she wanted him, she got him. She didn't care who she hurt. She's never cared who she hurt. She's—and this is a terrible thing to say about your own child, and obviously, I've been far from perfect myself, but I really think Josie has a heart of stone. A heart of pure stone."

The screen turns black and then changes to Pat O'Neill sitting in a community hall.

She shakes her head slightly.

There are tears in her eyes.

6 P.M.

For a while after Pat leaves, Alix feels numb. Her mother comes over and cooks something for the children to eat, serves it to them, sits with them while they eat it, listens to their chatter, creates a sense of calm and peace which Alix is currently incapable of doing.

"I think he's dead," she says to her mother when they're alone together in the garden later on.

Her mother looks at her with concern and says, "No. Surely not."

"No. He is. I can feel it. All this time I've been thinking that Josie was weird because Josie was damaged. All this time I've been thinking she was crying out for help somehow. That she needed me. But now I realize she was never crying out for help. She never needed me. She did have a plan though. The whole time. And I was just a cog. And so was Nathan."

"But why? Why would she want to hurt Nathan? She barely knew him."

"Look. She made it clear to me that she thought very little of Nathan, that she thought I'd be better off without him. She even asked me once how I'd feel if he died and then seemed really disappointed when I said that I would be sad. And when she first suggested that I should make a podcast about her, she pretty much told me that she was embarking on a project of change and that she wanted me to document it."

"You think all this was deliberate?"

"I don't know how exactly, but yes, I think it was. I mean, she obviously knew that Erin had all that money in her bank account and then somehow found a way to get her PIN, to extract all that cash, to pay someone to lure Nathan to that hotel. She knew that Nathan was going to be out that night because he told her, and you know, when she left that day, I was surprised about how easily she went, how she didn't make a fuss or try to stay, and now I know it was part of the plan too. And I really think she took him to kill him, Mum. I really do. Every second we're sitting here is a second lost for Nathan. And I don't know what to do, Mum. I just don't know what to do."

Hi! I'm Your Birthday Twin!
A NETFLIX ORIGINAL SERIES

The screen shows Tim, Angel, and Fred.

The text underneath says:

Tim and Angel Hiddingfold-Clarke, current owners of Josie's dog, Fred

Angel is feeding Fred a small treat.

The camera zooms in on him eating it, then pans back again.

Tim starts to talk.

"We genuinely had no idea that Josie was a wanted woman. We'd been enjoying our honeymoon, hadn't watched any TV, read any news. It wasn't until we started messaging our friends about this crazy thing that had just happened, this

woman giving us her dog, that we started getting replies
going, er, you know that might be the woman who the police
are looking for? And we were like, what woman? And then
we went onto the internet and saw the photos of the woman,
Josie, and yeah, it was her. And yes, of course, we went
straight to the police. Absolutely."

Screen switches to DC Sabrina Albright.

"We got a call from the Cumbria Constabulary on Saturday
the twenty-seventh. They'd had a call from a couple of hol-
idaymakers who'd been handed a small dog to take care of
a couple of days before. They said the photographs of Josie
Fair they'd seen online matched the woman who'd handed
them the dog. They said this all occurred in broad daylight,
in an area busy with tourists; they said it happened in a flash.
But they were able to give us more of an idea of what Josie
was wearing, that she was trying to disguise her appearance
with a hood and sunglasses. They said that she left heading toward the main village of Ambleside, carrying a small
handbag.

"We immediately started a street-to-street, house-to-house
investigation. But it wasn't until very late on Sunday that
we had a breakthrough. A family dining in a restaurant in
the village told us that a woman matching Josie's appearance with a small dog had been staying at their lodge park.
They said she'd arrived the previous Sunday in the middle
of the day and had gone by Thursday morning. We con-
tacted the management and they confirmed that yes, Mrs.
Fair had booked a lodge online two weeks earlier. They
told us that the lodges were accessed via a keycode and
that they had not had cause to meet with Mrs. Fair face-

to-face and that they were unaware that she had left the park on Thursday as her booking went all the way through to the following weekend and she had not notified them that she had checked out. We dispatched a team there immediately and entered the lodge just before midnight on Sunday night."

The screen shows archive footage of police cars arriving at the lakeside park, late at night, their blue lights reflected in the dark surface of the water. The audio is a police recording from the night.

"Water rescue team are going in. I repeat, water rescue team are going in. Stand by."

Then the screen fades and changes to an artistic shot of the lake, with gentle music playing in the background.

It is daytime and the sunlight sparkles off the surface of the water.

A flock of birds swoops and whirls overhead.

The camera follows the arc of the sun until the whole screen is burnt white.

11 P.M.

Roxy calls Alix that night, just after Alix has climbed into bed.

"How's Erin?"

"Still nothing," says Roxy. "But they say her vitals are improving all the time. They reckon she'll wake up within the next few hours. What about you? Have you heard anything?"

"Not yet. I suppose it's getting a bit late now. But hopefully tomorrow." Alix pauses. "Your grandma told me about her and your dad today. That Walter used to be her boyfriend."

"Ew, yeah, I know. Gross, isn't it? The whole thing . . . my family. I'm sorry."

"Sorry? What for?"

"Sorry you got involved. Sorry she dragged you in. Sorry you ever had to know about any of it."

"It was my choice, Roxy. I went to her, remember? I didn't have to go to the alterations shop that day. I didn't have to agree to her suggestion to make a podcast. I didn't have to let her stay here after she claimed your dad had hit her. I could have pulled the plug on it at any moment, but I let myself be controlled by her. It was all me, ultimately. All of it."

There's a short pensive silence and then Roxy says, "What was it about my mum? Why did you want to do it?"

Alix stops and gives the question some thought. Then she says, "Honestly? I think I was bored, Roxy. I think I was bored and I was having problems with my husband, I was filled with anger and re-sentment, with this low-level rage, and your mum came along with her stories that made my problems pale in comparison and I think it just stopped me focusing on the shit in my own life. That's all it was. A distraction. I overrode all my instincts when I said yes. And I think I did that deliberately, because I've been following my in-stincts for so long and making good decisions for so long, and a bit of me just wanted to see what would happen if I ignored them. If I was a bit reckless. You know, like when you're driving down windy roads and you deliberately close your eyes for a second, just to see what happens. So that's what I did. And now, well, here we are."

They end the call and Alix slowly places the phone on her bedside table. She is about to pick up her book when the scream of a fox dis-turbs her. She gets out of bed and walks to the window seat overlook-ing the garden. Here she pulls her feet up under her and watches for a while as two foxes play in the garden in the warm moonlight. She and Nathan have sat here together before, watching foxes through the window, and she feels the echoes of those moments running through her, from her head to her feet. Nathan in boxers, a toothbrush in his mouth, coming over to sit next to her, the smell of him—what was it? A sort of solid smell, like cars, like books, like trees. And the sheen of the skin on his back. And the reassuring feel of his weight next to hers in the bed, which even though she always fantasized about having her own room, she always appreciated. And then she remembers a moment a few weeks ago, in the recording studio with Josie, when Josie had been telling her the untrue story of how she and Walter had got together and she remembers Josie saying, "Well, as we're birthday twins, it's only fair that you should tell me about when you met Nathan. What was it like? Where did you meet him?"

Alix quickly pulls on her dressing gown and heads quietly through the house and out into the garden, where the foxes stare at her boldly for a moment before disappearing into the foliage. She unlocks the doors to her recording studio and puts on her headphones, searches through the recordings until she finds the one she's looking for. And there is Josie's voice, that odd, hollow voice with no inflection and emotion, asking Alix, "Where did you meet him?" and Alix's reply follows.

Hi! I'm Your Birthday Twin!
A NETFLIX ORIGINAL SERIES

The camera pans back from the burnt white of the sun and on to drone footage of the calm, rippling waters of Lake Windermere.

The drone drifts slowly down the length of the lake as Alix's voice carries over the film.

The text below reads:

Recording from Alix Summer's podcast, June 2019

"I was almost thirty when we met. I was starting to worry that I was never going to meet anyone. I was working in publishing at the time, it's a notoriously girl-heavy industry, the chances of meeting anyone were slim to zero. I was living with my sister Zoe. We were perennially single. Zoe was two years older than me and had already given up. But I still felt like he was out there. You know? I could smell him, almost, hear him coming. So I just kept putting myself out there. Time after time after time. But nothing. No one."

Josie's voice interjects: "I can't believe that. A beautiful woman like you."

Alix says: "Ha. That's not how it works. Trust me, it isn't. And then, one night, just before my thirtieth birthday, I was on my way home, and I was drunk, and I remembered that I had something to collect from the dry cleaner's. I'd been meaning to pick it up for weeks, but for some reason I chose nine o'clock on a Tuesday night when I'd just had half a bottle of wine and a gin and tonic to do it. And there was this guy in front of me, collecting shirts, bright red hair, taller than me, nice shirt, nice body. But it was the voice. That was the first thing. This voice. So confident. But not arrogant. Just a really good voice. And then when he'd paid, he turned round and I saw this face. I can't explain it. I saw this face and I thought: It's you. *It's you.* Like I'd already met him? Like someone had already told me about him? But of course, nobody had. Nobody had told me. I just knew. I said something cringey like that's a lot of shirts and he stopped and looked at me and I was drunk and he was sober and I think he just thought he'd play with me a bit and he said, 'Yes. I eat a lot of shirts.' And then I said, 'Sorry, I'm a bit drunk,' and he said, 'Yes, I know.' And he just looked at me and his eyes were this color, I don't even know if there's a word for it. Just the most incredible shade of nothing. And I got my dry cleaning, and he took me to the pub. And that was that. Two years later we were married. A year after that I was pregnant with Eliza."

The soft drone footage stops abruptly.

The scene changes to a shot of the inside of an empty recording studio.

Josie's voice plays on the audio.

"Do you still love him?"

"Of course. Yes."

"But, like, really love him. Like you did back then, in the dry cleaner's? When you didn't know anything about him."

"It's a different kind of love. But yes, I do."

"You don't ever think that your life would be better if you were on your own?"

"No. No, I don't."

"And yet you call yourself a feminist."

"Yes. I do. And I am. You can be happily married and a feminist."

"I don't think so. I think that you can only be a feminist if you're single."

"Oh. That's an interesting counterpoint. Can you elaborate?"

"I shouldn't need to, Alix. You should understand what I'm saying."

A short pause follows.

Then Josie says, "You have to be free in order to be in control, Alix. You have to be free. No baggage. A clean break. Like your friend Mari le Jeune said, the one from your podcast. Remember what she said, about clean breaks. Remember?"

The audio fast-forwards and rewinds briefly, before another voice plays over the video.

The text on the screen says:

This is the voice of Mari le Jeune, the subject of one of Alix Summer's previous podcasts from her series *All Woman.*

Her words appear as moving text on the screen.

"And as awful as it sounds, death is a clean break. There are no gray areas. No ambiguity. It's like a blank canvas in a way. . . ."

The voice of Josie Fair returns.

"Don't you ever think, Alix, that everything would be easier if they were dead?"

The screen turns black.

12:45 A.M.

Alix presses stop and pulls off her headphones. She leans back into her chair, lets her head roll back, and exhales loudly. There it was. There it was, all along. She hadn't got it at the time. She'd had no recollection of what Mari le Jeune had said about clean breaks and death. She'd thought Josie was rambling. But really she'd been giving her her warped manifesto, laying it out for Alix to see. And she'd totally missed it. *This*, Alix realizes now, was what Josie had wanted to share with Alix when she approached her outside the children's school with that slightly desperate air about her. She'd had a revelation and she wanted Alix to be the depository for it. And she'd shown it to her during this interview and Alix had blown it. She'd totally blown it.

She thumps her fists against the studio desk and cries out in rage and frustration at her own stupidity. "Stupid! So stupid!"

And then she pulls herself together when she hears the ringtone coming from her phone and sees DC Albright's number on the screen. She glances at the time. It's nearly 1 a.m.

Her stomach rolls over and she breathes in until her lungs are full. Then she presses reply and waits for Sabrina to speak.

The drive is endless. The children are at Maxine's and it is now almost three in the morning. Alix thinks back to Sabrina's words on the phone, what feels like a lifetime ago, but was only an hour and a half. "He was definitely here, Alix. It looks like he was held by force in the lodge. There's evidence of restraint. Of struggle. And there are tracks leading down to the lake. So what we're doing, Alix, is we're going to launch a water-rescue operation, right now. We're also going to be sending boats out across the whole lake, in case they've taken off on water. I think, Alix, you should make your way up here, as soon as you possibly can. Is there anyone who can drive you?"

She and her mother have been on the road for over an hour and they're barely out of London. Alix feels jittery and hollow. She hasn't eaten all day. All that is in her stomach is the glass of wine she had with her mother in the garden at nine o'clock. She should eat, but she can't eat and she doesn't want to stop for food and make this journey take any longer than it already is. She scrolls through her phone, mindlessly, aimlessly, painfully. She looks at all the messages that she's been sent over the past few days from people she hasn't seen or thought about for years and years, but who all love her and care about her, and she wants to reply to them all, but she cannot, she doesn't know what words there are or how to arrange them or what use it would be anyway, so she shuts down her messages and stares instead into the darkness of the night, the occasional beam of light from oncoming cars heading into London as she heads away from it, and the miles go so slowly and the Lake District is so far and her husband is out there somewhere and she's about to find out where and she loves him so much and hates herself so much for bringing that woman into their world, their messy, grubby, broken, and perfectly imperfect world, the world she thought that she didn't want but which she now knows is the only thing, *the only thing* she truly wants: her family, her home, her bad husband, his benders, the desperate, inglorious, ridiculous normality of it all. She wants it, she wants him, she wants that, she doesn't want *this*, this endless journey, her mother's knuckles white on the steering wheel of her car, the blinding lights, the grinding hunger in her gut, the sickening nothingness of it all. She wants Nathan back. She wants him back. And then she feels her phone thrum under her hand and she switches on her screen, and there is a message from a number that she doesn't recognize. Her breath bunches up in her lungs and she presses on the message to open it up. And when she sees what it is, she knows, even before the call that follows shortly afterward from DC Albright. She already knows.

Hi! I'm Your Birthday Twin!
A NETFLIX ORIGINAL SERIES

The screen shows grainy footage of a female news reporter at dawn. Behind her is a sea of police lights and police officers and reporters holding microphones.
Beyond is Lake Windermere, with the rising sun reflected on the surface of the water. The text underneath says:

Lake Windermere, 5:27 a.m., 29 July, 2019

The reporter speaks in a reverential tone of voice.

"I'm here this morning just outside the beautiful Cumbrian village of Ambleside, on the banks of Lake Windermere, where overnight a grisly discovery was made. The body of North London man Nathan Summer, who went missing from a Central London hotel in the early hours of Sunday, the twenty-first of July, was found in shallow waters, just here, a few hours ago. Police had entered a lodge, just behind the lake, and discovered items belonging to Mr. Summer. This instigated a full-scale water-search operation overnight with the sad discovery made at around two thirty a.m. Mr. Summer's family have been notified and are on their way here as I speak. The hunt for Josie Fair is still ongoing. This is Kate Mulligan, BBC News, Ambleside."

The screen fades to a reenactment of a woman in the

passenger seat of a car at night pulling a phone out of a handbag at the sound of a text notification.

She turns on the screen and opens the text.

On the screen is a voice message.

She presses play.

The text below says:

This is the voice message that Josie Fair sent to Alix Summer. It arrived five minutes before Alix Summer was notified of the discovery of her husband's body.

"Alix. Hi. It's me. I'm not sure what to say. I don't know what happened. What I was thinking. It wasn't my intention. None of it. The whole thing. I was trying to be helpful, trying to show you how much better your life could be without him. I was just going to keep him for a few days and then leave him somewhere to find his own way back to you, but it all went wrong, it's all a disaster. It makes me look like I'm evil. But I'm not. You *know* I'm not, Alix. That's why I wanted to share my story with you, because we are alike, you and I. We're both idealized wives with disappointing husbands. We've both been living in the shadows of awful men who chose us because of what we represented, not for who we are. We both had more to give, more to offer. And now Erin will wake up and say things about me too, and those things won't be true, Alix, you have to believe that. They won't be true. Everything I told you was the truth. We know that. You and me. You're the only person in the whole world I can trust to know the real me, Alix. Please, tell the world that I'm not a bad person. That I'm just a normal person coping with bad things. Not just the bad things I told you about, but other things. The thing I wanted to tell you about, the *real* end of the story, the darkest, worst thing of all, but I lost my nerve, I couldn't do it, and I wish I had, because now, because of this stupid mistake with Nathan, I've blown it. Now nobody would believe me anyway. So please. Don't believe the things you'll hear. I'm so sorry, Alix. I really truly am. Goodbye."

MONDAY,
29 JULY

DC Albright steps back to allow Alix to peer inside the lodge. Alix wears paper covers over her shoes and has been told to go no further than the entry. The lodge is still a crime scene, but she had begged DC Albright to at least let her see it, the place her husband spent his last days. She has to know. And as she stands in the entrance she is comforted in some strange and probably inappropriate way by the fact that the lodge is beautiful. It is modern and stylish and airy, with large windows on all sides, incredible views of the lake from the front and the countryside elsewhere. It resembles, in some strange way, Alix's house in London with its aqua-themed cushions and copper kitchen taps and pastel-painted tongue-and-groove cladding. It even has a window seat in the kitchen area, overlooking the front balcony. It's gorgeous. Alix wonders at herself for taking comfort from this, wonders at herself and her values and every last aspect of herself as she has done constantly for the past week. Who is she? Why is she? What has she done? What should she do? Is she a good mother? Has she been a good wife? Good sister? A good friend?

A good woman? Does she deserve what she has? Is she shallow? Is she irrelevant? Does she want to be relevant? Is she a feminist? Or is she just feminine? What more could she have done for Josie? And women like her? What more could she have done for her marriage?

Her boy sits inside headphones every night with eyes wide staring at a screen. Her girl cries over mean things said to her by other girls on the piece of plastic and glass she allows her to have access to. Her husband hands her cash as if she had a gun to his head. She sits in her recording studio pulling words out of women who've had a much harder life than her, who have suffered and survived, who have worked so hard and succeeded against all the odds. And there she sits in a twenty-thousand-pound recording studio built for her as a birthday gift by her husband, whom she hasn't had sex with for over two months and who would rather go drinking in Soho with strangers than come home to her body offered to him like a cookie jar for good behavior—and what sort of feminist rewards men for not behaving badly with offers of penetration? She is not a feminist, she is not anything; she is a trinket, a flibbertigibbet; and for a moment, yes, she can see herself from Josie's perspective, she can see what Josie saw in her, the big gaping space in her soul that she filled with things that couldn't hurt her, and she knows why she agreed to work with Josie: because, subconsciously, she wanted something to hurt her, and here she is now, staring at the last four walls her husband ever saw, and she is hurting, she is hurting so badly it feels as if fingers are inside her gut shredding it into pieces and she grabs hold of the doorframe with both hands and curls into herself and howls.

8:30 A.M.

Erin groans and Roxy sits upright. She stares at her sister for a moment, to see if she does it again. A second later she does, and Roxy turns round to call for a nurse.

The nurse appears and watches Erin from the other side of her bed, takes her pulse with her fingers, peers into her eyes, calls another nurse, who looks at the stats on the equipment that surrounds her bed and then smiles and says, "Well, hello, Erin! How lovely of you to join us!"

Roxy leans forward, closer to Erin's face, and sees a small smile begin to break out. "Oh my God," she says. "Fuck. Erin! Hello!"

The smile grows bigger for a moment and then shrinks again as Erin takes in the details of her surroundings. "Where am I?" she whispers.

"You're in hospital. You nearly died."

Roxy sees a thousand pictures flood her sister's only-just-returned consciousness within the space of a few seconds. She sees the emotions play out as the memories flood back. "Mum . . ."

"Mum is—" Roxy begins, but then stops. She doesn't know what to say. Mum is what? Mum is where? "Don't worry about Mum," she says, taking Erin's hand in hers and squeezing it softly.

"And Dad. Is he . . . ?"

Roxy nods, tightly, and holds on to her tears. She needs to stay strong for Erin. "He didn't make it. But it's fine, Sis. Be cool. It's fine. I'm here. So's Grandma. She's just gone to get us something to eat. We're here. And the world—oh my God, Erin, you know how many people signed your vigil book on Glitch, when you went missing? Like a hundred thousand people. A hundred thousand people signed it. Hashtag SaveErased. You were viral out there for a while. And now I can tell them that you made it. You're back! *Erased* was not erased!" She's babbling and she knows she's babbling but she doesn't want Erin to fall into a dark pit of remembering, not yet, not this soon after waking up. She's pleased to see Erin smile at her words, and she squeezes her hand again. "You're a fucking legend, Sis. Seriously. A legend."

Her grandmother returns then with bacon rolls and bad coffee and immediately puts them down when she sees that Erin is awake. "Oh my God! Erin! You're awake! I can't believe it. I go away from you for five minutes and that's when you decide to wake up!" She sits on the side of Erin's bed and takes her other hand in hers, brings it to her mouth and kisses it. "I've missed you so much," she says. "So, so much."

"What day is it?" asks Erin.

"It's Monday. The . . . ?"

Roxy looks at the nurse, who says, "The twenty-ninth."

"The twenty-ninth."

"I feel funny."

Roxy and Pat both laugh indulgently.

"I feel hungry."

They laugh again and the nurse says, "We'll get something ordered for her. Soft food, isn't it, Erin? I hear you like soft food?"

Erin nods.

"We'll sort something out for you. Some soup maybe."

The nurses finish their examination of Erin and then leave, saying the doctor will come as soon as he can. Grandma passes Erin a cup of water. And then it is just the three of them, and Roxy and her grandmother chatter and burble, trying to keep the inevitable tide of darkness at bay for as long as possible. But then, a few minutes later, it comes.

"Oh my God," Erin says, her eyes filling with tears and terror. "What happened? *What happened!*"

"It's fine," says Roxy coolly. "I'm going to tell you exactly what happened. OK? I'm going to tell you word for word."

Hi! I'm Your Birthday Twin!
A NETFLIX ORIGINAL SERIES

The screen flicks to blurry footage of a garage door, then pans across a small London mews.

The text beneath says:

Shortland Mews, London NW6, 30 July, 2019

The audio is a crackly recording of a police phone call.

"We're approaching the garage now, with Mr. Roberts, the owner of the block. Mr. Roberts is opening the main gates and we're getting ready to go in."

The footage shows a hand with a key in it going toward a large, rusty padlock. The key has a tag attached with the number 6 written on it. The key turns slowly, and the click of the lock is magnified on the audio.

The film slows down and the screen goes black . . .

. . . The screen changes to footage of a BBC News report.

A newsreader announces the headlines as the familiar BBC theme music fades out.

"Good evening. Earlier today, at around eleven thirty a.m., the human remains of a young woman were discovered in the boot of a car in a garage in Kilburn, London, by the Metropolitan Police. They are believed to be those of Brooke Ripley, the young girl who went missing from her school prom in June 2014. The garage was leased by Walter Fair, the seventy-two-year-old man found murdered earlier this week in his flat, while his adult daughter Erin Fair was found barely alive and tied to a child's chair in a cupboard. Erin, twenty-three years old, had last been seen by friends online whilst gaming in the early hours of Saturday, the thirteenth of July. A hunt for her had been carried out by her legion of online followers after they heard something strange happening during her last live stream, and a global campaign was ongoing to find out what had happened to her. She has told of surviving her ordeal by sucking on the strands of a floor mop in a bucket of dirty water left on a shelf in the cupboard where she'd been abandoned. Meanwhile, Josie Fair, Erin's mother, is being sought in connection with the suspicious death of Nathan Summer, the London estate agent found in the shallow waters of Lake Windermere early yesterday morning. Anyone with any information about Josie Fair or her current whereabouts is urged to contact the London Metropolitan Police at the first possible opportunity."

The screen changes to DC Sabrina Albright.

She shrugs and shakes her head sadly, just once.

"When we found Brooke, she was still wearing her white prom dress. The fabric disintegrated when it was touched. Literally just turned to dust, like a butterfly's wing. Poof."

Sabrina Albright smiles tightly. Her eyes fill with tears.

"Sad," she says. "So very sad."

Hi! I'm Your Birthday Twin!
A NETFLIX ORIGINAL SERIES

The screen shows a woman of around forty. She has long dark hair and wears tortoiseshell-rimmed reading glasses and a white T-shirt.

She sits on a fold-out vintage cinema seat in the middle of an empty cinema.

The interviewer asks her off-mic if she is OK and she says, "Yes. I'm good. Let's do this."

The text beneath says:

Abigail Kurti, mother of Brooke Ripley

The screen changes briefly to the reenactment of a police officer turning the key in the padlock, with dramatic music playing in the background.

Then it flicks back to Abigail Kurti sitting in the empty cinema.

She begins to speak.

"Brooke left home at about six o'clock. She looked amazing. I mean, she always looked amazing, but that night, in that white dress . . ."

The photograph of Brooke Ripley in her prom dress comes up on-screen briefly.

"And then she just didn't come home. I mean, we didn't know what to think. Brooke was a dramatic girl, you know. There were always tantrums and noise with Brooke. She hated my husband, her stepfather; they rowed *all the time.* She was rarely at home, and she had run away before. But this—I knew this was different. I thought it was to do with a boy. I didn't know anything about Roxy Fair. I knew there'd been a fight at school, but I thought it was just another school hallway scrap, you know? Very Brooke. I didn't know that Roxy and Brooke had been friends, or, or *lovers*. I didn't know anything about Roxy, I didn't know where Roxy lived, and so I couldn't see any significance in the fact that Brooke got off the bus at that stop. And I had no reason really to think that that's where Brooke might have been heading that night. And God, I wish more than anything that I'd known. Then I could have told the police. They would have gone round and questioned them. That woman . . ."

Abigail's voice cracks. She puts the back of her hand to her mouth and smiles tightly.

"Sorry."

"That's OK. Take your time," *says the interviewer off-mic.*

"That woman would have been stopped. There and then. Before she had a chance to hurt anyone else. And Brooke might have been saved."

She begins to cry and the screen fades to black.

Hi! I'm Your Birthday Twin!
A NETFLIX ORIGINAL SERIES

Screen shows Roxy Fair sitting on the same sofa as in previous scenes, but this time Erin is sitting next to her.

Erin wears her hair long and parted down the middle. She has on a baseball cap with her gaming logo embroidered on it and a matching T-shirt.

The text beneath reads:

Roxy and Erin Fair

Then new text appears below, typed letter by letter.

Erin Fair was recently diagnosed as having ASD. To compensate for living with her disorder in a toxic and dysfunctional environment, she developed various habits and coping mechanisms. These include talking in a very soft voice. As some of her words are hard to pick up on, we have provided subtitles for Erin's spoken words which will appear below.

"Our mother didn't want our dad to like us and she didn't want us to like him. She wanted him all to herself and she wanted us all to herself. She wasn't happy when we went to him or had fun with him or loved him. She wasn't happy when he was with us and tried to show us any love or affection. She controlled every element of our relationship with our father and his with us. It became worse and worse as we got older and older. When we tried to bring friends home, she would make them feel really unwelcome, and when Dad tried to organize fun things to do as a family she would find ways to sabotage them. And obviously there were other challenges in our family too. The fact that Roxy had oppositional defiant disorder. My issues. She didn't let my father have anything to do with his first family in Canada. He used to have to sneak-ily Skype with them when she was at work, and one day, she pretended to go to work but didn't, she sat at the bus stop outside, and then Dad looked up from his Skype call with his sons and saw Mum staring at him through the window. She didn't talk to him for days after that, so my dad just Skyped them from my bedroom instead. She didn't like us seeing our grandma because she was the enemy. She told us all these lies about her, that she used to be a prostitute, brought tricks into the house, that she used to beat her and starve her and of course we were small so we believed her. But then our dad told us it wasn't true, that Mum was just jealous of Grandma because she'd been with Dad before her.

"But it got really, really bad when my dad got the job up north, when he was only home at the weekends, and we were alone with Mum. She couldn't cope with us. Particularly couldn't cope with Roxy. She took Roxy out of school when she broke my arm, which"—*she throws a playful look at her sister*—"by the way, was kind of an accident. I mean, she did it in anger during a fight, but it wasn't done maliciously, but the social services tried to intervene, based on things me and Roxy had said at school about our home life, and Mum pulled Roxy out of school for nearly two years and said she was 'homeschooling' her. Which was bollocks. She just let her watch TV all day. And then when Dad got back at the weekends, she'd leave all this fake 'learning' stuff around the flat to make it look like she'd been teaching her. And she'd leave Roxy tied up to the Naughty Chair in our bedroom. Sometimes for like hours. And she said if either of us ever told our dad that he would leave us and go back to his other family in Canada, and we'd never see him again. Dad would come back at the weekends, and she would act like everything was just so happy and wonderful. I think he knew. He *did* know. But he was trapped too. He had nowhere to go. He was getting old, and he'd already lost two of his kids and he didn't want to lose us too. He stuck it out, for as long as he could. Tiptoed round her. Did everything he could to keep her happy. And then one night Dad couldn't sleep, and he walked past my room and heard me online. I guess this was about four or five years ago—it was after I finished school anyway, when I was gaming full-time—and he walked in and all my followers were like, 'Oh my God, is that your dad?' And I was like, 'Yes, this is Pops.' And he said hi to everyone and he wanted to know what we were doing, and he pulled over a chair and sat down and watched and after about an hour or so he was totally into it. And it was great having him there, because I talk so quietly, it's hard for me sometimes to create the sort of energy that gamers want when they're watching online, and he was there giving it all the energy, all the vibes. He was so much fun, and everyone loved him, and so he started joining in more and more and of course no, we could not tell Mum about it. No way. She'd have put a stop to it, pronto. She'd have killed it dead. So Dad used to wait for her to go to sleep at night and then sneak in. And it was Dad who helped monetize it all, got me on Glitch, managed my subscriptions, opened my bank accounts. He did all of that for me. He was the one who made me famous. And we were planning a trip to Nevada for a convention that summer, the summer he died. I was going to play in front of a live audience, for the first time. Then when we got home, I was going to move out, move down to Bristol to live with Roxy. I was breaking free. It was all happening. It was all within reach. And I think she knew it. She could smell it. And that's why she latched on to Alix Summer, made up that whole crazy story about Dad beating her and Dad abusing me. She wanted to disappear from her life before she lost control of it completely. Wanted to stop all the freedom and all the escaping. Roxy had already got out; she wasn't prepared to let me and Dad get out too."

"And Brooke?" *the interviewer asks off-mic.* "What can you tell us about Brooke?"

Erin sighs. "I was home with my mum. It was just the two of us. My father wasn't in London that night. He was working away so it had nothing to do with him. Roxy was in Bristol, so it was nothing to do with her. And I was in my room, in another world. But then I heard voices. A girl's voice. And I recognized it. It was Brooke, Roxy's friend. She used to be over a lot in the months before but we hadn't seen her for a while. I went to my door and peered through. I saw Brooke standing by the living-room door; her body language was like she didn't want to stay. She was wearing this nice white dress. It was long. Down to her ankles. And my mum was saying, 'She's not here. She's run away. It's your fault.' And Brooke was saying, 'No. No, it's not my fault. I loved her. She was running away from you.' And then I saw my mum just . . .'"

Erin pauses, closes her eyes for a moment and then opens them again, smiles awkwardly, and continues:

"She hit her. She hit her so hard. Around her face. And Brooke just stood there. She touched her cheek. She said, 'See. See, that's why Roxy ran away. Because of you. Because you're fucking mad. You're just totally mad. Roxy hates you, you know. She told me that. She hates you.' And then Brooke picked up the hem of her skirt and turned, and I put my head back inside my bedroom and closed the door and I heard her stamping down the hallway toward the front door but then I heard this crack. This crash. And I heard this noise, this choking noise. I didn't dare look. I just stood there, my adrenaline pumping so hard I could feel it in my blood, listening to these sounds of struggle, of violence. And then . . ."

She closes her eyes again. Roxy reaches across and takes her hand, squeezing it.

"And then it went quiet. And I did not leave my room for a very long time. Not for a very long time."

Interviewer asks off-mic: "How long?"

"A very long time."

Interviewer: "Did you tell anyone what you'd heard?"

Erin shakes her head.

"Not even your father?"

She shakes her head again.

"Not then. No. But recently, I did. About a year before he died?"

"And what did he say?"

"He didn't say anything. He just sort of shook his head and sighed. I think he might have said *fuck*."

"And what happened after that?"

"Nothing. Nothing happened. Life went on."

"And you never said anything to your mother?"

"No. I never said anything to my mother. I just cut myself off from her."

"Why?"

There is a short pause.

The camera zooms in on Erin's and Roxy's entwined hands and then pans out again.

"Because I was scared. Scared that if she could do that to Brooke, she could do it to me."

"So what really happened that night?" *the interviewer asks off-mic.* "The night she turned up on Alix Summer's doorstep claiming to have been attacked by your father?"

Erin sighs.

The screen changes to a dramatic reenactment of the night.

An actor playing Erin is in a messy bedroom at night, her face lit up by her computer monitor. She has headphones on and is interacting with online friends.

She pauses and removes her headphones.

She goes to the door of her room and puts her ear to it.

Erin's voice continues in the background:

"They came home. I heard them at the front door at about ten o'clock. It was quiet for a while and then a few minutes later I could hear shouting. Really bad. I opened my door and watched through the crack. My mother was accusing my father of being an embarrassment. Saying that he'd shown her up. That she'd been ashamed of him, and my dad did what my dad always did, just sat and took it. But then, out of nowhere, my mum called him a pedophile. She was screaming it at him, over and over, saying that he had abused her and now he was abusing me, and then I heard my dad start to shout back. He was saying that he'd had enough of her, that he couldn't take it anymore, that it was the end of the line. And then he said she was mad—'You're actually mad'—and was telling her that he'd had enough of her, that she was stupid, and that was when I heard my mother scream, it was like an animal scream. And there was a bang and a crash and then suddenly it just went quiet. I walked in and I saw my father on the floor. I thought he was having a heart attack. His hands were up against his chest, there was blood running from the side of his head, and I ran over to him and was going to try and, I don't know, try and resuscitate him or something. My mum just stood and watched. She said, 'It's too late. He's an old man. It was always going to happen sooner or later.' And she turned away and I said, 'But we need to call an ambulance!'

"She said, 'I already did. It's on its way.' I said, 'Why did you call him a pedophile? Dad's not a pedophile.' And she said, 'He had sex with me when I was sixteen. He was forty-three. What's that if it's not a pedophile? You put him on a pedestal but he's nothing that you thought he was. He's nothing at all. Just a dirty old man. A sad, pathetic, dirty old man.' And that was when I went for it. I said, 'And you're a *murderer*,' and I picked up the remote control and I ran to her and I battered her with it. Just battered her and battered her and she didn't fight back, just put her hands up around her head, and then, suddenly, she made this weird noise and she pulled herself up and she pushed me, really hard, and I fell onto my bum, winded myself so I could barely breathe, and she put her foot into my guts and pressed down so hard and I couldn't push back against her and my father was groaning, trying to get to his feet, and she just kicked out at him with her other foot and he was still clutching at his chest, making the terrible noises, and my mother, she stood above us both, and her face—there was nothing there. And she kept saying, 'I am not mad. I am not stupid.' She said, 'It's you. It's you.

You two drove me to this. You two. All I do is look after you both and all I get is hate. I can do better than this. I can do better than all of this.' And then I don't remember anything after that. Just woke up and I was in the cupboard. Tied to a chair. And Dad was . . . well. We all know what happened after that."

Erin shakes her head sadly, and the screen fades to black.

PART FOUR

PART FOUR

FOUR WEEKS
LATER

Nathan's funeral was every bit as horrific as Nathan's funeral was always going to be. Nathan knew so many
people, and everyone who knew Nathan loved Nathan.
The atmosphere in the packed crematorium was febrile with pain
and shock. Unlike Alix, Nathan had known hurt in his life. His
mother had died when he was twelve. His little brother had killed
himself when Nathan was twenty-eight, just two years before Alix
met him. And Nathan had dragged himself out of pain and grief
and made a good life for himself. He hadn't gone to university;
he'd gone straight out to work and grafted hard for every penny he
ever earned and was generous to a fault with the money he worked
so hard for. And the drinking—it was so painfully crystal clear
now to Alix—it was not about her, it was never about her. It was
about him, about Nathan, about how he balanced out the delicate
ecosystem of his damaged psyche. He didn't want Alix to see that
dark side of him. He did not want her to see him that way. When
he drank like that, to the point of oblivion, it was self-medication,

it was relief, it wasn't good times and escaping-from-the-battle-ax. He hated himself like that and that was why he didn't come home. Not because he didn't want to be with her, but because he didn't want her to be with him.

Nearly three hundred people packed out the crematorium near Nathan's father's house in Kensal Rise. Beyond the gates of the cemetery and onto the main road, the press and paparazzi kept a discreet distance. Alix wore a dress that she'd chosen to match the color of Nathan's eyes. The shop assistant had called it *artichoke*. Alix didn't know what color an artichoke was; she just knew that the dress was the same color as Nathan's eyes and that was the most important thing.

The weather was pleasant that day, four weeks to the day after Nathan's body was brought out of the waters of Lake Windermere, not yet bloated, thank goodness, still recognizably Nathan. The month had been a blur, but that day felt sharp and clear to Alix, somehow. Being with so many people felt right, and afterward at the wake thrown by Nathan's company at a huge bar in Paddington overlooking the canal, with seats outside and bottomless champagne and a playlist put together by Nathan's best friends and the children dashing about in summer clothes, and lively urgent chatter and laughter and people looking their high summer best, it felt almost as if Nathan would appear at any moment, in his element, loving every second, and when he didn't appear it felt as though maybe he was at home waiting for her, and when he was not at home waiting for her it felt as though maybe he was away on a boys' trip and when, ten days after the funeral, he is still not home, it is then and only then that Alix collapses. She lies on her bed, the day before Eliza's first day at secondary school, wearing her artichoke dress and clutching a pillow, arching and un-arching her back as spasms of agonized crying rack her body at the realization of what she has lost.

Hi! I'm Your Birthday Twin!
A NETFLIX ORIGINAL SERIES

The screen shows footage of a BBC News report filmed outside a cemetery in Kensal Rise, northwest London.

The male reporter speaks respectfully and solemnly.

"Today Nathan Summer, the husband of podcaster Alix Summer, has been laid to rest at Kensal Green crematorium in North London. Dozens upon dozens of well-wishers, friends, and family have flooded through these gates this morning to say their final farewells to a man who, it appears, was loved by many. But today, still, a month after his body was discovered in the shallows of Lake Windermere, police are no closer to tracing the woman accused of killing him with an overdose of barbiturates in a kidnapping gone wrong. Josie Fair, forty-five, was last seen on Thursday, the twenty-fifth of July, in the village of Ambleside, where she handed her dog to a pair of strangers before disappearing completely. Fair is also being hunted in connection with the murders of her husband, Walter Fair, seventy-two, and sixteen-year-old Brooke Ripley, and the attempted murder of her daughter Erin Fair, twenty-three years old. Since her disappearance, police have been following leads of sightings of Fair as far afield as northern France, Marrakech, Belfast, and the Outer Hebrides, but still, to this moment, her whereabouts remain a mystery."

The footage shows a long-range shot of Alix Summer and her two young children exiting the cemetery.

Alix is in a green dress, with a black jacket slung over her shoulders, wearing dark glasses.

Mourners come to her as she walks and offer condolences.

"But for now," *the reporter continues*, "there is some small semblance of closure at least for Alix Summer as she says a final farewell to her husband. This is Matt Salter, from Kensal Green, for the BBC."

The screen changes to Alix Summer.

She is sitting in her recording studio, wearing a yellow sleeveless top. Her blond hair is tied back from her face.

The text beneath reads:

Alix Summer, January 2022

Alix speaks to an off-camera interviewer.

"I couldn't come in here"—*she gestures at her recording studio*—"not for months and months. It felt so . . . *full* of her. So full of Josie. So, I just abandoned it. Focused on the kids, focused on getting my daughter through her first term of secondary school without a dad, on persuading my grieving son that I could be fun too. You know? And then a few months later, of course, the pandemic hit and life changed and everyone started doing things differently. Getting dogs. Baking bread. Writing novels. All of that. And I realized that it was all on me now, all of it. There was no life insurance policy, no income. There'd been a few thousand in our joint bank account when Nathan went missing, but that wasn't going to last very long. I needed to get a job, but of course, how can you get a job in the middle of a global pandemic when you're a single parent homeschooling two children? I felt terrified, started making plans to sell the house, downsize. But then one night, a few weeks into the first lockdown, I looked out across the garden and there was this fox, sitting by the door to my studio, staring at me. And he looked like he was issuing me with a challenge. Like, a, you know, *what are you going to do now?* kind of thing. Like an *are you just going to sit around feeling sad about everything or are you going to fire up your engines and make something out of all this fucking awfulness?* Because believe me, it was truly awful. But I knew that I had the makings, if I could only stomach it, of a truly unbelievable story.

"So the next morning I made myself a strong coffee and took a deep breath and I unlocked the door to the studio and I thought: Right, Alix Summer, it's all there, everything you need to make this happen, hours and hours of recordings with Josie, with Roxy, with Pat. I had access to all the news reports online. I had recorded all my calls throughout, so I had my phone conversations with DCs Albright and Bryant. I had more than enough to create something completely unforgettable, something unmissable. I got in touch with Andrea Muse, the famous true crime podcaster, and asked if she would help produce and edit. My previous podcasts had been straightforward one-on-one interviews, all recorded in one sitting, just needed polishing and a light edit before they went out into the world. This was going to be hugely different, involving complex editing skills that I did not possess. So, with Andrea on board, I started, that day. By the end of the month we had the first episode, and it went live in late May. And yes, as you know, it went viral. Totally viral. After the first episode aired, I had people contact me directly wanting me to interview them. Brooke Ripley's mother. Josie's friend Helen from school. Walter's son in

Canada. So week by week the podcast was becoming more and more complex, more and more multilayered, more and more gripping. And then, midsummer 2020, close on a year since Nathan died, I got a message from Katelyn. You know—Katelyn Rand? They'd just relaxed the restrictions then, which meant I could meet up with her, face-to-face. So we arranged to meet in Queen's Park, just around the corner from my house. It was a Wednesday afternoon. I was quite terrified."

WEDNESDAY, 15 JULY, 2020

Alix pushes her sunglasses from her face and into her hair when she sees Katelyn approaching. Her heart races in her chest and she feels a sickening mix of nerves and excitement.

Then the woman's face opens up into a huge disarming smile and her pace picks up and she comes to Alix looking as if she might hug her, then quickly remembers that she's not allowed to anymore, so they sit six feet apart and Katelyn says, "Wow, you're beautiful. I mean, I saw you on the news, obviously. But you're much more beautiful in real life."

"You're beautiful too," Alix says, without the same warmth with which Katelyn had imbued her compliment. And Katelyn is spectacularly pretty. Her skin is clear and honeyed and her hair is a mass of soft blond curls, tied away from her face into a puffball. She has dimples and a small gap between her very white teeth and she is leggy in skinny jeans and a cropped fitted cardigan that clings to breasts at least three cup sizes bigger than Alix's.

Katelyn poo-poos the compliment, likably, and Alix feels herself being drawn against her will into liking this human being who played such a huge part in the death of her husband. She sets up her phone and portable microphone, ready to record their conversation. Katelyn chatters as she does so.

"I couldn't believe it when I saw you'd put a podcast out. It's everywhere! I mean, I don't even listen to podcasts, I don't even *know* what a podcast is, barely. But this one—wow!—I mean, inevitable, I suppose. It's not every day you get thrown into your own real-life crime. And I'm sorry, Alix, but I have to warn you in advance, I have no filter. I say words before I hear them in my head, you know? And sometimes it makes me sound insensitive? Uncaring? But really, I am not that person. Not *at all*. And I need you to know, Alix, how horribly, horribly sorry I am for what happened. And for the part that I played in it. I can barely sleep at night, sometimes, thinking about it all, wanting to turn back the clock, wanting never to have walked into that alterations shop that morning."

"You met Josie in the alterations shop?"

"Yeah. Well, I knew who she was already, she was kind of famous on my estate for being the girl who ran off with her mum's boyfriend, you know? But I hadn't seen her for years before that. But listen, Alix, please believe me, I thought I was doing something good, you know? I thought I was doing something for the sisterhood. The way she painted it, that you were stuck in this marriage with this guy who couldn't keep it in his trousers, you know? And she was helping you escape. And I wanted to help you escape too. Obviously, the money was a huge incentive. A thousand pounds is a thousand pounds, yeah? But mainly I just thought: Let's show this woman what sort of man her husband is. Let's show her and then she can be free of him. And then of course, it turned out that your husband was not that guy at all. Not at all. My God, Alix, that man loved you. He didn't come near me in that way. He was not interested in me in that way. He was just so drunk and I think he saw me as his drinking buddy, you know? He just wanted a drinking buddy. But all the while it was Alix-this and Alix-that. And showing me photos of you on his phone."

Alix glances up at Katelyn at this and says, "His phone. Yes. I always wondered, why didn't he call me? Why didn't he text me? Why didn't he reply to my calls? When he was with you?"

"He was too drunk, Alix. I'm not sure I can really convey to you what a fucking mess he was. I'm sorry for swearing. Can you edit that out? Sorry. But he was seeing double. So I took over his phone for him. I told him I was messaging you to come and get him. But all the time I knew that Josie was going to come and get him. I lied to him, Alix, and I am *so sorry*. I mean, really. He was such a nice person. Such a good person. And I lied to him. Told him he was safe. Told him you were coming. Told him I was looking after him. And all the while . . ." Katelyn shakes her head sadly.

Alix feels a slick of bitter bile at the back of her throat as she absorbs Katelyn's words. She wants to hurt her. She wants to scream into her face.

"You can hate me," Katelyn says, as if she'd been reading Alix's mind. "I want you to hate me. I really do. I'm not here to be your friend or look for forgiveness. I'm here for your podcast. To make it, like, the biggest podcast there ever was, to make you famous, to make you fly. Because that's what I thought I was doing that night, the night I lied to your beautiful husband and destroyed your life: I thought I was helping you to fly." She tuts quietly at her own folly and shakes her head again.

"Just know, Alix Summer, that you had a husband who adored you, adored his kids, adored his life. A husband who didn't want anyone else. Only you."

Alix nods and holds back tears. Then she smiles tightly and says,

"Right, shall we start from the beginning? From the day you met Josie at the alterations shop." And the interview begins.

Hi! I'm Your Birthday Twin!
A NETFLIX ORIGINAL SERIES

The screen shows Alix Summer in her recording studio, taking off her headphones, shutting down her screens, walking to the door and closing it behind her.

The camera then pans slowly around the detail of Alix's studio in her absence and the following text appears on-screen:

The last episode of Alix's podcast was released in August 2020 on the one-year anniversary of Nathan's funeral. This is Alix's closing message.

Alix's voice is heard as the camera carries on exploring her studio.

"And that brings us to today. I'm here, near the end of August, in the middle of a global pandemic, not sure what the world holds for me, or for any of us. I do know one thing, that tomorrow I am collecting our lockdown puppy from a breeder in Hampshire. She is an Aussie sheepdog with mismatched eyes, and she will be called Matilda, for obvious reasons. She will, I hope, bring joy to our small family as we learn to live with the absence, with the grief, with the questions, with the pain. And earlier today I also had a very exciting email from a US production company expressing an interest in buying the rights to this podcast in order to film it as a documentary, so you never know, before too long you might be watching *Hi! I'm Your Birthday Twin!* from the comfort of your own sofa. And just two days ago Roxy told me that she and Erin have found a place to live together, that Erin is moving in this weekend, and bringing her whole gaming universe with her. So there is lots to celebrate as we reach these final moments. But, frustratingly for me, as a journalist, and for you, as listeners, and as is so often the way for true crime podcasts like these, there is no real closure, no real THE END, because, of course, as I speak, Josie Fair is still out there somewhere. She may claim to have done all of this to secure her freedom, but the truth is, Josie Fair has no freedom. None whatsoever. She is trapped now in a prison of her own making, where she will forever be looking over her shoulder, on the run, lying low, hiding. And I am glad. And of course I nurse a secret fantasy that moments before I press end on this recording my phone will ring and DC Albright will be on the line telling me that they've found her, they're bringing her in, she's going to court, she's going to prison, she's atoning for her crimes. And what crimes they are. What shocking, unthinkable, unbearable crimes. A feisty, clever teenage girl with her whole life ahead of her, her battered body left to rot in a dirty, damp garage, for no good reason. No good reason at all. Josie's pensioner husband, whilst clearly far from a good husband, and by some accounts even a bad man but a good father to his children, beaten whilst having a heart attack and left to die in a bathtub. The attempted murder of her own daughter, her vulnerable, firstborn child. What? To steal her money? To keep her from living her own life? Pursuing her own dreams? My God . . . And lastly, the pointless, ridiculous, dreadful murder of my own husband. Nathan Summer. My boy. My man. My flame-haired partner in life. My children's father. Friend to dozens. Loved colleague. Just . . . God. Just a nice guy, you know? We had our problems, yes. We had our issues. And yes, in the weeks before Josie took him, I'd considered a life without him. I really had. I'd imagined what it might be like to go it alone and not have to live with those long, awful nights where he didn't come home to me and I lay in the dark sleeplessly, my stomach churning, my thoughts racing, wondering if he was dead, wondering if he was having sex with a stranger, wondering why he didn't just want to come home to me. And maybe one day I would have reached the end of the road, maybe one day I would have decided to live without him. But Josie took that choice from me. She took all the other possible paths our lives could have taken away from us. And worse than that, she took a good father from his children. And whatever her reasons—her psychosis, her childhood trauma, her mental health, her difficulties and issues—whatever reason she would give for what she has done, I maintain, whatever she herself might say, that she did what she did because she is evil. Pure and simple. So, Josie Fair, if you're out there somewhere listening, know this. Your fight is yours and yours alone. Do not claim to be fighting on anyone's behalf. Do not claim that you are a victim. Do not claim that you are anything other than what you are. An evil motherfucking basic bitch.

"My name is Alix Summer. And this has been *Hi! I'm Your Birthday Twin!* Thank you for listening. And farewell."

The audio plays the single click of a recording being ended.

The screen fades to black and the closing credits roll.

Series ends.

WEDNESDAY, 28 OCTOBER

In October of that year, just before the second national lockdown is imposed, DC Albright phones Alix.

"We're closing off most of the investigation now, clearing out some boxes of evidence, and I have something for you. The bits and pieces that Josie took from your house last year—I thought you might like them back? I can drop them over this afternoon."

DC Albright arrives just after four o'clock, when the children are both back from school and the puppy is in hyper mode, leaving hot puddles of pee in her wake as she turns circles of excitement at the appearance of somebody at the door.

"Sorry, Alix. I can see you're busy. I won't keep you. But I just wanted to say, I listened to your podcast, the whole thing, and it was amazing. It really was. You know, for a detective, it's rare to get that level of deep, deep insight into a criminal you're still trying to hunt down. And her voice—just listening to it, it put shivers down my spine all over again. It was like reading a novel, you know, I just couldn't stop listening. And that last line! My God! I did laugh out loud! And of course, it's sent lots more info our way." She rolls her eyes. "Most of which is total nonsense and time wasting. But a couple of leads worth following up. Someone who thinks they saw her in Northampton last week. We're looking into that. So yeah, we'll keep you up-to-date with everything. And fingers crossed. Soon enough. I mean, ten grand won't last her forever, will it? She'll have to plug back into the real world at some point, start leaving a trail again. It's just a matter of time. Anyway, here you go. Here's the things. We returned the other things to Brooke's mum, but she said only a couple of bits belonged to Brooke. The corsage. The hair scrunchie. She said she'd never seen the phone case before. And Roxy and Erin didn't recognize it. So yeah, that's a mystery. One of many."

She smiles warmly at Alix and then she goes. Alix goes straight to the kitchen to get pet spray and paper towels to mop up Matilda's accidents and then she sits at the kitchen table with the Jiffy bag in front of her. It takes her a minute to summon the will to open it. She pulls the objects out, one by one, and lays them in a row. She is horribly aware of where they have been, of what they imply, but also aware that these are small and important pieces of her that Josie had stolen, and suddenly the need to reinstate them in her home overrides her distaste about where they've been and she gets quickly to her feet and moves about her home, replacing each object in turn. She finds the small space on the corkboard where Eliza's drawing had once been and pins it back into place in the exact spot it had been taken from, feeling a strange satisfaction as the tip of the pin meets and inserts into the same hole. She puts the receipt back inside the *Livingetc* magazine and takes it to the front door and places it half-way down the pile in her recycling bin. She takes the Nespresso pod and replaces it in the jar in her recording studio, puts the teaspoon in the dishwasher and the hand soap in the guest WC beneath the stairs. She is about to put the passport photographs of Leon back in the messy drawer where they'd once lived, but decides against it. He looks so young, so awkward, so fed up in the photos. But they are him, caught at a moment in his life when he hadn't known pain, loss, or grief, and she wants to celebrate that, so she takes another pin and attaches the strip to the corkboard, and touches it tenderly. And then lastly there is the bracelet. The delicate golden bracelet that Nathan had bought her for her birthday, and as she stares at it she hears the echo of her voice, calling through to the husband who she no longer has: *Nathan! Have you seen my bracelet? The one you bought me for my birthday?* and then she rewinds fast past that moment to the memory of Nathan giving it to her a year earlier, clipping it together gently on her wrist, which she held against this table, right here, this very spot. And she upturns her wrist and she calls through the house to her son, her flame-haired boy, "Leon! Baby! Can you help me with something?" And he appears in the doorway, his pale eyes blinking.

"What?"

"Can you do up my bracelet for me?"

He puts his iPad down on the kitchen table and walks toward her. He smells of boy, of home, of hair, of love. She can hear his slightly nasal breathing as he stands over her, concentrating on feeding the loop in the clip, missing a couple of times and then saying, "There. It's in."

He's about to wander off again but Alix draws him close, her arms around his thin waist. "We're good, aren't we?" she asks him. "Us three? We're good?"

Leon nods, rests his chin against her head, and says, "Yes. We're good."

Hi! I'm Your Birthday Twin!
A NETFLIX ORIGINAL SERIES

Screen shows a dramatic reenactment of a postman dropping a pile of letters through the letter box of a Victorian terraced house.

An actor playing Alix Summer picks up the letters and takes them into a kitchen, where she begins to open one.

The text below reads:

On 2 November, 2020, two months after the release of the last episode of Alix Summer's podcast, Alix Summer received a letter in the post.

The screen changes to Alix Summer reading aloud from the letter in her recording studio.

" 'Alix. It's taken me a long time to know what to say to you and how to say it. I listened to your podcast this summer. *Basic bitch*? Really? I've been under attack all my life, Alix. All my life. And now from you too.'

" 'When I first met you, I thought you were special. I thought it was some kind of destiny. Finally, someone who got me, who understood me, someone who realized how hard my life had been. And I gave you my truth, Alix. And what did you do with it? Turned it into some tacky "true crime" rubbish, when not one minute of it was true. None of it. And as for Erin and all her lies, I knew she would lie. Of course she would lie. Her and Roxy, trying to make me look bad when it was them all along. The fact that you bought into their act makes me think less of you. I am so disappointed in you. I really am.'

" 'And I did not take Nathan from you on purpose; I told you that already. I explained: it was an accident. I was giving him the right dose but it stopped working and he was making so much noise and so I had to give him more. How was I supposed to know that it would kill him? But still you're holding it against me, acting as if I knew what I was doing, acting as if there's something wrong with me when there isn't. It's the world that's wrong—you and I both know that.'

"'Fate has brought us together twice now, Alix, once on the day we were born, then again on the night we turned forty-five. Maybe it will find a way to bring us together again and maybe then we can get back to where we were. I hope so, I really do.'

"'Please send my love to your lovely children, especially Leon. I had such a soft spot for him. A lovely boy. A delicate boy. Keep him safe.'

"'Josie.'"

Alix folds the letter in half and puts it down on her desk.

She looks at the interviewer and shakes her head wryly.

The text below reads:

At the time of broadcast, Alix Summer has not heard from Josie Fair again.

SIXTEEN
MONTHS
LATER

MARCH 2022

J osie adjusts her face mask and pulls her dyed blond hair over her face when two young women get on the empty bus and sit in front of her.

She stares resolutely from the window of the bus, watching the dark streets of the small Midlands city where she now lives pass by, keeping her face away from people's eyes as she always does.

The women in front of her chatter, an endless flow of words that passes through Josie's consciousness like a thick, meaningless fog, until one of them draws in her breath sharply and says, "Oh my God, have you been watching that thing on Netflix? The *Birthday Twin* thing?"

The other woman says, "God, yes, I watched the whole thing in one sitting. I mean, what even was it?"

"Yeah! Exactly! It was like . . . that woman! She was just creepy as fuck."

"So creepy. And what she did to her children. And kidnapping that woman's husband. I was just . . . like, what the hell?"

"What did you make of those kids, though? Roxy and Erin. Did you think they were telling the truth?"

"What do you mean?"

"I mean, just, like, they seemed a bit shady to me. And then what that Josie woman said in her letter to the podcaster at the end. I just wondered if they were maybe in on it all."

"God. I hadn't thought of that. But all of it felt sketchy to me. It was like, that Josie woman, she wasn't the only one telling lies, you know. There was more to it, I think. The whole thing was just so fucking weird. Hard to believe that people like that exist, you know, in the real world."

The two women fall silent for a second, then their stop approaches, and they ready themselves to leave.

Josie watches them, feeling her breath hot and urgent inside her mask, her heart thumping roughly against her rib cage. One of them turns and Josie switches her gaze quickly back to the window. When she turns back again, the women have gone, and she is once more alone on the bus.

Her fingertips find the golden bumblebee that hangs around her neck and she slides it back and forth across the chain, feels the skitter of her heart as her thoughts churn and roil, trying to make sense of the things that live in there, all the snapshots of her life, the mistakes she has made, the lies she has told, her own reimagining of a life that started as an unborn child ignored and unwanted in her mother's womb, brought into the world to feel every iota of her mother's mistake, a life that was always destined to end this way, in hiding, alone, a woman in a mask, and she remembers the things that she did, as a child, as an adult, all the things she did not tell Alix, and she thinks of the thing she *said* she had done, although she didn't. And the whole thing feels like a twisted, sickening knot of truths and untruths that she will never ever be able to unravel, that no one would ever be able to unravel, but one thing shines through. It feels like the truth and she hopes it is the truth, because it defines her in so many ways: the night she came home and found Roxy kneeling over the white-clad body of Brooke Ripley with tears coursing down her cheeks, wailing, "I didn't mean to do it, Mum, I didn't mean to do it." And Erin standing in the doorway, staring and rocking with her hand to her mouth, and Roxy saying, "What are we going to do? *What are we going to do?*" and the call to Walter in Newcastle, who talked them so slowly and so insistently through what had to happen next: the plastic sheeting in the store cupboard, the window in the bathroom that opened out onto the garage mews, the key, in a drawer, with the number 6 attached on a plastic tag.

She thinks of the days that followed, that key growing hot in the palm of her hand, staring at it, staring at it, turning it over and over, waiting for the doorbell to ring, waiting for something to happen, wanting to go to the police, wanting the whole thing gone, finished, and days later Roxy's disappearance, her hate-filled words as she left: "If you tell anyone, I'll just say it was you. I'll just say it was you."

She thinks of the row she had with Walter the night of the dinner at Alix's house, how she'd pulled the key from the drawer and told Walter she was going to tell Alix everything, right now, that she was going to tell the world about their dirty little secret locked in the boot of his father's old Morris Minor in the garage behind their house. She remembers him clutching his chest, the stricken look on his face, she remembers staring at him as he fell to the floor, staring and just watching as the color left his face, his fist against his chest. She tries to remember what happened after that, but even as the memories form, she's not sure if they are true or if they're dreams, hallucinations, but Erin was there, she is sure, hitting her and hitting her and hitting her. And then the memories bleach out into nothing.

She stares through the window of the bus, and for just a fleeting moment, Josie is sure, she is *so* sure that—yes!—that is what really happened and that she has been maybe not a good mother, but a *true* mother, that she has done what any mother would do and protected her baby girl, kept her safe, saved her child from herself and the consequences of her anger as she had always done and will continue to do, now, tomorrow, forever, whatever it might take. And she has done nothing wrong, not really, not ever. All she has done, in her own way, is take care of the people she loves, try to help people, try to be a good person.

She is so sure that that is the truth.

So incredibly sure.

ACKNOWLEDGMENTS

Well, this one was a dramatic delivery! I started it in March 2022 and finished it in September. You'd think that twenty-one books down the line you'd have a handle on how you write and how things happen and what it takes to get a book onto the page, but like children, every book is different, and everything that you learned writing the books that came before it counts for NOTHING when you're confronted with a new universe to corral. And thus it was with this one. I didn't know I could write this fast! I worried that I wasn't doing the things I normally do, like creating a dual time frame or flashbacks. I kept thinking: Where is my male character? Where are my teenage points of view? What is this book? And why am I writing it so fast?

So really I think I would like to thank Will Brooker first and foremost, who even though he wasn't writing a book about me writing a book this year was still keen to read my latest work in progress just for fun and who, at around the 30,000 mark, when I was feeling dizzy with uncertainty and fear, wrote back to me to say, "I don't know what's going on, but it's f***ing delicious." This single-handedly got me through the next 60,000 words. Thank you, Will.

I'd also like to thank my sister, Sacha, for the chat in her kitchen back in February when I said, "There's an old man in a window at a laptop, and there's someone in a room down the hallway behind a closed door and I don't know who it is yet," and she said, "What about a teenage girl, who's a gaming addict?"—immediately bringing the whole thing to life in my head. The littlest things can have the greatest impact.

Thanks as ever to my editor, Selina Walker, who went above and beyond with this one—I'm not sure how many times she read it, but it was a lot—and to everyone else at Century in the UK who works so hard all the time on my behalf, especially Najma (much-deserved award-winning publicist of the year, no less!) and to Claire Bush and Sarah Ridley for all the background bells and whistles that help make books successful. Thank you also to Claire Simmonds for working so hard on my sales. Thank you to Jonny Geller, my agent at Curtis Brown, for always steering the ship in a straight line and letting me sit at my desk making stuff up without having to worry about the other things, and thanks to the rest of the team—to Viola, Ciara, Kate, and Nadia. To Deborah Schneider, my agent in the US, thank you for every minute of everything you've done for me over the years. You are incredible and I am eternally grateful to you.

Thank you also to the excellent team at Simon & Schuster in the US, to Lindsay Sagnette, my fantastic editor, and to Ariele Fredman, my not-yet-award-winning-but-bloody-well-should-be-because-she's-amazing publicist, thank you for working so hard and tirelessly on my behalf and helping me build such a brilliant and loyal readership on the other side of the pond. Thank you also to Jade, Dayna, Karlyn, Camila, and Libby. You're all superb.

And the usual thanks to all the people who facilitate reading: the librarians, booksellers, bloggers, Bookstagrammers, and teachers. I am so grateful to you all. And to you, the readers of course, thank you for picking up my books and sharing them and talking about them and making me feel like what I do is important.

And lastly, thank you to all the people who make up my day-to-day world, the world that brings me these stories and allows me the time and space and inspiration to write them; to my friends, family, neighbors, fellow writers, and, mostly, to the intriguing strangers in windows, on beaches, and on the street who spark ideas and birth worlds and will never know that someone wrote a whole book about them.

Thank you!

A NOTE ON THE NAME GIOVANNI COMOLI

Nathan's friend's name, Giovanni, was given to me by the winner of an auction to raise funds for the charity Young Lives vs Cancer. Here is a little about what they do:

When a child is diagnosed with cancer it threatens everything, for them and their family. At a time when they should be busy being children, enjoying their roller-coaster teenage years, or finding their feet at uni, life becomes full of fear. Fear of treatment, but also of families being torn apart, of overwhelming money worries, mental health stretched to the breaking point, of having nowhere to turn, no one to talk to.

At Young Lives vs Cancer, we get that. We are the charity that helps children and young people (0–25) and their families find the strength to face whatever cancer throws at them.

We know everyone's different, so we work hard to make sure each family has what they need to get through cancer. It could be a financial grant for a parent struggling to keep their child warm through their treatment or for a young person who can't afford to get to hospital. Or helping a family stay together at one of our free Homes from Home close to the hospital where their child is having treatment.

And if we think families aren't being heard by the whole system, we're not afraid to raise their voices or shout on their behalf. Children and young people with cancer deserve the same opportunities as anyone else. We'll always have their back, because we've been there before.

Powered by the kindness of our supporters, we'll face it all together.

ABOUT THE AUTHOR

LISA JEWELL is the #1 *New York Times* bestselling author of twenty-one novels, including *The Family Remains* and *The Family Upstairs*, as well as *Then She Was Gone* and *Invisible Girl*. Her novels have sold over ten million copies internationally, and her work has also been translated into twenty-nine languages. Connect with her on Twitter @lisajewelluk, on Instagram @lisajewelluk, and on Facebook @lisajewellofficial.